I0665354

SURRENDER
Your Heart

FATED
HEARTS
SERIES
3

INTERNATIONAL BESTSELLING AUTHOR
AIMEE NICOLE WALKER

Surrender Your Heart (Fated Hearts Book Three)
Second Edition
Copyright © 2022 Aimee Nicole Walker

aimeenicolewalker@blogspot.com

This is a work of fiction. Names, characters, places, and incidents either are the product of the author's imagination or are used fictitiously, and any resemblance to the actual person, living or dead, business establishments, events, or locales is entirely coincidental.

Cover art, interior design, and formatting provided by Stacey Ryan Blake of Champagne Book Design—www.champagnebookdesign.com

Editing provided by Susie Selva—www.susieselva.com

Proofreading provided by Lori Parks—lp.nerdproblems@gmail.com

All rights reserved. This book is licensed to the original publisher only.

This book is intended for adult readers only.

Copyright and Trademark Acknowledgments

The author acknowledges the copyrights and trademarked status and trademark owners of the trademarks and copyrights mentioned in this work of fiction.

SURRENDER
Your Heart

CHAPTER
One

Jack Murphy

REALISTICALLY, I KNEW HE WAS GONE. I'D SAT BESIDE MY GRAND-dad's hospital bed ten hours before, holding his hand as he took his final breath. His death was peaceful, and he had been surrounded by the people who loved him, but it sucked. My heart refused to accept what my brain already knew—that I'd never hear his hearty laugh again or feel his firm slap on my shoulder. Of all the blows I'd been dealt, this one hurt the most. I was his namesake and his buddy, and he was the man I admired more than any other man —including my father, though I loved him dearly.

My granddad was gone, and the anguish I felt had sent me reeling. The last place I wanted to be was sitting in his lawyer's office, but Terry Perkins was Granddad's good friend, and he said it was extremely import-ant—Granddad's final wish. My German shepherd, Charlie, nudged my leg with his nose and let out a soft whimper. I reached down and ran my hand across the top of his head to let him know I was okay and also to seek the comfort the simple act always brought me.

Charlie had been a gift from Big Jack after I retired from the army and found myself unable to handle civilian life. Every single minute had been filled with the mental torment of trying to transition back to a world where I wasn't in constant danger. I had to live with the losses of my fallen brothers-in-arms, and sometimes the pain was more than I could take. It was something a person couldn't understand until they were faced with the ugliness and the loss left after fighting in a war. I couldn't even find refuge in my sleep. In fact, I had dreaded sleep the most because I knew the terrors that awaited me every night.

My amazing family was with me every step of the way, but even then, it was harder to find the will to live and recover than it would have been to just end it all. No more pain. No more nightmares. No more regrets and sadness over the loss of my friends' lives and the helpless feeling of watching them die. I'd thought about ending my life more than once, and just remembering the temptation was enough to make me feel ashamed.

Big Jack wouldn't give up on me, and he refused to let me give up on myself. He'd served in both the European and Pacific theaters in WWII and knew what I was going through. Back then, he'd say, they didn't put labels on conditions and didn't invest any time or money helping the soldiers get acclimated when they returned from the battle—not that there wasn't a lot of room for improvement when it came to veterans' affairs in the modern era.

Granddad read an article one day about emotional service dogs and all the ways they helped returning combat veterans cope. Next thing I knew, he showed up at my loft with Charlie in tow. He was the absolute best gift I had ever been given, but Granddad didn't stop there. He talked me into meeting with Dr. Noah McKinney, a psychiatrist who specialized in PTSD treatment. I owed my life to Big Jack, Charlie, and Noah.

"Big Jack was a really good man—the best," Terry told me from across his spacious, walnut desk. His gruff voice pulled me out of my thoughts and had me refocusing my attention on him. I couldn't understand what was so damn urgent that it couldn't wait, but Terry was a devoted friend of Big Jack's, and if he said it was important to my granddad, then it was. "I know this is the last place you want to be right now, but I promised I would carry out your granddaddy's wishes, and that's why I asked you to meet me today." Terry's hands were steepled in front of his chin. He lowered his hands and blew out a slow breath before he continued. "I'm not acting as Big Jack's solicitor. I'm acting as his friend."

"Okay." I was sure the confusion in my voice was accompanied by a matching expression on my face. "What's going on, Terry?" I felt the bite of intrigue in the air around me and it was a welcome change—if only a short reprieve.

Terry rolled back his chair so he could open the center desk drawer. He pulled out an envelope, then closed the drawer and scooted his chair forward again. Terry placed the envelope on his desk, and I saw my name written across it in Big Jack's handwriting. I'd recognize that masculine scrawl anywhere from all the birthday cards I had received from him growing up and the handwritten letters he'd sent me while I was serving overseas. I hoped I'd adequately told him just how much those letters had meant to me while I served my tours in Iraq and Afghanistan. It appeared I was receiving one final letter from my granddad, and fuck if that didn't have me fighting to keep my shit together.

"Take this letter, Jack, but don't open it in my office." The gravity in Terry's tone made me snap my gaze from the envelope back to his face. His furrowed brow over deep-set blue eyes and pinched mouth further testified to the magnitude of the moment. "By law, I should retain that envelope in case it contains anything of value, but I promised Big Jack I would give it to you upon his death, and so I am. I can't know what's inside. Do you understand, Jack?"

I did, but the only thing I could say was, "When?"

"I'm sorry?" Terry was obviously confused by the question, so I quickly clarified it for him.

"When did Granddad write this letter and give it to you?" Had he

3

been sicker than he'd let on? If we had gotten him help sooner, would he be alive today? I had a pressing need to know.

"Jack, I don't know what is in the envelope," Terry said. "It could be a letter or a treasure map. All I can say for sure is that Big Jack gave it to me two weeks ago."

Which was about the same time he'd refused further treatments. He'd said he knew that he had lost his war with lung cancer, and he didn't want to spend the rest of his days sick and weak from radiation and chemo. I honestly couldn't blame him.

"Big Jack asked me to come see him," Terry continued. "He handed me the envelope and gave me instructions to give it to you as soon as he passed away." He slid the envelope across his desk toward me.

It looked like my hand was moving in slow motion as I reached out and picked it up off the desk. As I did, I felt a small object—perhaps something metal—slide along the bottom of the envelope. I looked at Terry again and his expression was inscrutable. It made me question whether he knew more than he let on. Sadness slowly creeped into his features, and I quickly pushed aside my curiosity and suspicions. Terry was grieving too, and there would be time later for questions. I folded the envelope in half and slid it inside my pocket.

"I'm truly sorry for your loss," Terry said softly as his eyes misted over with tears.

"Our loss," I corrected. "He was important to you too. You've always been a good friend to Big Jack, and I've long considered you a part of our family, Terry. Please don't be a stranger, okay?"

The older man silently nodded, and his lips trembled with the sorrow he struggled to contain. I wasn't sure of Terry's exact age, but I figured he was in his late seventies, whereas my granddad had turned eighty-seven on his last birthday. The pair had shared many fishing and camping trips at Big Jack's cabin once they had both become lonely widowers. Seeing Terry's devastation took my mind off my own heartbreak for a few minutes. I reached across the desk and placed my hands on top of his and gave a gentle squeeze. Tears leaked from Terry's eyes and spilled down his weathered cheeks.

"Your friendship meant a lot to Big Jack too," I said. "You guys were inseparable over the last decade, and grandad was lucky to have a friend like you."

"Thanks, Jack," he whispered gruffly. He wiped the moisture from his eyes and face with shaky hands. Terry cleared his throat and said, "I was blessed to have a friend like him too. I'm feeling a little lost to be honest."

"One day at a time, right?" I wasn't a typical Irish Murphy male who easily expressed their feelings. Instead, I often stumbled over the right words to say, but I tried harder for Terry. "Granddad wouldn't want you to be sad, Terry. He'd want you to toss back a pint, or a shot of good Irish whiskey, or both in his honor."

"So true." A thin smile split his face. "I'll do just that when I get home. Thank you, Jack."

I ran out of things to say, so I stood up and warmly shook Terry's hand before Charlie and I left his office. My heart was crushed, and my brain and body were exhausted from lack of sleep. I needed to head back to my parents' house and grab a bite to eat, a hot shower, and crash for a few hours. Maybe then I'd find the courage to open the envelope Big Jack had left for me—if not, I knew where my dad kept some liquid courage.

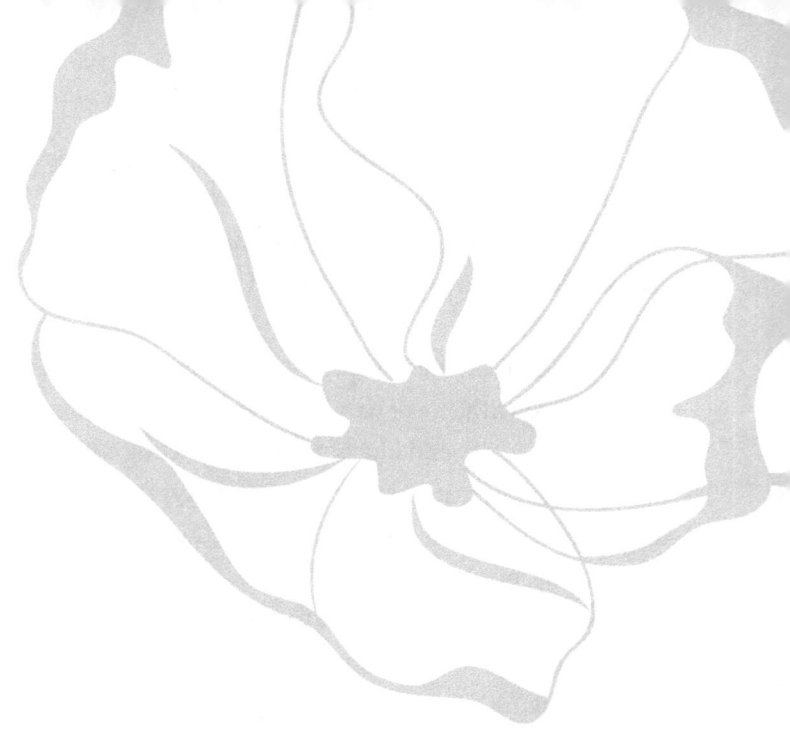

CHAPTER
Two

Liam Connelly

"**A**RE WE THERE YET?" I WHINED FROM THE BACK SEAT OF CHASE Wright's car. Chase was my good friend, sometimes coworker at Bottoms Up, and my half brother. Chase just didn't know the last part yet because I'd chickened out each and every time I tried to tell him since I'd met him eighteen months ago. I had to make my move soon because his best friend and adoptive brother, Xavier Cruz, had figured it out and approached me a week ago. Xavier had been kind enough to give me a little more time, but he wouldn't let me wait much longer. It would hurt Chase to know Xavier had kept such a big secret from him, and I refused to let their relationship become a casualty to my cowardice.

"Just a little farther," Chase said, playing along from the front passenger seat. I was looking out the window but still heard the smile in his voice. My brother was a good-natured guy, and I reminded myself of that every time I started to panic about telling him we shared a father.

"Don't make me pull this car over, young man," Chase's husband, Grayson, said in a mockingly angry tone.

My heart thumped heavily with dread, which suited both the circumstances and the joke, so I'd let the emotion seep into my voice. "Yes, sir."

Anxiety sat like a weighted brick against my chest. Blood sluggishly flowed through my veins, making me want to drag my feet as if being led to the executioner's noose. I wanted Chase to know I was his brother. We were already good friends, and I was confident we could get even closer if he knew the truth. That is if he didn't hate me for withholding the information for so long. I should have told him as soon as I'd tracked him down, but I let fear hold me back.

"It sure is beautiful here in West Virginia," Chase said, interrupting my miserable thoughts. "The leaves are starting to change, and all those shades of orange, yellow, and red just take my breath away. I bet it's equally beautiful in the spring when everything turns green with new growth after a long, harsh winter."

"Let's plan a weekend getaway for both spring and fall next year," Gray suggested. "I find the fresh air invigorating." He didn't bother to hide the suggestive sexual undertones in his remark.

Playing up the whiny kid role, I made gagging and retching noises from the back seat. "As if either of you need any help." My sarcastic comment was met with laughter from the lovebirds. "If you insist on getting away, you might want to talk to Jack because his family owns a cabin near the Monongahela National Forest. I'm not sure if they rent it out, though."

Chase twisted his upper body to look at me. "How do you know this?" He wiggled his brows suggestively, causing me to roll my eyes.

The common misconception among both the bar employees and patrons was that Jack wanted to have his way with me. According to my coworkers, he watched me like a hawk and scared off any would-be boyfriends. I often felt his presence in the bar and his eyes on me, but unfortunately, it didn't feel sexual. It was more like the protective stance a big brother would take. *Ick!* The insane level of lust I felt for Jack was completely at odds with how I thought Jack viewed me. I had brotherly love in my heart for Chase, but Jack? No. I wanted to wrap my legs around his solid body and never let go.

"There's a picture in his office of him and his grandpa standing outside the cabin holding up a line of trout they caught in the North Fork River." I pinned Chase with a steady gaze. "I know because I saw the picture and asked about it." Chase just grinned wryly with an *if you say so* look and turned back around in his seat. I looked back out the window and got lost in my dreadful thoughts again.

"We're here," Gray said sometime later. I hadn't even noticed we had slowed down and stopped. I had to tell Chase soon and deal with the fallout because it felt like the bitter acid caused by worrying so much was eating a hole through my stomach. I knew I couldn't go on living in a state of constant worry.

I stepped out of the car and looked around the funeral home parking lot. It was packed with people coming to offer their condolences and say goodbye to Jack's grandpa. My eyes landed on the horse drawn carriage-style hearse still used in a lot of military funerals. I knew from brief conversations that Big Jack Murphy, as his friends and family called him, was a decorated WWII veteran. His grandson, Jack Murphy, wasn't much of a talker, but he'd proudly told me about his grandpa's service on the anniversary of D-Day a few months ago. It had been just the two of us closing the bar when he'd handed me a shot, and we'd toasted in memory of the lives lost that day. I cherished those quiet moments we shared, even though I didn't think they would lead to anything other than friendship.

I didn't know much about Jack's military career except that he'd served as a US Army Ranger. He didn't speak about his service at all, but he spoke proudly of Big Jack's. I suspected Jack had seen a lot of horrible things during his service, which was the cause of his PTSD and the reason for his sealed lips. Maybe it was also the reason the man lived like a monk. It seemed impossible that he made time to date or even have sex with anyone. There were only so many hours in the day, and Jack spent most of them at his bar.

We waited patiently in line to offer our sympathies to the Murphy family. There were photos of Big Jack's life posted on boards throughout the funeral home as the line wound around to the front where the family waited to receive us. I had met all of them on more than one occasion when they'd come to visit Jack. The Murphys appeared to be the kind of wonderful family any kid would be lucky to grow up in. After an hour, or maybe longer, we reached the front of the funeral home. I followed behind Gray and Chase as they shook hands with the family.

"Sorry for your loss, Dec," I said to Jack's younger brother, Declan. He thanked me and shook my hand, offering me a weak smile.

"Thanks for coming, Liam," McKenna, Jack's younger sister, said. She gave me a loose hug and a quick kiss on the cheek. I shook hands with her husband, Darren, then found myself standing in front of Jack.

All the air left my lungs at the sight of him. He was wearing his army dress blues, and his chest was covered in colorful bars and medals denoting his valiant service. Jack had shaved for the occasion, and it was the first time I saw what he hid beneath the scruff. Holy hell was he beautiful. That square jaw begged to be nibbled on, and that dimple in his chin made me want to lick it.

"Liam," he said in his deep, gravelly voice, "thank you for coming."

His green eyes, a shade so light it never failed to take my breath away, were surrounded by ridiculously long black eyelashes and set beneath slashing black brows. Normally, I would get a tingly feeling every time I looked into them, but not that day. I saw pain and grief in their beautiful depths, and I wished I could do something—anything—to take that pain away. Jack offered his hand, but I ignored the gesture and wrapped my arms around him instead. I wasn't sure who I'd shocked more—him or myself—but after a second's hesitation, Jack hugged me back.

I tried hard not to think about how good he smelled or how right it felt to be in his arms. It wasn't the proper time or place to be having those thoughts, but they crept inside anyway. The smell of his soap had me thinking all kinds of naughty things—like what he would smell like at the juncture where his inner thigh and pelvis met. To me, that was where a man smelled the best. Yeah, not the right place or time for those thoughts. I stepped back and smiled at him compassionately.

"Big Jack was a good man. I'm going to miss his sense of humor." And I would miss his booming voice and the way he slapped the bar laughing at his own bawdy Irish jokes.

"Thank you. I will too."

I nodded at Jack and moved down the line to his parents, Patrick and Claire. I shook Pat's hand and hugged Claire, expressing my sympathy.

"You're a good lad," Pat said to me before I walked away. He might not be saying that if he knew the lascivious thoughts I'd had about his eldest son. I nodded at him with a small smile and continued down the line.

I caught up with Gray and Chase a few minutes later, and we took a seat to wait for the service. I tried to keep my eyes off Jack, but they kept wandering back over to where he stood with his family. He'd always had excellent posture, but it was even more pronounced while wearing his uniform. Eventually, everyone in the line cycled through, and the service began. I kept my ear on the speakers but my eyes on Jack. I had never seen anyone sit so still. I ached to sit beside Jack and offer him comfort, but I didn't have the right.

The trip to the cemetery was a beautiful ride through the countryside. Big Jack's final resting place was befitting a man of his caliber—up on a hill overlooking the valley he loved so much. Gray, Chase, and I stood in the back and watched the final tribute to a man loved by so many. Flags representing each branch of the military were carried by soldiers who served in those branches. "Taps" was beautifully played by a single soldier on his bugle. Seven soldiers lined up and paid their respects with a twenty-one-gun salute. The final ceremony was to remove and fold the American flag draped over Big Jack's coffin. It was performed crisply, precisely, and with the utmost respect for the country and the WWII veteran who had passed away. I had expected the flag to be handed to Patrick, who was Big Jack's only child, but instead, I saw them place the flag in Jack's white-gloved hands.

His hurt was so palpable I could feel it. I wished he had Charlie by his side to bring him comfort. Jack was a very strong man, and he had come a long way in the short time I'd worked for him. Not because of anything he said or did; I knew from the changes in his facial expressions and body language. There were more smiles and more emotions in his eyes, even if I was seeing humor and mirth in their green depths and not the desire I hoped to see. I didn't want to see him regress after the loss of someone he loved so much.

As I made my way to Chase's car after the ceremony, I felt Jack's eyes on me. I turned my head and our gazes connected. I gave him what I hoped was a reassuring smile and a small wave before climbing into Chase's car. I had to believe Jack would be okay, that he could work through his grief. Jack had his family to support him and Charlie's unwavering loyalty. God, he had me too if he wanted me.

CHAPTER
Three

Jack

DAMN THAT LITTLE SPITFIRE. LIAM MADE ME WANT AND FEEL THINGS I had squelched for a long time—two decades to be precise. I attended an Irish Catholic church growing up, and they were adamant that homosexuality was a sin. Then I chose a profession that didn't exactly roll out the welcome mat for gay men and women. Sure, DADT had been repealed, but people still feared for their jobs—and sometimes their lives—if they lived openly. The armed forces couldn't openly discriminate against us, but that didn't mean they couldn't find other ways to make life miserable or even deny promotions for some trumped up reason. My very life depended on my fellow Rangers when we were engaged in a mission, and although I wanted to believe they'd have my back regardless of my sexual orientation, it wasn't a chance I was willing to take.

Things had improved greatly, but there was still a long way to go before true equality became reality—both in and out of the military.

I had accepted my decision to live my life as a straight man and had even been engaged to my high school sweetheart, Kristen Donahue. I was home on leave a few months before the wedding when Big Jack asked me to stop by the house, a home he had built for my grandmother with his own hands. I thought he just wanted to visit and toss back a few shots of whiskey, but that wasn't his intention at all.

"Jack, I love you with all my heart. I want you to have an amazing life filled with love and laughter, but I'm not convinced you'll find that with Kristen."

You could have knocked me over with a fucking feather. Granddad loved Kristen—everyone did—so I was shocked when he expressed doubt over my impending nuptials. I think I sat there blinking at him for several minutes before I either asked why or he read the question in my expression.

"Kristen is an amazing young lady, and I love her dearly, my boy. She also deserves a life of happiness, but will she get the unconditional love she deserves from you? I see the way your dad looks at your mom as if the sun rises and sets in her eyes, but I don't recognize the same emotion when you look at Kristen. I know you love her, but I don't think you're *in love* with her. I'm simply asking you to think about it and pray on it before you commit your life to one another."

I was shocked by his request. There was no censure in his voice or accusation in his eyes, but it felt like I had disappointed him nonetheless. Behind Granddad's compassionate light green gaze, I thought I saw something else, but I wasn't sure what. It seemed like maybe he'd wanted to say something more but wasn't sure if he should.

I told Big Jack I would think and pray on it, but I didn't. I had made up my mind to marry Kristen and had no intention to change it. I was sure I didn't look at her the same way my dad looked at my mom because he wasn't hiding his true self from the world. Yes, I had guilt and questioned my ability to make Kristen happy for the rest of her life, but Big Jack's talk hadn't motivated me to walk away from her; it inspired me to commit harder to giving her the life she deserved. Kristin was my best friend and confidant, and I loved her. I was positive we could make it work, but Kristen didn't agree. She came to me tearfully a few days later and asked to be released from our engagement for the same reasons my grandfather had given me. As painful as it was to hear that I could never be enough for Kristin, I let her go.

For twenty fucking years, I had ignored what I'd known about myself since I was sixteen. I was a gay man trying to conform to a straight life, and I had been able to avoid all temptation until *he* came along. Liam Connelly changed everything. The things I noticed about other men but pushed aside hit me ten times harder with him. He changed me with one look into his oddly colored, hazel eyes. I started noticing how his dark chestnut hair picked up natural golden highlights from the sun. I became addicted to Liam's shy grins and timid chuckle, which turned into full smiles and infectious laughter once he got used to me. I found myself mesmerized by every move he made, every subtle flirt he threw my way, and especially his snarky remarks. Oh, the things I wanted to do with Liam's sassy mouth. I'd been able to keep him at bay for a year and a half, but that was before he hugged me. Now I knew the fresh scent of Liam's shampoo and what his smaller frame felt like pressed against mine.

I stood in the cemetery and watched him walk away, and a feeling of loneliness hit me so hard that it took my breath away. Then Liam turned and smiled at me, and I felt warmth in my soul. Once he broke eye contact and turned away, Liam took his warmth with him. I could've really used that warmth as I sat in my old bedroom at my parents' house, holding Big Jack's envelope. I had a feeling whatever it contained would change my life forever.

It had been a very long day, I was exhausted, and I debated putting off opening the envelope until I returned home, but I decided to deal with it the night of Big Jack's funeral as an attempt at closure. Charlie was on the bed beside me and shifted so his head rested across my right thigh. I dropped a hand and scratched his ears in appreciation.

"You're such a good boy," I cooed. Charlie let out a little doggy groan as if he heard my praise and approved. "All right, boy, let's see what we have here." I slowly tore open the envelope and pulled out a letter. I could tell by the weight of the envelope that the small metal thing I'd noticed the other day was still inside. I peered into the envelope and saw a small key tucked into the corner. I set the envelope aside, inhaled a deep breath through my nose, and exhaled through my mouth. It was one of the breathing methods Noah had taught me to use whenever I felt nervous or anxious. I opened the letter, and my eyes welled up with tears just from seeing Big Jack's handwriting.

Dear Jack,

I know you weren't ready to say goodbye, and neither was I, but we're not calling the shots. You've been my boy since you drew your first breath, and that won't change just because I took my last. Look around you, and you'll see me everywhere. You'll find me in the snowflakes that fall from the sky, the wind that blows through the trees, and the rising sun that casts its adoring light on a new day. I'll be with you everywhere you go.

You always made me feel ten feet tall, brave, and strong enough to do anything I set my mind to. How I wish those things were true. I wish I had been strong enough to tell you the secrets I carried in my heart for decades because I think it would have made your life happier. Had I been honest with everyone and lived my life the way I wanted to, then maybe you would have felt you could too. The truth is even hard to write about now, but I wouldn't be able to rest in my afterlife if I left this unsaid.

Jack, the real reason I asked you to break off your engagement with Kristin was because my heart told me no woman would ever be able to complete you, to be the other half of your soul that makes you whole. I know that even right now a part of you is trying to deny my words are true, but I know what it's like to live half a life, and I don't want that for you. I loved your grandmother with everything I had, and I gave her the best life I could, but half of my heart— my soul—had already been given to Jeremiah Merritt on our first day of basic training, and I never got it back. I could only give her half of me, and that wasn't fair to either of us. I wouldn't allow regret to rule my life because if not

15

for my decision, then I wouldn't have had your father or you and your siblings. However, there was never a day that went by that my heart didn't call out for Jeremiah and wonder where he was and if he was happy. Did he have a family of his own? Did he still think of me?

Shocked? Yes, I imagine you are. So just imagine how that would have gone over in the 1940s. Had Jeremiah and I been found out, we probably would have been killed and no one would have looked into it. Times have changed a lot—not that it's a perfect world for a gay man now—but it's a vast improvement over my generation.

Jack, I think it's time you live the life that will make you happiest. You've been through hell and back with each tour you served. You deserve the peace and tranquility that only living your truth will bring you. I could be wrong about you, and you could be seriously pissed off right now, but I don't think that's the case. Am I right? Instead, you're wondering how I knew. The answer is simple, my boy: I saw myself when I looked at you.

Your military career is over, and you no longer have to worry about the repercussions of coming out while wearing the uniform. So that only leaves the fear of how your family will respond. They love you, and they will accept whoever you love. I think your dad might be shocked, of course, but he has loved you since you took your first breath. I'll never forget the look in his eyes when he placed you in my arms for the first time. That depth of love will never be lost, no matter how confused or concerned he might be. Your dad might need some time to come to terms with things, but he will. I know Patrick Murphy, and he'll do right by his oldest son.

The hardest thing to do in life is to be yourself. There is always someone who will want to tear you down and make you feel like less of a human, regardless of your situation. I wasn't brave and courageous, but I know you are. Live the life you were meant to live, be the person you want to be, and by God, surrender your heart when you meet the person who makes you feel what it truly means to be alive.

Inside this envelope is the key to a small storage unit on Shylerville Rd. That unit holds every memory I have of Jeremiah Merritt—things I held near and dear to my heart for a lifetime. I am trusting those possessions to your safekeeping, my boy. You'll also soon learn that I left the cabin to you as well. I only ask that you let Terry use it as often as he'd like when you're not using it. He was my best friend during some of my darkest and loneliest days after your grandmother passed away.

I love you, Jack. I always have, and I will carry that love with me into my eternal life. I'm not afraid of going to hell because I lay with another man. There's no sin in loving someone, despite what the church says.

I'll see you on the other side, but hopefully not for many, many years. Find your happiness, Jack. Don't wait!

Love,
Granddad

I sat on my bed staring at the letter for a long time, maybe even hours. I was shocked by Big Jack's confession and equally stunned that he knew the secret I had been hiding. *Could it really be as easy as he said? Could I really come out to my family and still have their love? If not, would being with another man be worth the sacrifice?* Those questions kept turning over and over in my mind on an endless loop. Charlie whined as if to say he'd still love me, and I rewarded him with a belly rub.

An image of Liam's gentle smile in the cemetery came to mind, and I closed my eyes, clinging to the memory. Alone in the room, I allowed myself to remember how he'd smelled and felt in my arms. I wasn't sure if I was ready to embrace the part of me I'd kept hidden for so long, but Big Jack's confession certainly made me feel less alone and had me thinking about my future. Would that future now include an impish, hazel-eyed guy who made me feel scary things?

CHAPTER
Four

Liam

A FEW DAYS AFTER THE FUNERAL, CHASE AND I WORKED THE CLOS-ing shift with another bartender, Trevor, and two waitresses, Hayley and Melissa. I was off my game and had been ever since the funeral. I couldn't get the sad look in Jack's eyes out of my mind, nor could I vanquish the memory of how his arms had felt wrapped around me.

"Customers want refills down at the end of the bar, pretty boy," Melissa said, breaking into my thoughts. I smiled at her, but it wasn't my usual megawatt grin, and I could tell she noticed by the concern in her light blue eyes. "Are you okay, honey?"

"I'm just tired, Mel."

She reached across the bar and squeezed my arm. "Not much longer, honey."

I pulled my head out of my ass and focused on the job at hand, except every time I looked at Chase, I was hit by another wave of guilt that felt like a blow to my solar plexus. I had to bite the bullet and tell him the truth; it was the right thing to do. The worst that could happen would be that he'd never speak to me again. I'd really hate that because Chase had become a good friend, but not telling him was just plain wrong. I already had to explain to him that I'd known he was my brother for almost two years, allowing myself to be welcomed into Chase's home and never once telling him the truth. What was that well-known saying? Something about preparing for the worst but hoping for the best?

The last few hours went by quickly, and soon we were shutting down the bar. I was locked inside my brain while working up the courage to speak to Chase. Normally, I would've been dancing and talking while I cleaned the bar to make the tasks go by quicker, but I didn't that night, and it didn't go unnoticed. Had I been smarter, I would've faked it.

"Seems to me someone is missing his shadow," Trevor said from the other end of the bar. It took a few seconds for his words to penetrate my thoughts. I looked down the bar at him and he stuck his bottom lip out in a pout and pretended to wipe tears from his eyes. He threw in an extra sniffle for effect. I'd never had a problem with Trevor before, but I had noticed that his normal teasing held a bite to it lately where it hadn't before. "The boss man said he'd be back tomorrow." His smirk had me pondering what the hell was going on with Trevor. Did he have a thing for Jack and see me as competition? I didn't think he had anything to worry about if that was his issue. I took a lot of teasing from the crew about the way Jack watched me, but never once had the silent sentinel given me any indication that he viewed me as anything other than an employee.

"Okay," I said nonchalantly. I had far more important things to worry about than a potential pissing contest with Trevor.

"At least you've been hit on more while Jack's been away," Hayley added with a wink. "The big guy really puts a damper on your ability to get a date around here." There was no passive-aggression in Hayley's words.

"I didn't see Liam take anyone up on their offers, though." Trevor looked away from me and began drying off glasses so he could put them away. "Why is that?"

"I didn't even notice." Which was partially true because my focus had been mostly elsewhere during Jack's absence.

"You never do, sweetie," Melissa chimed in as she came around the bar with a broom and dustpan. "Someone will have to knock you over the head or snatch you up and plant a kiss on you before you notice their interest."

"Is this a multiple-choice question?" I asked with my first hint of humor that night. "If so, I take the second option." I blew playful kisses in her direction.

"Or maybe you just like playing hard to get?" This time Trevor made no attempt to disguise the irritation in his tone. And what was with the sneer on his face? I didn't get what the hell I had done to him. *Why? What changed?*

"Knock it off, T," Mel said firmly. "We're a family here, and there's no place for your passive-aggressive bullshit. If you have something you want to say to Liam, then say it, otherwise keep your mouth shut." Trevor looked like he was going to say something but changed his mind. He just shook his head and went back to his task. "Fine, then let it go."

I gave Mel a grateful smile. "Is Chase still in Jack's office? I wanted to talk to him before he left." I had decided if I didn't say something right then, I'd chicken out again and drive myself crazier.

"Yep, he was putting the night's deposit together when I got the supplies out of the closet twenty minutes ago." Melissa gave me a kiss on the cheek before saying, "I'm heading out. I'll see you tomorrow."

"Night, Mel."

The dreadful feeling returned as I made my way to Jack's office. I guess I should more accurately say that it had never left, but it was definitely stronger that night. I paused and took a deep breath before I twisted the knob, opened the door, and looked into the vivid green eyes of Jack Murphy.

"Oh. You're back." I was both pleasantly surprised and frustrated to see Jack where I expected to find Chase. My confusion must have been evident in my voice, and it gave him the wrong impression. Jack's black brows slashed down as he frowned at me and ran a hand over his smooth, shaved head. He'd shaved it in solidarity when his mom was fighting breast cancer, and he'd kept shaving it long after Claire had won her fight.

"That's a bad thing?" Jack's voice was gruffer than normal, and his eyes were as troubled as they'd been the day in the cemetery.

"Not at all," I quickly amended. "I was just hoping to talk to Chase before he left for the night. I'll just, um, call him tomorrow." I took a step back and started to close the door.

"Wait!" Jack's commanding voice stopped me in my tracks. "What's wrong?"

"Nothing." I gave him a quick smile as a punctuation to my statement, but if it looked as awkward as it felt, then Jack wouldn't buy it. He missed absolutely nothing.

"Come in here and shut the door, Liam." Try as I might, I couldn't stop thoughts of Jack using that commanding, dominant voice on me in bed. "Let's try this again, and this time I want you to tell me the truth," Jack said once I shut the door and approached his desk. "What's wrong, Liam?" He leaned back in his chair, crossed his thick arms across his wide chest, and raised an arrogant brow at me.

"Jack," I began in a pleading tone, "this has nothing to do with you or my job. It's something personal that I wanted to discuss with Chase." I needed him to understand and not press me because resisting him would be hard—maybe even impossible.

"Spill it." There was no give in his voice.

"I can't, Jack. I don't want to make you complicit." I pleaded with him using my eyes because my words hadn't worked.

"Complicit?" Jack snorted sarcastically and asked, "Were you planning on knocking over an ATM or something? Being complicit usually involves something illegal, Ace." *Ace?* That was new, but I really liked it. Jack cocked his head to the side and studied me closely. My nerves began to fray and I balled my hands into fists to keep my fingers from twitching. Would it be so bad to tell someone about all the turmoil spinning around in my brain?

His shoulders looked really broad and strong like maybe they'd be able to carry my burdens for a bit so I could have a break. "Liam?" Jack pressed.

All the fight left me, and I flopped down in a chair. I dug my elbows into the knees of my jeans and laid my forehead in the palms of my hands. "I really screwed up, Jack, and I don't think he's going to forgive me."

"Who? Chase?" I didn't need to look at Jack's face to know he was confused because I heard it in his voice. I mumbled my answer and nodded. "Chase is a really nice guy, and I can't see him withholding forgiveness for anything other than sleeping with his husband, but I know that's not what this is about. It can't be that bad."

I raised my head and looked him square in the eyes. "Chase is my half brother."

"Oh." Jack collapsed against the back of his chair in surprise. "Wow."

"I learned that we shared a father some time ago, and Chase was the sole reason I moved to DC, but once I met him, I couldn't find the words to tell him. Next thing I knew, more than a year and a half had passed, and I still haven't told him." I ran my hands through my hair, tugging slightly on the ends. Jack watched my every move with unreadable eyes. "How do you even tell someone they're your half brother? Do I have it written on a cake and invite him over for dinner? I know... How about I hire a skywriter or a singing telegram?" My voice ratcheted up a notch with each suggestion until I was starting to sound hysterical.

"Or"—Jack paused for effect—"you could just sit him down over coffee and tell him exactly what you just told me. If you are honest with Chase, he'll at least respect you, even if he's mad at first. Once he has time to think about it, he'll calm down and reach out to you to talk some more." I liked Jack's drama-free version better than my drama-laden freak-out.

"I hope you're right, Jack." I offered a small smile in appreciation. "Thank you for your advice." I wanted to ask how he was doing, but he was such a private man. I knew I shouldn't ask him personal questions, but I had been worrying about him during his absence, and I could at least put one of my concerns to bed that night. "Are you and your family doing okay? Is there anything I can do?"

His expression was unreadable for several seconds, and I started to regret my boldness. "One day at a time," he finally replied. "It meant a lot to me and my family that the three of you made the trip to pay respects to a man you hardly knew. Thank you."

"Big Jack was a sweet man, and I appreciated the time spent in his company, but we made the trip to West Virginia to support *you* more than anyone. We care about you." Jack's eyes widened, and his nostrils flared slightly. Once again, I wondered if I'd said too much when the room fell into awkward silence. I stood up quickly and produced an exaggerated, fake yawn. "I'm just going to head on home now."

"Liam," Jack said firmly once I reached for the door. I turned around slowly and his green eyes made my insides quiver like my nanna's Jell-O salad. The expression in his eyes was different from any I'd ever seen before, and it was difficult to place. Grateful? Hopeful? "I... um... Thank you."

I nodded and smiled at him once more before I left. The look in his eyes followed me home and stayed with me as I laid my head on my pillow to sleep. *What exactly had I seen, and what did it mean?* I tossed and turned for a long time before succumbing to sleep. At least the exchange with Jack had given me a short break from my angst over the situation with Chase, and though confused about Jack, I was grateful for the momentary relief.

CHAPTER
Five

Jack

I STARED AT THE DOOR FOR A LONG TIME AFTER LIAM LEFT MY OFFICE. His confession about Chase was a big surprise, and I hadn't been sure how to respond. Several questions about when and how he'd found out played through my mind, but it was obviously not the right time to ask him. I believed what I told him; Chase might be hurt at first, but there was no way he would reject his brother. I took small comfort in the fact that Liam looked slightly calmer when he'd left than when he had first walked into my office.

We care about you.

Liam's words lingered as I finished the deposit and placed it inside the safe in my office. I knew he'd said "we" and not "I," but I changed the pronouns around to suit my wants. It had been a very long time since I wanted someone, other than my family, to care about me. As I progressed further into my PTSD recovery, I found myself wanting to experience a connection like I'd had before everything went to shit. Except now, I didn't want to settle, and my urge to be with a man was only made stronger by Big Jack's confession and encouragement. It wasn't just any man I wanted to be with either; it was Liam.

My muddled thoughts churned around in my brain while I double-checked the locks on all the doors, then exited out the back. I walked along the rear of the building until I came to the entrance to my private garage. I fished out my keys and let myself inside the garage where I kept my Jeep Wrangler and my Harley. I'd bought the old warehouse after my retirement in hopes that renovating it would keep me busy enough that the anxiety, depression, and hellish nightmares would go away on their own. I had been wrong; only addressing the issues head-on with Noah had helped me, but I ended up building one hell of a business and home in the process.

I had turned two thirds of the large warehouse into a bar and private garage, and I rented the third space to a body shop that specialized in motorcycle repair. The entire top floor was my loft-style personal residence. It may not have been the wilderness that I grew up with, but my loft was still my home. It was the first place I could call my own since leaving the family homestead at eighteen. It had taken me a long time to get the loft exactly how I wanted it, but the place was perfect for me.

Charlie was waiting for me as soon as I opened the door. "Hi, boy. Miss me? I was only gone for an hour." I knelt and gave Charlie's ears a good scratch to ease his tensions since the dog worried about me when I was out of his care. I tossed my keys onto the table next to the door where I kept a jar for keys and mail.

It was going on three in the morning. I needed to get some sleep, but the WWII footlocker I had retrieved from Big Jack's storage unit called my name. I had decided to bring it home and open it after the funeral. It wasn't the right time to explore its contents, but the gravitational pull was too strong to ignore—sort of like the tug I felt toward Liam.

I blew out a quick breath and went into my bedroom before I once again lost my nerve. I opened the trunk and found what appeared to be photos and journals inside. I wasn't ready to look at Big Jack's pictures yet. The pain was too fresh, and I just wasn't ready to feel that searing stab in the heart when I looked at his smiling face in pictures. The journals weren't dated on the outside, so I chose the one on top. I flopped down on my bed and opened it up to the first page, which was dated December 27, 1963.

I was scared shitless when I stepped onto the base at Fort Benning in Georgia exactly twenty years ago today. My parents didn't approve of my choice to enlist, but then again, they didn't approve of most things about me. I could only imagine what would have happened if they knew the real reason I refused to propose to Mary Lou Markum.

The army shuffled us through like a herd of cattle as we got a quick medical exam, a haircut, and a uniform to wear. I was standing there rubbing my newly shaved head when I lifted my head and met the prettiest blue eyes I had ever seen. I later learned his name was Jeremiah Merritt, and he would become the person I loved most in the world.

I was afraid to stare too long, afraid he and everyone else would be able to see the reason why I was so captivated by his baby blues. It was while I was staring at him that a sense of calm washed over me, and I knew I was going to be all right. I was meant to live this moment and meet this man. He would become the beating of my heart, the air I breathed, and I stupidly thought I'd get to keep him forever.

Life rarely works out the way we want it to, though. The challenge is to accept that as truth without losing hope that maybe, just once, there might be an exception. In the end, I wouldn't have traded one single second in his arms for all the money in the world. Twenty years later, I can still smell his cologne and hear his laughter echoing through my mind. Losing Jeremiah hurt me badly, but thinking I could've gone my entire life without knowing him hurts even worse.

My eyes were heavy from exhaustion, and my vision had started to blur, so I decided to call it a night—or morning considering the time. I shut the journal and laid it on my bedside table then stripped down to my boxers before I climbed beneath the covers. The books were more like memoirs than journals since they'd been written after the fact. Granddad probably wouldn't have felt comfortable writing those entries while in the army. He would have been afraid of them being discovered and getting outed. Charlie jumped on the bed and curled into a ball at my feet where he lay every night. I turned off the lamp, throwing my bedroom into complete darkness, the only light coming from the digital alarm clock.

I lay in the silence and thought about Granddad's words and how similar our lives seemed. My emotions were less tumultuous, the nightmares were less frequent, and I hadn't had a bout of depression or anxiety in a very long time. I could finally tolerate the touch of another human being. In fact, I was starting to crave intimacy with a certain hazel-eyed man like a drug. Yet I still lived in fear. I was afraid of rejection I could experience if I took what I wanted. Was living in the open worth the risk?

Granddad had lost Jeremiah, though I didn't yet know how. Big Jack went home after Japan surrendered in August of 1945 and married Mary Lou Markum, my grandmother. Granddad appeared to live a happy life, and no one would have guessed the secret he'd kept hidden. I didn't want to continue living a lie, but I had to think it through before making a move.

I thought of what Big Jack had written about Jeremiah's calming presence, and I recalled how I'd felt the same peacefulness with Liam the day of Granddad's funeral. Could I really risk not exploring my feelings for Liam? Could I really risk the rejection of my family and friends to claim the life I wanted?

All the muscles in my body relaxed when smiling hazel eyes filled my thoughts and sleep started to claim me. My heart was leading the charge, but only time would tell if it won the battle.

CHAPTER
Six

Liam

GRAY WAS OUT OF TOWN ON BUSINESS, SO I CALLED CHASE AND invited him to a late dinner at Louie's. It was a fifties-themed diner that was really popular with locals and tourists. I used to work there part-time until Jack was able to move me up to a full-time bartender. Louie's had been a fun place to work, but I was grateful to have the full-time gig at Bottoms Up. My schedule was pretty consistent, and I made killer tips I was saving for culinary school.

On the way to Louie's, I practiced all the different ways I could tell Chase we shared a father. "Yo, bro," wasn't right. "Chase, we share the same father," I said aloud using a Darth Vader voice. "Once upon a time, there was a man named Matthew Rivers." That was one fucked-up fairy tale. "You complete me," but this wasn't a *Jerry Maguire* moment, and

I doubted he'd come back with "Show me the paternity." All I accomplished on the drive over was to make myself even sicker and cause people in other cars to look at me funny for talking to myself.

My knees bounced beneath the table of the corner booth I'd chosen in the back of the restaurant. I wanted as much privacy as I could get for the conversation we needed to have. I didn't have to wait long, as Chase walked through the door a few minutes later. His eyes searched the diner, then landed on me. He greeted me with a warm smile, which I tried to return, but I could tell I had failed miserably by the concerned look in his warm, brown eyes.

Chase must have looked like his mother because he looked nothing like our father, whereas I was Matthew's spitting image. I had the same hazel eyes and chestnut-colored hair as our sperm donor.

"What's wrong?" Chase asked as soon as he sat down.

"Hmm?" My voice shook because my legs were bouncing so hard.

"My gram would say you look as nervous as a whore in church," Chase said. "I've never quite understood that phrase until now." He smiled wryly at me, but it only helped a little. "Come on, Liam. Tell me what's wrong."

I dropped my eyes to look at the table, too ashamed to look my brother in the eye. "I, um… I've been meaning to tell you something, Chase. I should've told you when we first met, but I didn't know how, and then time slipped away from me, and I couldn't figure out how to tell you." I blew out a shaky breath and chanced a look at his face. All I saw was concern, but I knew that was about to change.

"Knew what?" Chase asked. "What should you have told me as soon as we met?" The concern in his voice matched the kindness and encouragement in his eyes.

"Oh, Chase. I'm sorry, and I hope you will forgive me someday." I took a fortifying breath and leaped. "I moved here for one purpose, which was to find you and tell you that we're brothers. Well, half brothers to be exact." I looked into Chase's shock-widened eyes. His lips parted as if he were going to say something, but he didn't, so I continued to speak while I had the courage. "Matthew Rivers is my father too. He met my mother not long after he and your mother split, and I'm the result of their very brief relationship." Chase just kept staring at me with his mouth hanging open. "Please say something. Yell at me. Throw something."

"I need time to think." Hurt made Chase's voice thicker and tears welled in my eyes. "I can't believe you've known for nearly two years and didn't tell me something this huge. Why?" I opened my mouth to speak, but Chase waved me off as he stood up from the booth. "No, never mind. I can't do this right now." He turned and left the diner without another word.

I felt like he took all my hope for having a happy life in DC with him. Fear gripped my heart in its gnarled fingers, squeezing until it felt like the organ would explode. A waiter—I couldn't tell you which one—approached the table to ask if I was ready to order. I told him no and left the diner without saying anything else. A cold chill seeped into my bones while hot tears slid down my face as I numbly made my way to the car.

I felt lost and more alone than I had ever been in my life. I knew where I wanted to go, but I couldn't say why, except something—an unknown inner voice—told me to go to Jack, that he'd know what to do and say to make it better. I listened to the voice and aimed my car in the direction of the one person I wanted. I used my key to go in through the back entrance so the other employees wouldn't see me and ask questions. I opened the door to his office without knocking, which isn't something any of us did. He demanded and deserved our respect, and we gladly gave it to him.

Jack stood in his office with his back to me, and his arms were raised up over his head as he pulled his shirt off and tossed it aside. I temporarily forgot my own problems and even how to breathe as my eyes raked over his naked skin, taking in every detail of the elaborate black and red dragon tattoo that took up nearly his entire back. The dragon was curled up in midflight with its fierce talons ready to rip the heart right out of its enemy. The dragon's mouth was open wide, and a forked tongue angled up toward the top of Jack's broad shoulder. The tattoo was so realistic I half expected the dragon to breathe fire at any moment.

Charlie realized I was there before Jack, and he came running to me, a soft whine escaping from him as if he sensed my distress. Jack turned to face me, and I saw his bare chest for the first time. I tried not to stare at the black hair that lightly covered his chest or the happy trail that bisected his abdomen and disappeared into the waistband of his worn blue jeans. Charlie whined again, and I tore my eyes away from Jack's torso to look down at the dog. Charlie cocked his head to the side, and I bent over to give his ears a scratch like I had seen Jack do many times.

"What's wrong, Liam?" The concern I heard in Jack's voice caused me to jerk my gaze back to him as he pulled a different shirt over his chest. "You talked to Chase tonight, didn't you?" he asked, correctly guessing the reason why I was upset. The grief struck me anew, and I could do nothing but nod at him as new tears threatened. "Oh, man. Please don't cry." Someone telling me not to cry only made me want to do it harder. "No. No. No." Jack paced a few steps as if he wasn't sure what to do. Next thing I knew, he pulled me farther into his office, shut the door, and wrapped his arms around me, holding me tightly against his chest. I held on to him for dear life as grief and fear battered my heart from all sides. "It's going to be okay," he whispered huskily into my ear. "I know Chase, and he'll come around."

"I hurt him by being a coward, Jack." I sniffled against his chest and twisted my fingers into his T-shirt where they rested just above his ass. "You'd never act so cowardly. You would've done the right thing and told Chase right away." I felt Jack's heart thumping beneath my cheek, and the steady rhythm helped to calm me a little.

"I'm not always very brave, Liam." There was such sadness in his voice that I pulled my head off his chest and looked into his eyes. "There have been plenty of times I didn't act on the things I felt, spoke

31

the things I should've said, or taken chances when they were presented." The way he studied my mouth made me think he was talking about something a little more personal. My heartbeat quickened in response to the hope that Jack might notice me as someone other than his employee. But, quick as a snap, the heat in his eyes was gone. He blinked and dropped his arms from around me and stepped back.

"Jack." I couldn't keep the want from creeping into my voice when I said his name. He shook his head and took another step away from me, and the coldness I felt from before creeped back in, but this time it was worse. Somehow his rejection was worse than Chase's hurt, and I just needed to leave so I could lick my wounds in private. "It was a mistake for me to come here. I see that now. It was stupid and selfish, and I'll just leave. That will make it right again for everyone." Jack's office was a blur when I spun around and opened the door. I meant what I'd said, coming to DC had been a mistake, and I could fix it immediately by going back home.

"Wait, Liam," Jack called after me, but I didn't stop. I didn't want to see pity in his eyes. It was a blow I just couldn't take at the moment.

I nearly collided with Trevor who must have been on his way to see Jack. My fellow bartender looked at my tear-stained face, then at Jack, assessing the situation. A nearly cruel smile spread across his face when his eyes reconnected with mine. I was seconds away from punching him right in the mouth, but I shoved past him so I could leave.

"Liam," Jack called my name again, but I didn't stop.

"Jack, we have a problem out front," I heard Trevor say. I sensed Jack's hesitation as if we were somehow connected and felt his intense eyes watching me as I strode away.

"I'll be right there," I heard Jack say to Trevor as I pushed open the door.

I took a deep breath as soon as I stepped out into the fresh air. Humiliation heated my skin, but the cool autumn air eased the burn. I was thankful for Trevor's interference, even though I knew I would pay for it the next shift I worked with him—if I stayed here.

"Don't take another fucking step." The anger and command in Jack's voice stopped me dead in my tracks. His footsteps crunched in loose gravel as he approached me, and the heat coming off his big body made me shiver. Jack wrapped his large hand around my bicep and held me firmly in place. "You're not driving anywhere this upset. Do you hear me? I'm going to take you upstairs to my loft and get you settled while I see what Trevor needs. Then I'm going to come back upstairs, and we're going to talk about the situation with Chase." *And us.* Those two words went unspoken, but the tone of his voice and the tension in his body told me he was thinking about a more personal situation than the one between my brother and me. "Okay?"

I nodded, too afraid to do anything more. Jack let go of my arm and walked away, leaving me to follow him.

Jack unlocked the next door down from the bar entrance and let us into his garage. I saw his Jeep parked there and a motorcycle I didn't know he owned. I followed him up the metal staircase and waited while he unlocked and opened the large steel door. The beauty of his home was enough to make me temporarily forget my situation.

Jack's loft was a beautiful mix of dark wood and black metal. One entire wall was windows, which overlooked the Potomac River. The view during sunrise would be breathtaking. The designated living areas were separated by warm rugs on the floor and furniture groupings. I wasn't sure how much entertaining Jack did, but he could fit ten people around the large dining room table made from repurposed barn wood.

"Make yourself comfortable." Jack gestured to the living room where the furniture faced a large flat-screen TV mounted on a rustic brick wall. "I won't be long, okay?" Jack had replaced his controlling voice with a cajoling one. "I want you to be here when I return." He paused for a second and then said, "Look at me, Liam." I did as he asked. "Will you be here when I get back?" Jack asked.

I should not have wanted to stay, but I did. A stubborn part of me wanted to know what he had to say, even if it was bad. If they were to be the last moments I had with Jack, then I'd take them. "I'll be here." It seemed like some of his tension left his body once I agreed. He gave me a quick nod, then left his loft.

It felt odd to be in his private space without him there too, and I hoped that he handled the situation at the bar and came back quickly. I had been running on fumes all day due to my nerves, and it seemed my tank was nearly empty. I walked over and sank down on the dark gray couch. All the fight left me as I stared out at the inky darkness through the wall of windows. My eyes started to feel heavy and my body relaxed into the sofa. My last conscious thoughts were of Jack's sexy tattoo, his stunning physique, and whether his chest hair was as soft as it looked.

CHAPTER
Seven

Jack

WHAT THE HELL HAD I BEEN THINKING WHEN I INVITED LIAM UP to my loft? My damn libido was screwing with my brain and making it impossible to think whenever Liam was nearby. I took one look at his grief-stricken face and wanted to lay everything I had at his feet to make the pain go away. I shook my head as I stomped down the stairs to the garage below.

There were other reasons I should stay away from Liam besides the fact that I wasn't ready to accept who I was and live openly. One, there was a twelve-year age gap between us. I felt like I'd lived four lives already, and Liam was just getting started. It didn't matter that he was really mature for his age; he was still only twenty-four to my thirty-six.

Second, we worked together, and it could spell disaster. I had never taken any of my employees, or patrons, up on their propositions, and I had received a fair share. I didn't have any rules about workplace relationships at Bottoms Up, and I was kicking myself in the ass for not establishing them. I was excellent at following rules and wanted to believe I would've been better at keeping that sassy little imp out of my mind if a no fraternization policy existed.

And what if I had sex with Liam and later decided I wasn't willing to come out to my family? What then because hurting him wasn't an option.

I didn't have answers, just more questions. I needed to talk to someone about this, but I had no one to turn to that I could trust to keep my secret. It occurred to me as I let myself in through the back of the bar that I did have someone I could talk to. I could trust Noah. Not only was he sworn to secrecy by doctor-patient privilege, but I instinctively knew that I could tell him anything, and he'd listen and be objective. He had stopped by Granddad's funeral to offer his condolences and told me to call him anytime if I needed to talk. I decided to call his office in the morning and make an appointment.

"What's the problem, Trevor?" I hoped he could tell by my firm tone that I wasn't in the mood for bullshit. Lately, he had been throwing small hints that he'd like to be more than my employee, but I'd thwarted all his attempts. He was a good-looking guy, but his cockiness and sense of entitlement made him unattractive to me. Trevor was the exact opposite of the hazel-eyed sweetheart who was waiting for me upstairs.

"Remember that guy, Devon Bellows, who used to date Chase's husband?" As if I could forget the one date Chase had gone on with Devon Bellows and the events that happened afterward. Thinking of the way Chase had crashed that birthday party never failed to make me smile.

"The guy is a tool and not a very sharp one. What about him?" Liam was waiting for me, and I wanted to get back to him, not mess around with that dickhead.

"He's back and causing trouble for Michael. He doesn't want to take no for an answer." Michael was my newest bartender and had only worked at Bottoms Up for a few months. Michael was shyer than most bartenders and didn't really know yet how to play flirty games with the customers. Some patrons saw that as Michael playing hard to get and ramped up their attention. It really upset him and brought out all our protective instincts. My staff wasn't just employees to me—they were family. Maybe I didn't tell them how I felt, but I showed them by always having their backs. No one was permitted to harass my bartenders and waitstaff.

"Let's go." Trevor practically had to jog to keep up with my long, angry strides. I rounded the bar, and sure enough, Bellows had his hand on Michael's arm, trying to detain him when it was obvious the bartender had other customers vying for his attention. It didn't help matters that Trevor had left him by himself when he'd come to get me. "Maybe next time you can send me a text or ask one of the waitresses to get me instead of leaving Michael to the wolves." It was fucking packed for midweek, and I'd have to stay and help them get caught up before I could return to Liam. I walked right up to Devon the Douche and placed my hand firmly on his shoulder. "Let go of my bartender and get the hell out of here." I wasn't even trying to be subtle. I *hoped* I lost that dickhead's business.

"Relax," Devon said calmly. He let go of Michael's arm, and I stood back so he could climb off the stool. He threw up his hands as if surrendering and smiled arrogantly at me. "There's no problem here, chief." I followed behind him until he walked out of the bar and disappeared into the night.

I helped Michael and Trevor get caught up behind the bar and delivered drink orders to Hayley's and Mel's tables. There was no task I was unwilling to perform at my own bar, which I hoped was part of the reason most of my employees had been with me since the very beginning. It was nearly an hour later before I was able to tear myself away and return to my loft.

I walked into my place, but Liam was nowhere to be seen. I dropped my keys on the table, placed my hands on my hips, and released a frustrated groan. I was in such a hurry to get back that I hadn't looked to see if Liam's car was parked where he'd left it. I should have texted him and let him know what was going on and that I'd be later getting back because of the situation at the bar. Liam would've understood and probably would've waited for me. He wouldn't have thought that I had just tucked him out of the way and forgotten about him.

I heard a soft whimper coming from the living room area and walked over to see what had upset Charlie. I walked around the back of the couch and found Liam fast asleep on his side with his hands tucked beneath his cheek. He looked so peaceful in sleep, and it stirred something deep inside me, a feeling I hadn't felt before and couldn't put a name to.

Charlie sat beside the couch with his head resting on the cushion next to Liam's hands. It was something he had done for me when nightmares ravaged my dreams, turning my peaceful sleep into memories of a bloody hell I still couldn't fully escape. It made me wonder if Liam was experiencing disturbing dreams, even though he appeared to be at peace.

I crouched down beside Liam, which was probably a big mistake. I noticed every fine detail of his face from his long, dark eyelashes to the tiny freckles on his nose and his lush lips. I told myself to leave Liam alone, but that isn't what I did. His skin looked so perfect, and I just had to know if he was as soft as he appeared.

I slowly raised my arm and ran the back of my hand over his cheek. Liam's skin was soft and smooth, and just that little touch wasn't enough. I ghosted my fingertips across his forehead, down his nose, and over his pouty lips. I was so busy staring at the mouth I wanted to taste and didn't realize Liam had opened his eyes until he said my name in a breathy whisper.

My gaze flew to his, and I saw sleepiness mixed with arousal in Liam's steady stare. It tempted me—*he* tempted me beyond reason to take a quick taste of his lips. His eyes dropped to my mouth as if he wanted the same thing. Slowly, Liam untucked his hands from beneath his face and sat up. He swung his body around and made room for me between his spread legs. Nothing had ever felt so right, and it spurred me to do something I swore I wouldn't. Not until I'd sorted out my feelings, anyway.

I raised my arms and gently cupped his face, noticing how big my hands looked cradling his head. I knew what I was about to do was wrong—unfair even—but I couldn't seem to stop myself from lowering my head and taking what I had wanted for so long. My eyelids drifted closed at the first touch of his lips against mine. They were soft and firm and immediately molded to my mouth.

Liam sighed, and I breathed him in. It was just a small kiss, the slightest pressure of his lips pressed against mine, but I knew I was irrevocably changed. I felt that kiss on a molecular level, and it shook me to the core. Liam's fresh scent penetrated my nostrils and tickled my senses, urging me to get closer and take more. It was Liam who boldly took the next step by licking the seam of my lips with his inquisitive tongue. I couldn't deny Liam what he wanted and opened my mouth to receive his gift.

He was restrained at first as if he instinctively knew it was a big moment for us—for me—but I doubt Liam knew just how big. My hands trembled against his face. Liam's tongue slid seductively against mine and curled, then he sucked my tongue into his mouth. My heart started to speed up, and my dick throbbed to life, hungry and seeking relief. It had been a very long dry spell, and my dick wasn't feeling all that conscientious about hurting someone's feelings. I was in control, and there wouldn't be anything more than a kiss, no matter how badly I wanted to lay sweet Liam down on my couch and ravish every inch of his slender body.

I heard moaning, but I couldn't say for sure if the sounds were coming from one of us or both. Arousal thrummed through my body and crackled in the air around us. I kept my hands around Liam's face, knowing I would break the promise I had made to keep this at just a kiss if I moved them. Liam must not have made such a promise because he roamed his hands up and down my chest.

I needed to stop. I was fast approaching the point where I would give in to what both of us so plainly wanted with no regard for the next morning, but Liam deserved better. Still, I found myself pressing against him until he fell back on the plush cushions. My hands slid from his face down to his legs where I cupped the backs of his thighs and lifted until he wrapped his legs around me, bringing our erections into contact. I was acting on pure instinct and adrenaline as I ground my hips against his. Liam broke our kiss and arched his neck.

"Jack." My name was a whispered plea for me to make it better, to make everything right. He was so damn beautiful and all I ever wanted but never believed I could have. "Oh God," he cried, then bit his lip as I thrust my hips into the inviting vee of his parted thighs. Liam released his lip, and I leaned over him and licked at the indentation his teeth had left behind.

I was so worked up after such an innocent act that I was afraid I was going to spill inside my briefs. We still had all our clothes on, and we were keeping our hands above the belt. Well, until Liam slid his hands down my back and squeezed my ass through my jeans. I was about to give in and give us both what we had been itching for, deciding we could work the rest out later, but a ringing phone stopped me in my tracks.

"It's Chase's ringtone," Liam said, answering my unspoken question. The lust vanished from his hazel eyes and was replaced by fear and insecurity. I hated that he felt that way and wished I could help, but he and Chase had to work through their issues together.

"You better answer it." I pulled myself off Liam and rose to my feet. I turned my back and walked over to the wall of windows just as he was reaching for his phone in his pocket. I willed my body to get itself under control, but it didn't listen. My dick was hard enough to drill for oil, and it was pissed at the delay in the action.

"Hello." Liam's timid voice pulled on my heartstrings—strings I didn't know I still had. War had changed me and made me look at the world differently. I didn't find joy in the simple things like I had before, and I felt like it had killed off a lot of the empathy I felt for others. Liam made me feel those things again—simple pleasures and compassion. "Hi, Chase." It got so quiet for a few minutes that I could've heard a pin drop, but then Liam's soft sniffles penetrated my brain. I turned to find him smiling in relief with happy tears trailing down his face. "Okay, that sounds good. I'll meet you there tomorrow at noon. You too. Goodnight."

Liam slid his phone back into his pocket and rose to his feet. "That was Chase." He smiled, and it was so nice to see the lines of stress removed from his face.

"So you said." I attempted to keep the moment light and to steer us away from the mistake we'd almost made. "Are things good now?"

"Better." Liam's expression was optimistic. "He didn't want me to go to bed thinking he hated me or that he was angry. He told me he was shocked and disappointed I hadn't said something sooner, but he understood it was probably harder for me to do than he realized. Chase invited me to lunch tomorrow, and I accepted."

"I'm really glad, Liam. I was sure he would come around, but I'm glad it didn't take him too long." I wasn't sure what to say or do next. The air had turned thick with an uncomfortable tension between us, and we stared at each other with apprehension in our eyes.

"I shouldn't have kissed you, Jack," Liam said. "I would like to say that I was feeling vulnerable or blame it on me being half-awake, but that would be a lie. I've wanted to do that from the first moment I saw you, and although I shouldn't have done it, I'm not sorry."

"I'm not sorry either," I said. If Liam could be brutally honest, then so could I. "I'm not sure I can be what you need from me, or that I'm ready to face things I shoved aside for so long. I don't want you to be an innocent casualty of me giving in to a moment of weakness only to find out later that I can't handle it. I won't hurt you that way."

Liam studied me closely, his confusion plain on his face. He was probably thinking I was referring to being in a relationship and had no idea I was referring to having sex, or anything other than friendship, with a man for the first time. That was something I wasn't ready to share with him. I suddenly found myself wanting to be alone to think.

"Do you want me to walk you out to your car?" Damn, that sounded harsh and dismissive even to my insensitive ears.

Liam stiffened briefly, then seemed to relax a bit. If his smile was meant to appease me, he failed. It looked more like a grimace than a smile. "Not necessary. I can find my way." Liam wiped his hands on his jeans several times as if he was nervous again. "I'll see you tomorrow night during my shift, yes?"

I nodded. "Tomorrow." My one-word replies didn't do anything to lessen the awkwardness.

"Night, Jack." Liam took a few steps backward and gave me a little wave.

"Night."

I watched him leave without another word. My loft suddenly felt lonely after having Liam there for only a short time.

CHAPTER
Eight

Liam

CHASE WAS WAITING FOR ME OUTSIDE THE ITALIAN RESTAURANT when I pulled up. He looked calm and relaxed, which was the exact opposite of the emotions running through me. I hadn't slept much the night before for obvious reasons, and it was taking its toll on me. I looked like an extra on the set of *The Walking Dead* as I shuffled up to the restaurant. Chase had put me at ease with our brief phone call, but nothing and no one could put me at ease over the abrupt way my night had ended with Jack.

What did he mean when he'd said he might not be ready to face things he had shoved aside? Was he referring to past hurts from relationships or his PTSD? Jack was so hard to read that it was impossible to know what he was thinking. The one exception was the look in his eyes when he'd touched my lips when he thought I was still asleep. I saw the same raw need sparking in his gaze that had been lashing at my guts for a long time. It's what prompted me to make an ass of myself and kiss him. I'd like to think I would've come to my senses before things had gone too far, but I doubted it. I wanted Jack more than anything, and I would've given in to him, consequences be damned.

"That's not an *I'm happy to have lunch with my brother* look," Chase teased as I approached. "We've connected as brothers for less than twenty-four hours and you already dread hanging out with me." I smiled a little, and he laughed. "Just wait until I drag you to all of Gram's shindigs," he added with mirth. Chase held open his arms, and I walked into them for my first brotherly hug. "I've always wanted a brother," he said. Hot tears of relief burned behind my eyes and stung my nose.

"You have Xavier," I reminded him, although I'm positive Chase hadn't forgotten X just because he found out about me.

"He is my brother, and no blood test will tell me differently." Chase ruffled my hair in big-brother fashion. "Speaking of Xavier," Chase said with a mock scowl on his face, "he told me last night when I called him that he had figured out our connection and confronted you about it a week ago. He said you wouldn't tell me that he already knew to spare him from my anger. I asked him how the hell he figured it out, and he said..."

"We have similar mannerisms that became obvious when we worked side by side at the bar," I finished for him. "I wasn't about to throw Xavier under the bus. He wasn't the one who'd kept the secret for eighteen months." I looked Chase in the eyes, man to man like he deserved. "I really am sorry for not telling you sooner. It was a really shitty thing to do and being afraid isn't an excuse."

"Breathe, Liam. It's going to be okay." Chase held open the door to the restaurant and followed me inside. The hostess showed us to our table, and we settled in with fresh rolls while we waited for our server to appear. "Will you start at the beginning?" Chase asked.

"Well, it was a rainy day in May 1991 that I came kicking and screaming into the world. I honestly don't remember much, but that's the story my mom told me." Chase tilted his head slightly and narrowed his eyes at me. "Sorry," I said, followed by a short laugh. Not everyone appreciated my sass. "My mom doesn't talk much about Matthew Rivers. I think he bailed on her during her pregnancy. She met my stepfather, Jamie, who later adopted me when I was about five." I paused as the waiter approached our table and nearly tripped over his tongue when he laid eyes on my brother. The red-faced guy nearly spilled a glass of water on Chase's crotch, and I couldn't smother my laugh, which earned me another dirty look from my brother.

"It's fine, Ryan," Chase said, peering at the name tag our server wore. "No harm done." Chase looked back at me. "Are you ready to order?" I hadn't even looked at the menu, but neither had Chase, so he must have eaten there often enough to have the menu memorized. I gestured for him to order first, then ordered the same thing for myself. "You were saying," Chase said once Ryan left our table.

"Anyway, I had never talked to or interacted with the man in my entire life. Matthew just showed up on our doorstep February of last year and asked to talk to me. He said he'd been diagnosed with a progressive brain tumor, and he wanted a chance to tell me he was sorry that he was such a lousy father. Matthew also asked me to find you and pass those words along. Apparently, he didn't have the courage or the time to tell you himself. Matthew told me where I could find you and said I had the right to know I had a brother."

"Wow." Chase sat back in his chair in a deflated fashion as if all the air had left his body in a whoosh. "I'm not sure how I feel about that." Chase ran a hand through his blond hair, and I felt sorry for the distress I caused him. He had asked, and I felt I had to be completely honest. I owed Chase that. "Why didn't Matthew want to apologize directly to me?"

"He said he'd run out of time and was being admitted into hospice. Matthew provided me with your name and address, so he must have looked you up. It just seems like he ran out of time before he could contact you himself."

"He just drove up to your house and told you these things?" Chase sounded as incredulous as anyone would be upon hearing the ridiculous tale. "Forgive me, Liam, but it sounds like a soap opera—and not a very good one."

"He came in a cab, and it stayed running in the driveway while he turned my world upside down. There stood the man I had wondered about my entire life, even though my family had told me he wasn't worth my time. And this stranger apologized for abandoning me, told me I had a brother I never knew about, and asked me to track said brother down and pass along his dying apology for being a lousy father. It was frigging surreal." I shook my head at the memory. I looked at Chase and smiled wryly. "Holy hell, it sounds like one of the movies my mom watches on the man-hater channel."

"Man-hater channel?" Chase sniggered at my description. "What the hell is that?"

"Just like it sounds, bro." The nickname just slipped out, but it came naturally to me. Chase smiled widely in acceptance. "It's this channel that she's always watching. In every movie, the man is a cheater, killer, or abuser—and sometimes all of the above before the first commercial break." We both laughed at my silly joke. "Anyway, I know it's hard to believe, but my mom was there when he showed up, and she confirmed the stranger was in fact my sperm donor."

"That's quite a story," Chase said, disbelief still resonating in his tone. "Can I ask you some questions?"

"You can ask me anything, Chase." I meant it. I was willing to tell him anything he wanted to know to make things right between us and so we could get to know each other better.

"You moved here a month after daddy dearest came knocking at your door. Did you apply at Bottoms Up only because I worked there?"

"Yes," I said without hesitation. I fiddled with the napkin in my lap, wondering if he thought I was some psychotic stalker making up this story to get close to him. "I had plenty of bartending and kitchen experience from working at the country club where my family has a membership."

"Country club?" Chase's question was followed by a quirked brow. "Really?"

"I didn't exactly fit in with the Biff and Tiff crowd if that's what you're asking." I gestured to my coifed and gelled hair.

"I was thinking more about the expense of belonging to a country club rather than you not personally fitting in. I can't imagine anyone not liking you."

"Believe me when I say there were plenty of people who didn't think I belonged." I didn't keep my voice modulated enough to keep the bitterness out. I could tell he heard it by the frown on his face, but I just shrugged in hopes that he didn't ask more questions. I guess I wasn't ready to tell him quite everything about my past. "Anyway, I did know you worked at Bottoms Up and it was the reason I applied for a job there. You probably remember that I also worked at Louie's Diner from the one time I waited on you and Gray."

"It was our first date," Chase said with a wistful smile.

"Oh, I didn't know."

Chase burst into laughter across from me, and I could only stare at him because I wasn't privy to the joke.

"What?" I asked.

"You kept coming to our table at the worst times." The memory of it made Chase laugh some more. "I thought Gray was going to throttle you. Every time we brought up an important subject to talk through, you'd come over and…"

"Do my job?" I supplied for him with a grin. "It wasn't deliberate, but I was curious about the guy my brother was dating."

"Gray thought you wanted me or something by the way you always kept an eye on me. I thought you were just lonely and wanted a friend." Chase got really quiet, and his eyes turned as serious as his thoughts. "You were so solemn when you first came to town, Liam. You had a lost, sad look in your eyes, and I wanted to be your friend. I never would've guessed the reason for your solitude." Chase cocked his head slightly and offered me a genuine smile. "The more time I spent in your company, the more I liked you. It seemed like you were opening up more as you got comfortable and began showing us your feisty personality."

"Is that why you started inviting me places? Because you felt sorry for me?" My heart sank that he had only been kind to me out of pity.

"No." Chase was quick to answer. "That isn't why I invited you to hang out with me, my friends, and my family. I asked you because I liked it when you smiled, and I wanted to see you smile more often. You seemed to have a good time around us, and I liked seeing you happy. It wasn't pity."

I blew out the breath I had unknowingly held. Ryan chose that moment to bring our food and Chase was lucky not to be wearing his Italian sampler of lasagna, fettucine Alfredo, and chicken parmesan. Ryan's hand shook something fierce as he placed his plate on the table. Chase's blond hair and big brown eyes had that effect on people.

"Whoa there," Chase said good-naturedly, grabbing hold of the plate before it spilled onto his lap. "There we go," he added when it was safely *in front* of him and not *on* him. "Thank you, Ryan." Chase offered a comforting smile to Ryan, who nearly tripped over his feet as he backed away. "Um, Ryan, could you leave my brother's plate so he can eat too?"

"Oh shit!" The red-faced waiter nearly choked on his own saliva after he cursed. "Sorry, sirs." Ryan plopped my plate onto the table and fled for the safety of the kitchen.

Chase watched him leave with a smile. "Poor kid." He looked back at me and pointed to my plate with his fork. "Eat. We have plenty of time to get to know each other, right? You're not planning on leaving town or anything, are you?"

"No." But I had thought about it. "I'm staying put," I said.

"Good. I have dozens of questions swirling through my brain, but they can wait for another time. I can't think when I smell food this good." He closed his eyes and inhaled the aroma appreciatively. "Gray gets home tonight, and I'm going to need all the protein, calories, and carbs I can get my hands on." Chase punctuated his statement with an exaggerated eyebrow wiggle.

I happily dug my fork into the delicious food and felt grateful for the moment I had with him. Sure, things weren't completely resolved between us, and there would be details to flesh out. I just told Chase that his father had most likely died last year, and even though Matthew Rivers didn't have an active role in his life, he'd probably feel a little regret that they ran out of time before they had a chance to reconcile the past. I'd gotten to hear Matthew's apology, but Chase hadn't. It might hit him hard later, and I wanted to be there for my brother if it did.

Brother. It felt so good to be able to publicly claim him. The happiness I felt when Chase told the waiter I was his brother was almost indescribable. Euphoric might come close, but probably still not good enough to explain the way my heart had swelled with pride and joy. I was plenty happy to experience it and not worry about putting a label on my emotions. I shoved all my concerns aside and focused on enjoying lunch with Chase. A small worm of discontent regarding Jack tried to inch itself into my happy thoughts, but I shut it down. I would see Jack when I worked my shift later, and I'd deal with the fallout from my behavior then and not let worry rob me of my time with Chase.

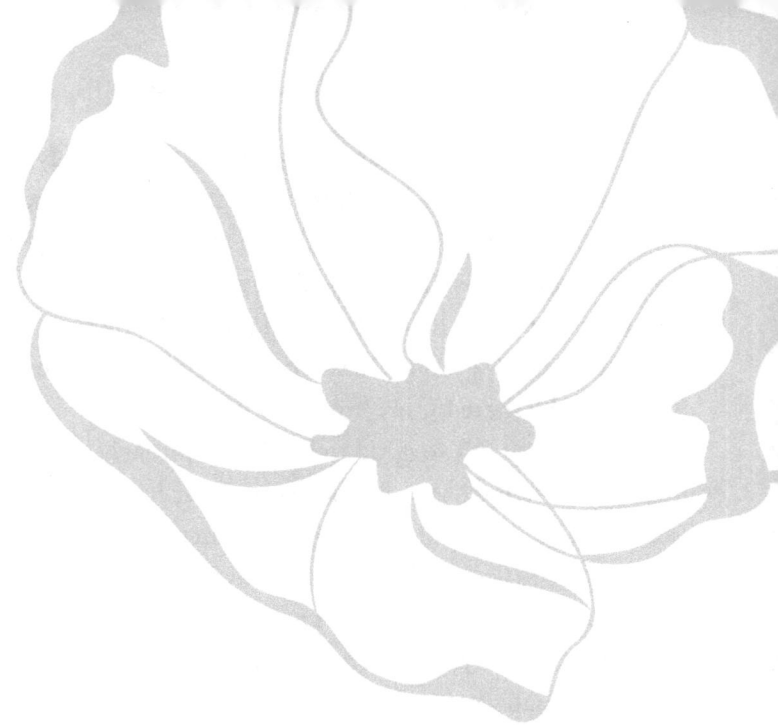

CHAPTER
Nine

Jack

March 14, 1964

    We let our fear of getting caught delay the inevitable, so it was about three months after we met before I first felt Jeremiah's lips on mine. That kiss was everything a kiss should be: earth-shattering, sweet, and life-altering. I was never going to be the same after having the tiniest taste of Jeremiah's lips, and I didn't want to be. The world said we were wrong, but something so right, so pure, couldn't be wrong.

    I refused to believe that I wouldn't have him for the rest of my life. I took for granted the fleeting moments we shared until they were gone. I would've given anything for just one more kiss from Jeremiah. As badly as it hurt me, I wouldn't have changed a single second of my time with him. The joy of really loving

someone and being loved in return was worth the agony of losing Jeremiah—
of losing my heart.

I sat in Dr. Noah McKinney's waiting room and recalled every word
of the journal entry I'd read the previous night. It just so happened to be
the same evening I first kissed Liam, and it felt like my heart was being
squeezed by a vise as I read Big Jack's words. Hadn't I experienced the
same emotions when I felt Liam's lips pressed against mine? Hadn't I felt
that kiss deep inside my soul? Yes, and it had rattled me so much that I'd
forgotten the late hour and dialed Noah's number.

Noah had become so much more than my psychiatrist; he had become a valued friend. He hadn't hesitated for a second, and he didn't send
my call to voicemail. Noah made sure I wasn't in a crisis, then told me he'd
meet me at his office before his other appointments since he was booked
all day. The world was a better place because of people like Noah.

His office was the perfect balance of comfort and practical. Even
though he was contracted to work with veterans, Noah kept his office
away from the nearby military bases because he said just stepping onto
them was a trigger for some veterans.

Noah's methods might have been viewed as unorthodox by other
practitioners, but they worked for me. He insisted I call him by his first
name. He always wore jeans, a button-down shirt, and a pair of boots to
every appointment I'd ever had with him. Noah's relaxed demeanor made
it possible for me to be comfortable around him and open up. He was
there to help me, and I desperately needed his help.

Saying my truth out loud would make it real, then I'd have to act upon
my confession because I knew I would no longer be able to straddle the
fence, walk the tightrope, or live in denial. I was either going to accept
this part of me and live openly or continue to live a lie and not have what
I wanted—no, what I needed.

Noah's demeanor shifted slightly when I entered his office as if he
could sense the turmoil lurking inside me. Honestly, the angst I felt that
day was just as severe as my first visit when I'd looked him in the eye and

told him I needed his help. I'd wanted to live that day and didn't know how, or even if I could. I sat in my usual spot on the couch and met his blue-green gaze, which always seemed to see into the heart of me.

"Do you want some water or coffee before we get started, Jack?" His concerned voice propelled me to make the leap, to tell the truth.

I looked down at my hands in my lap because I didn't want to see rejection in his eyes. "I think I'm gay." There, the words had been spoken, but they weren't exactly true. I looked up to see his reaction, and Noah's eyes didn't even widen. There was no outward indication of what he thought. "I don't *think*," I amended. "I *know* I'm sexually attracted to men." *Breathe in, breathe out. Breathe in, breathe out.*

"And you're worried about what others might think?"

I swallowed down the emotional lump lodged in my throat and nodded. "I'm not sure how my family and friends would feel if they knew I had feelings for a guy."

"Are you referring to guys in general or a specific person?" Noah's voice remained calm and compassionate, and there wasn't a hint of disgust anywhere. I didn't realize how badly I'd wanted his acceptance until I had it. If only the rest of the world could be so accepting. I raised my head and met his gaze head-on.

"I've been attracted to other guys since I was in high school, but I never acted on it until recently. Well, it was just a kiss." But it wasn't just a kiss. It was *the* kiss to end all other kisses—if Liam wanted me. I recalled my granddad's words about Jeremiah, and they warmed me from the inside out. "It's a specific guy, and it felt like a lot more than a kiss."

"What are you afraid of? What is the worst thing that could happen if you allowed yourself to love this man?" Noah struck right at the heart of my anguish like he always did. Perceptive bastard.

"I could lose my family and the friendship of my surviving unit members. They could turn away from me in disgust, and I'm not sure that's something I can handle. That's my dilemma—live openly and fully, possibly at the expense of my family and friends, or continue to live a lie. I've been with women, but not even one of them has ever made me feel like he does. I've tried to be what people want me to be, but it just feels all wrong." I blew out a shaky breath, feeling so much better for having spoken the truth to someone at long last.

"Can I be very frank with you?" Noah asked gently. I nodded for him to continue. "Is going through the motions really living, Jack?" I could only shrug because I didn't know if I could take the risk. "It's obviously a huge decision for you to make, and it isn't something that has to be decided today. You have to do this at your own pace."

I didn't want to hurt everyone I loved or the person I was falling for, the *guy* I was starting to think had been sent to me. No, I wouldn't do anything that would hurt Liam, even if it meant maintaining my distance. It physically pained me to think about not being around him as much, not seeing his sweet smile or hearing his laughter ring out as he talked to a patron or a coworker. Could I really go for too long without his sass? He was a temptation I wasn't sure I could resist.

"Jack," Noah broke into my thoughts, "I want to warn you that these tumultuous feelings might trigger night terrors. I don't want you to be caught off guard by them." I nodded, grateful for his warning. There was nothing worse than one of those evil things gripping me by the throat when I least expected it. Noah tilted his head to the side, and his eyes took on a faraway look as he contemplated what to say next. After a few moments, his eyes locked on me again. "Would it help you at all if I told you my coming out story? I don't usually share my personal life with my patients, but if you've never talked to a gay man before about his experiences, then it might make your decision easier. It's up to you, Jack."

It didn't surprise me Noah was gay. I'd stopped drawing conclusions about peoples' sexuality a long time ago. It did surprise me that he was going to open up and tell me his story. All I had to refer to were Granddad's journals, and he never came out, so I was curious about Noah's experience, even though I knew it didn't mean mine would be similar. I gave him a slight nod and my full attention.

"It wasn't easy telling my gunnery sergeant father that his only son liked other boys. I think my mom knew, as a lot of them do, but Dad was clueless. He kept pushing every pair of boobs he came across at me." A wry smile spread across Noah's face, so I guessed that it didn't go all bad. "I searched for the right way to tell him, Jack. I tried to find a way I could let him know without shocking him, but I just couldn't come up with anything creative. In the end, he forced my hand by giving me a *Playboy* magazine for my eighteenth birthday." Noah's expression told me that he had at no time found himself curious about the opposite sex. Noah broke into a laugh over the memory, and I found myself chuckling along.

"I was really aggravated and fed up that I had let this drag on for so long. I marched right into his study and tossed the magazine on his desk. 'No thank you,' I told him. 'I'm not into girls, Dad.' I think I even did a dramatic shiver in front of his desk, too grossed out to be afraid of his reaction. 'Besides, I already have my own porn stash,' I said. Then I watched as the truth dawned on him." Noah's smile slid from his face for a brief moment, then returned. "He was shocked at first. He didn't believe it was possible that his son could be gay. I held my ground just like he'd instructed me my entire life, and he realized I wasn't joking, unsure, or being rebellious. I was who I was, and he could love me or not."

"I hope he loved you anyway." Noah was a great man, and I couldn't imagine a father not being proud of him.

"He did." Noah nodded slowly. "It took some time, and things were a little awkward between us, but eventually, we got back to the way we were. I take that back. Our bond was stronger because the truth was out there. It seemed like it was no time at all before Dad started echoing my mom's sentiments and asking when I was going to settle down with a nice young man. They want grandkids," Noah told me.

"There's no Mr. McKinney, then?" I don't know why I asked such a personal question, and I wished I could take it back.

"Not yet," he sighed wistfully. "I'm still hoping, though."

It was entirely possible I wasn't giving my folks enough credit, and the thought really gave me pause. The only way to know would be to tell them the truth and let the chips fall where they may. I wouldn't give my family up without a fight.

"Thank you, Noah. You've helped me out more than you know." I saw the clock behind his desk and realized I had been there longer than I'd expected. "My time was up ten minutes ago," I said wryly. "I hope it doesn't mess up the rest of your day."

"Not at all," he said with certainty. He stood and walked around his desk, offering his hand to me. "You call me if you need anything else or just need to talk," he said after we shook hands. "My door is always open."

"That means a lot to me. Thank you."

I drove away from my meeting with Noah feeling a lot better. I still hadn't figured out what I was going to say to my parents or Liam, but at least I was ready to acknowledge that not being honest wasn't a viable option.

Maybe it was cowardly, but I stayed in my office for the majority of Liam's shift. I'm sure the staff and customers wondered what the hell was going on because I usually watched him like a freaking pit bull. No one said anything to me, but I felt their questioning glances when I was briefly behind the bar. I was aware of how everyone perceived my focus on Liam—everyone *except* Liam. I couldn't look at him without remembering the way his mouth had felt against mine or how he tasted. I had to adjust myself several times beneath my desk when I'd caught sight of him on the monitors in my office. I rarely used them because I liked to be behind the bar, but that night I had to take a break or risk making a fool of myself.

I looked down at my dick and willed it to behave, but it had a mind of its own. My sex drive had been pretty much nonexistent during the worst of my depression and PTSD recovery. But after a hint of the passion Liam could bring to my life, my cock wanted more, more, more. It was sick and tired of my hand and wanted to be buried in the tight heat of Liam's lithe body.

I turned the monitors off when the bar closed and the last customer left. I retrieved the tills from the registers and tried not to notice how stiff

Liam was, but it was impossible to miss. The air felt stifling and tense, and it made me wonder if there was something else going on with Liam. I decided to ask him about it later because I wasn't going to let another day go by without at least trying to explain my behavior. I just hadn't decided how much I was willing to share.

I took the tills back to my office to put the deposit together. I ran the end of day reports so I could balance the cash and credit card transactions, but throughout my work a nagging suspicion took root and wouldn't turn loose. There was something going on at the bar that night, and I needed to find out what. I placed the reports and tills in the safe, deciding to tackle them in the morning. I left my office and quietly walked down the hallway, feeling all kinds of stupid for spying on my own staff. I would've turned on the monitors, but it was video feed only. It had never been a problem before, and I hoped it wasn't then, but my gut said otherwise. I made it to the edge of the hallway and stood just inside the doorway, remaining hidden in the shadows and out of sight of my staff. It didn't take me long to hear what was going on.

"Oh, how the mighty have fallen," I heard Trevor sneer, and instantly, I knew who he was talking about. "I caught your little weepy act when you left the boss's office last night. Did he get tired of your little games, Liam?" How long had this been going on? "Not so golden anymore? What's the matter, honey? Not man enough to handle all that?" I'd heard enough and was about to make my presence known but stopped when Melanie spoke up.

"Leave him alone, jackass. Mind your own damn business. He doesn't deserve your petty bullshit just because Jack doesn't notice you're alive. You hit on the boss, and he didn't take the bait, so let it go and leave Liam alone."

"It's pretty pathetic, Trevor," Hayley contributed. I was mighty proud of my girls. "Liam, do you want to come to the movies with me and Mel? They're playing that new horror movie with the killer clown in 3D."

"Uh, no. I don't do horror movies," Liam said with a smile in his voice.

"You're such a Mary Poppins," Trevor said sarcastically.

"Yeah, maybe so, Trevor, but I learned that a spoonful of sugar helps me swallow down more than just medicine." There was the feisty guy who'd wormed his way into my heart and made it beat again.

I suddenly imagined Liam on his knees, taking my cock in his mouth and swallowing down my release. The image was so vivid I felt the pull in my gut as my cock tightened painfully behind my zipper. I wanted to call Trevor back to my office for the ass chewing he deserved, but I knew Liam would be long gone before we finished our talk. It was more important that I talk to Liam, so I poked my head around the corner.

"Liam, can you come to my office before you leave?"

He jumped when he heard my voice and jerked his head in my direction. I saw the uncertainty in his pretty hazel eyes, and I hated the way I'd made him feel. I offered what I hoped was a reassuring smile but wasn't sure I remembered how. I couldn't remember the last time I'd really smiled, most likely before everything went to fucking hell in Iraq. Liam nodded and returned to his task. I switched my focus to Trevor and hardened my eyes to let him know I'd heard what he said and wasn't going to let it slide.

"Trevor, you need to report to my office thirty minutes before your shift tomorrow," I said. "Is that clear?"

"Yes, sir." It was said sarcastically and not with respect, and that didn't sit well with me. I raised my eyebrows at him, and he quickly backed down. "I'll be there."

I returned to my office and paced while I waited for Liam. It seemed like an eternity before his soft knock came at my door. I called out for him to enter and held my breath until Liam was standing in front of me. I stalked toward him, and the intensity on my face had him backing up, but I didn't let him get far. I shut the door soundly behind him and locked it. There would be no interruptions. I kept my eyes locked on his as I pressed him against the door's hard surface.

Liam's gorgeous eyes closed briefly as his body trembled against mine. When he reopened them, I saw so much desire and confusion in their depths. "I missed you out front tonight, Jack. I missed the way you make me feel safe. Did I ruin everything by kissing you?" Liam's tortured whisper tore at my heart.

"I've thought of nothing else but the way your mouth felt against mine since you walked out of my loft last night, Liam. I'm going to kiss you again unless you tell me not to." I inched my mouth closer to his, allowing him time to tell me no or push me away. He chose to do neither, so I closed the distance and kissed him, capturing his moan in my mouth through our parted lips.

My heart thundered in my chest, and blood rushed through my veins to my happy dick. I slid my tongue into Liam's mouth and claimed his lips and tongue with my own. This wasn't a simple kiss; it was a mating of mouths. Liam mewled deep in his throat while I growled with the need for more. I kissed him long, hard, and deep, the same way I wanted to be buried inside him. How in the world would I be able to walk away from Liam Connelly after I experienced this connection?

CHAPTER
Ten

Liam

I HADN'T IMAGINED JUST HOW GOOD JACK'S LIPS HAD FELT AGAINST mine. In fact, it was better than I had allowed myself to recall. The weight of his body and the heat rolling off him made my eyes roll back in my head, and we were still completely dressed with our hands far away from any of the good parts.

Jack had been giving me mixed signals, and I shouldn't have kissed him back, but I couldn't resist the feel of his tongue sliding against mine. I couldn't think of a single valid reason why I shouldn't take a chance when I had pined for this man from the moment our eyes met. Maybe I was borrowing trouble, but I couldn't care less in the heat of the moment.

Our kiss escalated from lazy and sensual to scorching really quickly. I shook all over with the need to touch and be touched. I had thought

I could just be happy with another kiss, but my body said differently. It craved more. I placed my hands on his broad shoulders and began to run them over his strong body, memorizing every muscle as I went. I resented the shirt he wore because it kept me from touching his skin. I wondered if he'd let me trace the lines of his sexy tattoo or run my fingers through his chest hair.

Jack followed my lead and began touching me through my shirt. It was still pretty innocent stuff for two grown men, but it was a huge fucking turn-on. The anticipation of sliding my hands beneath the cotton of his shirt and touching his hot flesh for the first time had me shaking in his arms. It was a good thing he had me pressed so tightly to the door or I might've melted into a puddle of goo in his office.

I dug my fingers into the tight muscles in his back, causing Jack to tremble. Was he thinking what I was thinking? Was he wishing I was digging my nails into his bare flesh while he was inside me? If he was, then why weren't we doing more than sharing a scorching hot kiss and some innocent groping? My pucker clenched tightly in the cleft of my ass cheeks. I wanted—needed—to be filled by him.

My hands wandered upward until they were touching his smoothly shaved scalp. The skin was as soft as it looked, and my soft sigh was captured by Jack's mouth. The feral growl vibrating in his throat told me he liked my touch, so I kept it up. At least when I fantasized about Jack kneeling between my thighs again, I would actually know what his skin felt like beneath my fingertips.

Jack tightened his hold on me as if he couldn't get close enough, and my mind chose that moment to interject doubt. Damn it. I wished my brain would shut down and just let me enjoy what Jack was offering. The erection grinding against mine said Jack wanted this as badly as I did, so why were we in his office and not in his loft getting horizontal? As much as I wanted this, I couldn't go into it blindly. I had too much to lose, and contrary to my dick's wishes, I had learned my painful lesson years ago when I was a naïve young fool who thought stolen kisses and groping meant more than just quick gratification.

I reluctantly broke the kiss and searched Jack's green eyes. He looked so lost in lust that I figured a coherent conversation wouldn't be had, but I needed to try. "Talk to me, Jack. Tell me what's going on with you. I keep getting these mixed signals, and I need you to be completely honest about what you want and expect from me."

Jack stared at me for several long moments as he worked to get his breathing under control. "Not here." His rough voice was a heady cocktail of hunger and awe. "Let's go to my loft."

I swallowed hard because I was weak for him. If I went upstairs with Jack and he wanted to have me, I'd let him. Then what? Jack correctly read my hesitation because he gently touched my face with the back of his hand just like he had the first time. Somehow his gentle touches rocked me harder than the passionate ones.

"We can just talk, Liam. Nothing physical needs to happen between us, okay?" I read the sincerity in his eyes along with the concern that I might refuse him. *As if.* I didn't trust my voice, so I nodded my agreement.

I helped Jack double-check the locks on the doors and turn the lights off before following him up to his loft. Charlie greeted us both with a huge doggy grin and wagging tail. It was easy to see why Jack loved him so much, and I only understood a fraction of their bond.

"Would you like something to drink? I have beer, water, and ginger ale," Jack tossed over his shoulder as he walked toward the huge stainless-steel refrigerator in the kitchen.

"Ginger ale sounds good." My eyes devoured his tall body while he was turned away from me, and I didn't bother to take my eyes off him during the return trip. I wanted Jack, and I didn't believe in subterfuge or bullshit games—another painful lesson learned from my past.

Jack gestured for me to have a seat. He handed me a bottle of ginger ale and set his water on the coffee table in front of the couch. Jack sat beside me, but it was an awkward position for a conversation, so I angled myself in the corner of the sofa and curled my leg up beneath me so I was facing him. Jack did the same, and we just sat there staring at each other for several moments before he finally spoke.

"Today was the first day I ever admitted out loud to anyone that I'm attracted to men." Jack expelled a shaky breath, and the urge to comfort him was overwhelming. I set the ginger ale on the coffee table and took both his hands in mine. Jack visibly relaxed beneath my touch, and I knew it was what he needed from me. "I've known I was attracted to other guys since high school, but I was afraid to come out. I grew up in an Irish Catholic family, and my path had been laid out for me: college or military, wife, then a family. I tried, Liam. I really did." I squeezed Jack's hands to let him know I was right there with him. I wanted to crawl into his lap and hold him tight, but that would have to wait.

"The military was both a blessing and a curse for me. It kept me on the straight and narrow because fear of getting caught made it easier for me to live in denial." Jack cocked his head slightly to the side and said, "I didn't have the courage to even watch gay porn for fear someone would find out, so you know I wasn't having secret bathroom hookups at clubs." I couldn't imagine living like that and hated that anyone felt they had to. "Even when DADT was repealed, I was too afraid to be honest about what I wanted. My career and my unit meant everything to me, and I wouldn't jeopardize either, so I kept burying my head in the sand."

"What changed?" I asked softly.

"You." There was playful accusation in his words and a sly smile on his face.

"Me?" The incredulousness I felt leaked into my voice.

"You." There was no playfulness in his expression or his voice, only a green-eyed intensity that set my insides quaking. The urge to climb onto his lap grew tenfold. "The temptation to know you and have you for myself is stronger than anything I have ever felt. Everyone who sees us in the same room together knows how much I want you. Well, everyone *except* you." A coy smile split his face, and it was getting harder and harder to sit still.

"So what are you willing to do about the situation?" I asked. "This leads us back to the question I asked in your office about what you want and expect from me." My pulse raced and I felt lightheaded. I had so many questions and hoped I'd get the chance to ask them.

"First of all, I don't *expect* anything from you, Liam. I want to be strong enough to be the man who goes home and tells his family the truth, then comes back and claims you. You make me want so many things."

"Like what?" I had to know what he hoped to have with me.

"Breakfast in bed, a long soak in the bathtub after a rough night, the sight of you on the pillow next to mine in the morning." I thought Jack was done, but I was so wrong. "I want to know your favorite movie, your favorite music, the one food you can't live without, and I have to know the noises you make when you come for me."

I was speechless for long enough that Jack got uncomfortable and looked like he was second-guessing his honesty. "Don't pull away," I pleaded with him. "I... um, I've never had anyone say anything so beautiful to me, Jack. It shocks me that someone as stoic as you was hiding such lovely words."

"I honestly didn't know I was capable of saying those kinds of things until now. You make me want to be brave enough to risk everything, and it scares me to death." Jack chewed his lips nervously.

Honestly, I was scared too. What if he upset his family and things between us didn't work out? That was a lot of pressure on me—on us. Fear of rejection wasn't something I'd had to face, so I couldn't relate to his situation, but I could definitely sympathize. I wasn't willing to be an experiment for him, though. Been there, done that. Jack was being honest, so I needed to do the same.

"I crave all those things you mentioned too, but wanting them and acting on them are two different things," I said. Jack's brow furrowed, and he looked like he wanted to protest, but I wouldn't be deterred. "I've been in this very same position before, and it didn't end very well for me. I'm not willing to repeat it, especially not with you. It would hurt me a lot more if you were the one to tell me I wasn't worth the risk." I didn't want to push my memories between us, but it was the only thing I could think of to keep me from making an idiot of myself again.

"He was a fool." Jack's deep voice resonated with conviction, and it helped to soothe the hurt from drudging up painful memories. "I'm many things, Liam, but foolish isn't one of them." Jack's thumbs rubbed hypnotic circles on my hands, but it was his voice that drew me in. "I'm not going to take this to a physical level until I've had the courage to do the right thing. I'm not willing to hurt you like he did." Jack released one of my hands and cupped my face. I leaned into his warmth and savored the connection with him. I wanted to believe it would be different with Jack. "Will you just let me hold you for a while?"

"How about we hold each other?" I asked.

Jack's answering smile made my heart stutter. "Even better."

I uncurled my legs and leaned into him without question. I soon found myself in Jack's lap, which was where I'd wanted to be from the moment we sat on the couch. His strong arms held me tight against his chest, and we pressed our foreheads together. I wanted to kiss him, but I knew if I started, I wouldn't want to stop. It wouldn't take much for both of us to forget the promises spoken. I needed this time to be different, so I held firm and just let Jack's embrace be enough.

CHAPTER
Eleven

Jack

I SPENT THE FOUR-HOUR DRIVE TO THE FAMILY CABIN IN WEST Virginia thinking about recent events. We decided to have one last private memorial for close friends and family. My heart couldn't reconcile that I wouldn't see Big Jack in his favorite place or that he'd left the cabin to me.

As my tires ate up the asphalt, my mind was busy spinning out the events of the previous days. Liam and I had spent some time getting to know each other better in the days following my confession, but I had been very careful to keep my hands to myself. I needed Liam to know my feelings were genuine and encompassed more than sexual desire. The only way I thought to do that was by talking, texting, and spending time with him. My need for Liam didn't lessen; it only grew stronger until he was all I could think about.

Noah had been right. My night terrors had returned due to my emotional upheaval, but I was recovering faster, and they weren't as intense as they had been before I started treatment. Of course, having Charlie helped me more than anything. There was something so relaxing about petting him while I struggled to get my breathing under control. I reached over to the passenger seat and gave his ears a thankful scratch, and he gave me a doggy grin in return.

I'd spent more time reading Big Jack's journals and had learned how his relationship with Jeremiah had developed. It was bittersweet to read about their secret dates and stolen kisses. It was wonderful to read my granddad's words about finding love with his soulmate, but it was sad they couldn't be open and honest about who they were and who they loved. Times had changed drastically since the forties, and people were more accepting. I just hoped I would be saying the same thing about my own family and friends when I left the cabin the following day.

I spent a lot of free time thinking about the reference Liam had made to being someone's secret in the past. I wanted so badly to ask for more details, but it would just lead to anger. It wasn't fair of me to judge a situation I knew nothing about, but I wasn't always reasonable where Liam was concerned. He brought out my protective instincts, which left me stumbling over what to say or how to act.

I did know Liam deserved to be loved openly and honestly, and I wanted to be the man sharing his life. Today was the first step in the right direction for that kind of future. I had decided to come out since everyone I held near and dear would be gathered in one place. Most of the family arrived before me since they lived in West Virginia. All except my two best friends from my Ranger unit, Garrett "Sully" Sullivan and Hunter Allen. Sully lived in Pennsylvania, and Hunter lived in Ohio, but both were making the trip for the weekend to say a final goodbye to Big Jack, whom they both loved like their own. I stepped out of the Jeep and sucked the crisp mountain air into my lungs. It was always fresher and purer in the valley, and the extra nip of chill in the air helped me clear my head and focus. Right then, I needed all the assistance I could get.

Charlie climbed out of the Jeep, and we were swarmed by family and friends. I was hugged, kissed, and even pinched to within an inch of my life. Everyone was affectionate toward Charlie but respectful of his service dog stature. We gathered for a delicious meal prepared mostly by my mom, sister, and aunts. We ate until we nearly exploded and reminisced about my granddad's life. We laughed until we cried, then cried until we laughed. It was the sendoff Big Jack would've wanted. Most of my extended family lived locally and went home that evening while my parents, siblings, great-aunt, and best friends stayed at the cabin with me. I figured it would be the best time to tell them the truth.

My dad broke out the good Irish whiskey and passed shot glasses around. We tearfully toasted my granddad with a few rounds, and I started to feel a little warm from the alcohol. I decided there wasn't going to be a better time to make my confession. I had liquid courage coursing through my veins and a captive audience. I set my shot glass on the end table, stood up, and walked to the front of the great room, feeling every set of eyes on me. I turned and faced the people I loved most in the world, feeling more scared than ever.

"I'm in love." Those weren't the words I'd rehearsed during the road trip. *Love? Could I honestly say I was in love with Liam Connelly after a few heart-to-hearts and some kisses? Yes, I could.* This connection had been building for nearly two years, and I was no longer willing to suppress all the wonderful things he made me feel.

"Great! Who is she?" Mom asked.

"When can we meet her?" Declan's girlfriend, Keri, asked.

Panic was starting to set in, and the frenzy nearly made me laugh out loud at their assumptions. Then again, why would they assume anything else? I looked around the room and cataloged the expressions my loved ones wore on their faces. It only took a few seconds, but it seemed like an eternity. I saw knowing and acceptance in McKenna's and Darren's eyes. I saw confusion and a bit of suspicion on Sully's and Hunter's faces. Aunt

Bea had a smirk on her wrinkled, ninety-year-old face. My mom looked up at me with a glowing smile, while Declan looked perplexed as to why I'd make such a big deal about meeting someone. Lastly, I looked into my dad's wise eyes and saw absolutely no expression or emotion. I had never seen my dad locked down so tight, and it scared me. I didn't want to lose his love or respect.

I took a shaky breath and recalled Big Jack's encouraging words. I'd come this far, and there was no turning back. It was time to rip off the Band-Aid and start living. "I'm in love with a guy." I didn't take my eyes off my dad while I spoke. The room went completely still and silent. Nothing and no one stirred, not even the air.

"Take a walk with me, son," Dad said.

I scanned the room once again to see how my announcement was going over. Sully and Hunter didn't meet my eyes as I walked across the room, and it felt like someone had taken a knife to my heart. My mother, bless her soul, reached out and took my hand as I approached her. She kissed the back of it and offered me a watery smile. Declan, Keri, McKenna, and Darren all gave me encouraging smiles.

"I knew it!" Aunt Bea's loud exclamation bounced off the high ceiling of the great room. "That damn Stella died before she had to pay up." The mention of her nutty best friend made me smile. Bea snorted in a very unladylike way before adding, "I wonder if her lazy, no-good son, Carl, will pay up the twenty bucks she owes me. Doubt it." The last part was mumbled under her breath.

I stopped by her chair where she sat covered in an old afghan. I leaned down and gave her a kiss on her paper-thin cheek. "I love you, Aunt Bea." She patted my hand where it rested on the arm of the chair. Granddad would've been so proud of his older sister for breaking the tension and creating a little humor. I didn't linger by her side because I had to meet my father and face the consequences of my announcement.

I fell into step beside my dad as we wound our way around the front of the cabin and headed toward the small creek running through the property.

Summer hadn't quite relinquished her grasp, and the sun hadn't set over the trees yet.

"I convinced myself you were just looking out for the young man and that's why you could never take your eyes off him, but I should've recognized that look. Lord knows I've been gazing at your mama the same way you stare at Liam for forty years now." Dad let out a soft snort. "I could have done without the huge announcement in front of the entire family, my boy, but I guess you wanted to say it once and be done with it, right?"

"Yes, sir." My dad and I were going to come out of this okay. I refused to believe differently.

"Do you feel better now that you've told the truth, Jack?" Dad stopped walking, and I did the same. I turned to face him and was relieved to see curiosity was the primary emotion in his dark green eyes. "How long have you been keeping this to yourself? Have you always been attracted to guys?"

I was more than willing, grateful even, to have this conversation with my dad, regardless of how uncomfortable it was for us both. "I've known I was attracted to guys since high school, but I never acted on the feelings. Still haven't," I confessed. "I know you're probably wondering how I could know what I want before I've even… um…" I stumbled over my words, and luckily, my dad took pity on me.

"That isn't what I'm wondering at all, Jack." My dad shook his head as if he was disappointed that I'd read the situation all wrong. "I didn't need to be with your mama like that to know I loved her. I'm wondering why you felt you couldn't tell us the truth. What did we ever do or say to make you think we'd love you less or somehow see you differently because you loved a man?" Dad's brows slashed into a deep vee, and the scowl extended to his eyes and firmly set mouth. "You're my son, Jack"— his voice cracked—"and I love you. I will love whoever you bring home to meet our family."

Seeing my dad so upset cut me to the quick. "I'm sorry I hurt you, Dad. It wasn't anything you or Mom ever said or did. I'd convinced myself I was happy in my denial until I met Liam." I shrugged my shoulders and continued, "Sure, I'd found other guys attractive, and I was curious, but

I was able to push aside the temptation because my military career was more important to me at the time." I shook my head and smiled wryly as I recalled the punch to the gut I'd felt the first day I met Liam. "I couldn't say I'd feel the same way if I had to choose between Liam and a career."

"It's fate, then." Dad's pronouncement was said with finality as he wrapped his strong arm around my shoulders. "We better get back so your mama can fuss all over you. She might be sad if she thinks too hard about not getting grandchildren from you, but she wouldn't sacrifice your happiness to suit herself."

"Dad, gay men get married and have families." I smiled at him so he'd know I wasn't mocking him. "If I choose to have kids, I'll adopt them or find a surrogate."

"Adoption I understand," he said, turning us around to face the house. "I'm not sure what a surrogate entails, but your mama and I will support you no matter what you choose. You'd make one hell of a father, Jack."

I didn't yet know if fatherhood was in the cards for me. It wasn't a decision I could make on my own, but my heart swelled from his high praise. "Thanks, Dad."

Sully and Hunter were on the front porch when we returned. Their eyes met mine and held when I climbed the steps. Their wounded expressions were a far different reaction from the one my announcement had received in the house. Dad patted me on the back and nodded at the guys before he went inside.

"You could've told me, Dragon," Sully said as soon as the door closed behind my dad. Dragon was the nickname they'd given me in the army. "Sure, I would've been surprised, but I still would've had your back. Always."

"Thanks, Sully. The truth is I didn't feel comfortable enough being gay. I was in denial for a very long time, and it was easier to live the lie than tell the truth." I looked over at Hunter. "How about you? You okay with this?"

"I'm shocked, Dragon. There're a lot of things I thought you might say but loving a dude wasn't one of them." Hunter shrugged and smiled. "You were still the bravest badass in a Ranger uniform, and I'm proud to have served under you." His face turned bright red when he realized how his words could be misconstrued. "Under your command, that is."

"Relax, Hunter," I said with understanding. "I know what you meant. I wasn't going to tease you and make you uncomfortable." I reached over and slugged his upper arm playfully.

"Why not? I would," Sully said with a sneer.

"Fuck you, Sully." Hunter's words held no heat, and it looked like we'd weathered the storm pretty well.

"Be honest, Dragon. Which one of us did you fantasize about the most? I'm taller with bigger muscles, but Hunter has a bigger dick by a few inches."

"Christ," Hunter blurted rather loudly. "Quit looking at my dick."

"You swung that thing around like a prize ribbon, asshat." Sully strutted around the porch and imitated swinging a dick. "How could we not look?" Sully then turned to me with imploring eyes. "It was me wasn't it, Dragon. Be honest."

"No way, Sully," Hunter argued and shoved their friend to the side. "I smell way better, and I do have a bigger dick. It was me, right?" He batted his eyelashes at me playfully.

"You were both too much like brothers, so no." I gave them my best apologetic smile.

"That's what I'd say too, Dragon," Sully said, then blew me a kiss.

They bantered back and forth for several minutes before we bro-hugged and went inside to rejoin my family. Whiskey and beer were passed around for several more hours, but I chose to drink water. I didn't want to be hungover and feeling like shit the next day because I would be driving back to DC and staking my claim on Liam. I lay in bed that night and sent up a prayer of thanks to Big Jack for writing his letter and sharing his secret with me. He'd given me the courage to be honest and live the life I wanted.

I fell into a peaceful sleep and dreamed of a hopeful future. No more fear. No more hiding. Just love.

CHAPTER
Twelve

Liam

I DROVE TO MY PARENTS' HOUSE IN SOUTH KENSINGTON LIKE I DID every Sunday. I forced myself to listen attentively to my dad talking about the things going on at his dealership and the charity golf tournament he'd just won. I complimented my mom on her delicious food and heard all about Leah's upcoming cheer competition. Even though I had commented in the right spots and nodded when appropriate, my mom still sensed my distraction.

"What's going on, honey?" she asked as soon as I'd followed her into the kitchen to help clean up. Leah had also offered, but Mom had waved her and Dad off. "Did you finally have that talk with Chase?" Lisa Connelly might have had her heart broken by Matthew Rivers, but her disgust with him didn't extend to his oldest child. She'd encouraged me to go to Chase and had advocated for me to tell him the truth as soon as possible. I knew it disappointed her that I had allowed Chase to get to know me without being honest with him, even though she never let on.

"Yes, I finally told Chase he was my brother." Her eyes widened in surprise, and I could tell she had a hundred and one questions. "It was rough at first. He was obviously hurt I hadn't told him sooner." I grinned when I remembered that it had only taken a few hours for Chase to reach back out to me. "It's amazing how close we've become in a short time. I mean, he had already invited me to his and Gray's house for barbecues and swim parties, but this is different. This is texting funny jokes at eleven at night on a Wednesday for just the hell of it. Oh"—I laughed—"he refers to me as Uncle Liam when he's talking to his cat about me."

"I'm so happy for you, baby," my mom said as she cupped my cheek. "He sounds like a wonderful young man. Do you like his husband?"

I thought of the man my brother had married and couldn't keep the smile off my face. "Gray is perfect for Chase. They're amazing together. I can't wait for you to meet them, Mom. It's so cute when they finish each other's sentences or start speaking at the same time. They're connected like nothing I've ever seen before—including you and Dad—and I hope to have that for myself someday." My voice trailed off toward the end because I had started to think about Jack. I was too afraid to hope for a future with him, but my heart hadn't gotten the message.

"Where'd you go just now, Liam?" She sure didn't miss much. A subtle change in the tone of a voice or a slight expression and she was all over it. "Have you met someone?"

I had never talked to my mom or dad about my feelings for Jack, but not because they wouldn't have supported me. They always had my back, and I knew that. I was one lucky guy to have such awesome, supportive parents. I didn't have a big coming out moment when I was younger. My mom knew I was gay, and she didn't want me to stew or worry over how they'd feel.

One day we were at the mall shopping for school clothes when she nodded to a boy my age and said, "He's cute, don't you think?" That had been the opening I needed.

"Not my type," I'd replied casually.

"Oh, how so?" She had looked confused like maybe she was wrong about my orientation.

"I prefer the more athletic type," I'd said jokingly.

"Ahh, jocks," she'd said, nodding. "You want to hit up the sporting goods store and scope the place out?" She wiggled her eyebrows, making me laugh.

I always knew how lucky I was to have such a supportive mother, and I never took it for granted. If I could, I'd clone my mom and share her with every lonely kid who felt the sting of their family's rejection.

"Annnd, I lost you again," Mom teased.

"Sorry," I said with a laugh. "I was just remembering the shopping trip when you made it easy for me to admit I was gay. I don't think I ever thanked you enough for the way you handled that." I looked into her compassionate blue eyes and smiled broadly. "I wish I could gift a mom like you to every kid on the planet."

"That's the nicest thing anyone has ever said to me, Liam." She placed her hand over her heart and smiled brightly. "So, what made you relive that moment just now?"

"I have very strong feelings for my boss, Jack, but he's not out." God, it felt so good to tell someone about the situation. I couldn't talk to Chase and Gray about it because they both knew Jack, and it would've betrayed his trust. My mom felt like a safe option—my only option—to get some things off my chest.

"Oh, I see," she said kindly, "Are you thinking about how things went down with Kenner Wilcox?"

Kenner was the son of our family friend. Our families did everything together, including vacations, so we were thrown together a lot. Our sisters were the same age and stuck like glue also. Kenner also happened to be the first boy I had given my heart and body to, but he was too afraid to tell his parents he was gay. Bart and Jillian Wilcox wouldn't have been as understanding as my parents.

Kenner had held me tight and whispered words of love during sex, but he'd never really intended to tell his parents. He made me feel used and dirty, not good enough to love openly. I wouldn't wish that horrible feeling on anyone. I became depressed and withdrawn when I figured out Kenner's game, and my parents grew concerned. They'd approached me one evening, and I told them the truth, even if it had been awkward. A small part of me worried they would tell me to suck it up and get over it, but they didn't do that at all. They were angry Kenner had used me and started making excuses to the Wilcoxes as to why we couldn't hang out with them. It didn't take the other family long to get tired of being pushed aside before they found another set of friends to spend time with.

The Wilcoxes started making trouble at the country club where I worked by hinting around to other members that I had hit on Kenner, and he'd rejected me. Oh, he'd rejected me, but not until after he fucked me ten ways to Sunday. I could've confronted them about their lies, but it wouldn't have done any good. They would have said I was lying, and it was my word against theirs. The job wasn't worth it. They weren't worth it.

"It reminds me a lot of how I felt when Kenner and I were together," I confessed to my mom. I blew out a frustrated breath. "Jack wants me physically, but that doesn't mean he wants more from me. I won't be a dirty secret again."

"Baby, I don't want you to lose hope, but I respect that you're holding your ground. You're a beautiful person, and you deserve someone who wants to show you off to the world, not hide you."

"Thanks, Mom." I hugged her tight. "I always feel better after talking to you."

"I'm here anytime you need me, Liam. You'll always be my baby no matter how old you get." She pulled back and kissed my cheek. My phone buzzed with an incoming text. I pulled the phone from my pocket and saw the message was from Jack. "Is that him?" she asked.

I nodded and unlocked my phone to read the message.

Can I see you tonight? Jack asked.

Yes, I replied without thinking and then typed, *I'll stop in after my shift.*

I wasn't good for much after that brief text exchange with Jack. I hung out with my family for a little while longer, then drove back to my apartment to do my laundry and cleaning. My mind was on Jack and our upcoming night together. I rolled every possible scenario around in my brain while I showered and took extra care in grooming myself—just in case.

Nerves ate at my insides as I made the drive to Bottoms Up. It seemed like a waste to drive my car such a short distance, but I didn't like the idea of walking home at two in the morning. I sat in my car for a few extra minutes, chewing my bottom lip as my thoughts churned until I felt sick with worry and dread. Why did I have to think such anxious thoughts about Jack rejecting me before we had a chance to see what we could have? Why couldn't I think positively and remember that Jack Murphy was a hundred times the man that Kenner Wilcox could ever hope to be?

I reluctantly got out of the car and went in through the rear entrance of the bar, which opened onto a long hallway where Jack's office was located. I thought about stopping by his office to get the conversation over with. I didn't want to work an entire shift with my stomach tied in knots, especially if Trevor was behind the bar. My distress would be like blood in the water, and he'd be the circling shark waiting for the right moment to chomp the hell out of my leg. I was waffling back and forth on whether to stop when the decision was made for me.

Jack's strong arm snaked out and pulled me into his office before I could pass. I found myself pressed up against his closed office door once again—a familiar position but not an unpleasant one. Jack captured my mouth in a ravaging kiss, and it was like pouring gasoline on a flame, igniting my lust and longing for him. I was going to cave, regardless of my tough talk at my mom's house. His animalistic aggression had my cock hard and leaking in the confines of my underwear. Being taken by him was all I could focus on at that moment.

My hands touched him everywhere, roaming over his broad back, his smooth head, and cupping his firm ass. I was ready to wrap my legs around his waist and give myself over to him right then and there. Jack wasn't fairing any better if the growls and groans coming from his throat were any indication. He slid his strong hands into my hair and tugged my head back, arching my neck.

"I told them I was gay. Everyone, Liam. I made a huge announcement because I'm not willing to spend another damn day without knowing what you taste like, how you feel naked in my arms, and how you look lying on the pillow beside mine." His kiss-swollen lips almost distracted me from comprehending the words coming from them. I looked up into his light green eyes and saw the truth in his words. "I promise I will wine and dine you later, but this has been building up between us for too long for me to push aside another night."

My zeal dimmed somewhat out of concern for how his family had re-acted to the announcement. I placed my hands alongside his neck and felt his pulse thundering beneath my thumbs. "How'd it go? Are you okay?" A huge smile lit up Jack's face, mesmerizing me. I relaxed against his broad chest because he wouldn't be that happy if his world had just been turned upside down.

"It was unbelievable." Each word was said between kisses on my neck. I felt the scruff along his jaw scraping my sensitive skin, but it felt incredi-ble. Plus, I knew I'd be wearing his mark for the rest of the night. "My par-ents were upset that I hadn't come to them sooner and were disappointed I didn't have more faith in them, but they also understood my hesitation." Jack cupped my face in his large hands and looked at me tenderly. "I'm a very lucky man, Liam."

"I'm so happy for you." My heart pounded in my chest because the potent look in his eyes told me he was ready to move our relationship past a few relatively innocent kisses.

"Will you come home with me after your shift is over? Can I re-move your clothes and get to know every inch of your body?" Jack low-ered his head, pressed his mouth against my ear and asked, "Can I have you tonight?"

I closed my eyes and let his words wash over me. Need buzzed beneath my skin like ten thousand bees; there wasn't a single part of me that didn't vibrate with anticipation. I wanted to feel him all over my body, to have his warm, naked skin pressed against mine. I opened my eyes and saw the same want and need in his gaze.

"God yes." My breath left in a rush as I was once again crushed against his chest, but I soon forgot about the need for air when Jack's lips touched mine again. He invaded all my senses and touched me everywhere with just a kiss. I was left wondering how I'd be able to work knowing my fantasies would come true soon.

Eventually, Jack sent me to the bar to work my shift with kiss-swollen lips and scruff marks on my neck. If that wasn't obvious enough, then the obnoxious smile I wore gave me away. My face started to hurt from grinning so big and so much. I wanted my mouth to be deliciously sore from a completely different activity and then my mind went there—to lying on sweat-soaked sheets with Jack's hands tangled in my hair while I worked his dick in and out of my mouth. I knew I had to pull myself together when I almost dropped a mug of beer.

I caught Trevor's annoyed expression a few times, but I didn't let him get to me. In fact, his annoyance made me smile even brighter. I wasn't sure what Jack had said to him after he had overheard Trevor giving me shit, but it had worked. I couldn't be sure my luck would hold forever because it had to be obvious to everyone that there was a difference in the way Jack watched me that night.

He was a silent sentry, watching every move I made. I felt his hot gaze boring through my clothes and warming my flesh. It felt like hours of torturous foreplay, and it kept me on edge the entire shift. The buzzing sensation I'd felt in his office returned and had magnified until I was practically levitating by the time my shift ended.

No words were spoken when I placed my hand in Jack's and followed him to his loft. Once inside, he turned and faced me, his eyes so full of heated promise that I thought I might die from the pleasure he would give me. I half expected to be tossed over his shoulder and hauled to his room, but instead, he pulled me into a tender hug and held me against his chest.

"It feels like I've been waiting for you my entire life, Liam, and I am scared to death of messing this up. Please don't let me do that."

His concern warmed my heart. "Okay, Jack."

"And tonight isn't about getting off," he said. "I don't want to rush you and ruin everything. The intensity that I'm feeling worries me. I might hurt you or—"

I cut him off with a quick kiss. "We're going to be amazing." I waggled my brows playfully. "Now take me to your bedroom."

Jack gave me a wicked grin, took my hand, and led me to his bedroom.

"Stay, Charlie," Jack commanded as the dog began to follow us. "We don't need an audience," he told me. "I don't think either of us wants to be surprised by a cold, wet nose pressed against our asses." Charlie whined but complied, throwing himself down with a dramatic thump beside the couch.

"What about my hot tongue on your ass?" I asked.

Jack's eyes darkened with lust, and he nearly tripped over his own feet. His mouth opened, but no words came out, and I loved that I rendered him speechless.

Jack's bedroom was hidden behind a tall, decorative wall. I wanted to look around to get a feel for his private space, but I only had eyes for his king-size bed.

"So, this is where the magic will happen?" I asked, hoping to keep the mood light and curious.

When Jack didn't answer, I looked at him. The raw lust from earlier was still present, but it was tempered by nervousness.

Recalling this was Jack's first time with a man, I said, "Everything that happens between us will be amazing and beautiful."

Jack inhaled deeply and briefly closed his eyes. "I don't want to disappoint you."

I snorted playfully. "As if." Releasing Jack's hand, I slowly lifted my shirt up and over my head, tossing it to the floor. "Your move."

CHAPTER
Thirteen

Jack

"**G**OD, YOU'RE SO BEAUTIFUL," I WHISPERED. "AND I'M A LITTLE worried about your safety."

Liam smiled and crooked his finger. "I'm not afraid."

I closed the small gap between us and placed my shaking hands on his bare skin for the first time. Liam was my living, breathing dream come true and finally standing before me. My palms rested against the curve of his pectoral muscles and his heartbeat thundered beneath my hands.

I glanced up and smiled when I saw the blissful expression on Liam's face. He'd tilted his head back, closed his eyes, and let his mouth part slightly. The tip of his pink tongue darted out to moisten his lips, and that simple little action held me spellbound. Liam must have sensed my intense gaze because his ridiculously long eyelashes fluttered and parted.

The raw ache and need I saw in his hazel depths encouraged me to be bolder. I teased his already pert nipples with my thumbs until they became hard nubs. Liam made needy sounds in his throat, which made my erection throb in its cotton prison. His eyes closed again, and his head fell back as if it had become too heavy for his neck to hold up any longer. His sexy lips parted even more as he began to breathe heavier.

"Jack."

The hungry whisper sent an electric current of need zipping straight to my dick, and I was concerned I wouldn't last as long as I wanted. I had jacked off earlier so I wouldn't come too soon and make an ass of myself. I was too old for premature ejaculation, but then again, I had never been so worked up by such simple touches before either. Liam had the power to unman me and bring me to my knees.

"Liam," I said softly. "Can you possibly know what this means to me? I… We've been trying to fool ourselves for a long time." I took a deep breath while searching for the right words to say. "Expressing my feelings isn't easy for me at all." It never had been, and I didn't expect that to change just because I was falling in love for the first time.

"I don't need pretty words," Liam said tenderly.

"I don't have a lot of experience." To say I was a little rusty in the sex department was putting it mildly. Not only was I worried about rushing things, I was also afraid my performance would be less than memorable.

"Is that what you're worried about? That you won't please me?" Liam smiled seductively. "Oh, Jack, I'm positive you'll give me more pleasure than my heart can handle. As far as it being your first time with a man, I know there are differences, but your body will take over and do what comes naturally. If you're not ready, we can wait, but I have no doubts about making love with you tonight."

Making love. He was right that this felt entirely different from what I had experienced before, and *making love* felt appropriate for what I wanted to do. "I don't want to wait."

"Listen to your heart, and it will guide your hands and body. It won't fail you, and neither will I."

My hands roamed over Liam's lithe torso, memorizing every detail and appreciating the taut skin over lean muscles. His beautiful body was so different from my larger frame, and I found myself enthralled with the differences. My heart urged me to take things slow and learn every part of him while my body demanded I take and possess. I wanted to do both but wasn't sure how I could ravish and savor at the same time.

Follow your heart. Worship him with your entire being. I lowered myself to my knees and his hands instantly went to my shoulders. I looked up and found Liam watching me intently. I placed soft kisses along his abdomen and dipped my tongue into his navel as I worked his fly open. It felt like I was slowly unwrapping a gift. Liam was my gift to enjoy and treasure, and that's exactly what I planned to do.

The nervousness I'd felt earlier had been replaced with the rightness of being with him. My body trembled from anticipation, not hesitation. My hands steadied once I touched his body again. I slid them into the back of his jeans and slowly worked them down his legs, loving the feel of his crisp hair rasping against my palms. I worked his shoes off his feet, and he used my shoulders for balance as I stripped off his jeans and socks before returning my attention to the cotton-covered bulge in front of my face.

Slow. Go slow. Show him how he makes you feel.

My body took over, doing what felt natural and right to me. I placed my hands at the backs of his thighs and slid them upward until the round curve of his ass cheeks pressed against my palms. I kneaded the firm flesh there and rubbed my nose along his erection. Liam's hands went from gently massaging my shoulders to caressing my shaved head as I continued to tease him through his sexy black briefs. Liam's confident fingers traced my brow and teased the curve of my ears. God, who knew such innocent caresses could make my skin tingle all over?

I'd never blown a man before, but I had been on the receiving end, so I decided to do what felt good to me. "You'll have to tell me if I'm doing this wrong." My voice was so rough and raw I barely recognized it.

"You'll be perfect," Liam said confidently. He looked down at me with so much tenderness in his gaze. God, I hoped he was right. I wanted to ruin him for anyone else but me.

I eased Liam's underwear down his legs and tossed them aside. Finally, he stood completely naked in front of me, and he was so much better than my fantasies. Liam's dick stood proud and erect, tempting me to taste him, but I wasn't done exploring yet. I wrapped my hand around his cock, slowly working my fist up and down while pressing kisses to his pelvis. Then I nipped his tender skin, causing him to jump and cry out my name.

His precum smeared on my hand, which pulled my focus back to Liam's glistening cockhead. I couldn't resist tasting him another second. I placed one hand on his hip and fisted his dick with the other. I swirled my tongue around his crown, capturing his pearly essence in my mouth.

Liam's taste exploded onto my tongue, leaving me hungry for more and making me forget about my first-time nerves. I circled my tongue around the swollen head again, teasing his slit until he rewarded me with more of his essence. Liam's fingers tensed against my scalp, and I thought about growing my hair out again just so I could feel his hands tugging on the strands.

"Jack." There was a little more urgency when he called my name.

I kept my gaze locked on Liam's, acting on pure instinct when I rubbed the broad head of his cock against my lips, smearing his precum on them before licking it off. Liam's pupils were blown until only the thinnest circle of his hazel irises showed. Giving him pleasure gave me the courage to take more risks.

I wrapped my lips tightly around the crown and lowered my mouth as far as I could take him. I figured giving good head was something I'd learn with practice. I sucked hard, hollowing my cheeks as I pulled back up to his crown. The trembling in his legs told me I was doing something right.

"More, Jack. Please."

I worked his cock with my mouth, gaining confidence with each physical and verbal cue. I felt more in tune with his body than I ever had with my own, and I didn't let up until his entire body quaked with pleasure.

I let his dick slide from my mouth, then stood to pull my clothes off.

Liam moved as if to reciprocate the oral delights I bestowed on him, but I stopped him with a gentle hand. "I want your mouth on my cock very badly, but I don't trust my control right now."

Liam raked his lusty eyes all over my body and licked his lips. He looked like he wanted to touch me but was hesitant. I reached for his hands and placed them both on my chest. My heart beat a staccato rhythm as I felt his intimate touch for the first time.

"Anything you want," I said.

Liam's long fingers sifted through my chest hair, and he let out a purring hum. Fuck if I didn't want him to pet me and stroke me until I purred too, but that would have to wait. I was dangerously close to climax from what we'd already shared.

I led us over to my bed and pulled Liam down beside me. He immediately turned into my arms, pressing his lithe frame against mine. I'd let my body lead the way up to that point, but I started to panic once I had him on my bed. I had to outweigh him by fifty to sixty pounds, and I worried about hurting him. Theoretically, I knew Liam would stretch to receive me, but I had never done that before, and I wasn't sure of the proper technique. I mentally kicked myself for not doing a little bit of research.

"Relax." Liam's whisper ghosted across my lips. "We're going to be amazing."

Liam pressed his lips to mine and pushed me onto my back. He lay on top of me, and I loved the full-body contact of our bare skin pressed together. His confidence helped overshadow my concerns until he began to grind his erection against mine, and I felt my body preparing to release at his slightest touch. The feisty imp grinned wickedly at me, relishing my reaction to his touch. It seemed Liam would be just as feisty in bed as he was out of it.

I grinned and accepted the challenge I saw in his smile, willing my body to stay under control. "I refuse to come all over myself like a randy teenager now that I am finally living out my fantasies," I said, then rolled him over onto his back, fitting myself between his spread legs.

I pinned Liam's arms above his head and tortured him in return by rubbing our erections together, slowly and without mercy. I captured his sighs and fevered whispers with my mouth, drawing out our pleasure and teasing him until neither of us could take it any longer. I rolled back over so he was once again sitting astride me, and I let him take the lead.

"Where do you keep the lube and condoms?" It was a simple question, but my lust-fogged brain found it hard to formulate the words I needed. I finally pointed at the bedside table that housed the supplies I'd purchased. Liam climbed off me long enough to retrieve the items and lay them on the bed beside us. "I'll tell you how to prep me, then you're going to lie there and watch as I take your dick deep inside my body."

His words painted a very sexy visual, and it ratcheted up my desire until I felt like my heart might explode in my chest. "Liam," I groaned.

"We're going to be so good together, Jack. My body was made for you, and I'm going to love every second of it." Liam kissed me as he scooted his body up to straddle my waist. "Hold up your hand."

I obeyed his command, and he squeezed a generous amount of lube onto two of my fingers before rising to his knees.

"Slip your hand between my legs and tease my pucker with the lube. You'll feel it respond and quiver at your touch." Liam tossed the bottle aside and leaned over until his mouth hovered above mine. "Start with one finger, and you'll be able to tell when I'm ready for more. Then you'll add another finger and move them in and out to stretch me wider." His words were like an incendiary device, burning me up with the picture he painted. Liam angled his head and looked down at my cock. "It will take three fingers to prepare me for you. Are you ready?"

"Yeah, Ace." Liam smiled sweetly at the use of the endearment and gave me a few kisses before releasing my lips. He looked down between our bodies and watched as I touched him so intimately for the first time.

I reached between his legs and circled his tight hole until it quivered beneath my touch. I slid my middle finger in all the way with the first push. Liam grunted, and I jerked my gaze up to his face to see if I'd hurt him. The blissed-out expression on his face told me he liked the sensation as much as I did.

I was fascinated by how silky smooth and hot Liam felt inside. I worked my finger in and out several times, paying special attention to the spot inside him that made Liam purr every time I grazed it. His head fell back on his shoulders, his mouth gaped open, and his eyes drifted closed. I roamed my gaze over his exultant face and beautiful body.

"Two fingers, babe," Liam urged with a hint of desperation in his voice.

I'd never cared for the word *babe* and surely didn't think I'd want someone to use it on me, but it sounded so right coming from Liam's mouth. I carefully slid two fingers inside him and watched as he bucked his hips to ride my digits, and I couldn't wait to watch him take my cock.

Liam's gorgeous eyes had lost their focus, and it looked like he had floated to a different realm of pleasure. I couldn't wait to join him there. My three fingers met with a bit of resistance, and I feared I was hurting him, I began to pull back. "No, Jack. Don't stop," Liam urged. His eyes locked on mine, and I only saw need and want, no pain. "Give me your mouth."

I cupped the back of Liam's neck with my free hand and pulled him down for a wet, hot kiss. His body relaxed, and I eased three fingers inside him, turning and twisting them while I captured his lustful cries in my mouth. Liam broke the kiss and rose until he was kneeling over me once again. He gripped my wrist and pulled, easing my fingers from his tight passage.

My breath snagged in my throat when Liam scooted back down to straddle my thighs and make quick work of rolling the condom onto my erection. Then Liam moved up until his ass hovered over my erection. "Watch us," he said seductively as he coated my cock with more lube. "Touch me, Jack. I need to feel your hands on my body." I wanted to touch him everywhere at once but settled my hands on his hips.

Liam lowered his body until I felt the tip of my cock pressing against his puckered opening. He eased down until my crown breached the first ring of muscle. His heat and tight clench were like nothing I had experienced before, and the sensation overload threatened to crash the party before it really began. I watched, spellbound, as my cock slowly disappeared inside Liam until his ass cheeks were pressed firmly against my upper thighs, and I was buried to the root inside his body.

Liam sat there for several moments while adjusting to my girth. He rocked his hips back and forth to test his readiness, making us both groan. With a wicked smile, Liam slowly lifted off my cock until only the tip remained inside. He kept his gaze locked on mine as he lowered himself back down, sighing blissfully as he took my dick to the root again. Liam closed his eyes and let his head fall back as he repeated the slow rise and fall on my erection. His thumbs found my nipples and began to tease them while he gradually increased his pace. Small sighs became hungry growls as he gave in to his body's needs. Liam moved his hands up to my shoulders, using them for leverage as he began to ride me in earnest.

The slap of his flesh against mine and the animalistic sounds he made drove me wild. I dug my hands into Liam's tender skin and began guiding his hips up and down my dick. I didn't know how I hadn't lost my load already, but it was close.

Liam met my gaze once more. "Stroke me, Jack. I'm so close." I pumped his cock, and he lost his rhythm for a few seconds before he found it again. His nails bit into my shoulders, scoring my flesh while his ass tightened around my cock seconds before the first jet of his cum splashed on my hand and lower abdomen. "Oh, Jack," Liam cried out. I pumped his cock until the last drop of his milky essence dripped onto me. "So good," was all Liam managed to say before he started to collapse on my chest.

I caught him and rolled, pinning him beneath me. Liam automatically wrapped his long legs around my hips as I began to move inside him. I started out slowly because I was still worried about hurting him, but his grunts, pleas, and the way he dug his heels into the back of my thighs told me he wanted it harder. I was more than happy to oblige him and began to slam our bodies together, finding a perfect rhythm that took me right to the edge in just a few thrusts. Liam grabbed my ass and pulled me deeper inside him, and I lost it.

Pleasure spread like wildfire throughout my body, erupting into the most powerful orgasm I had ever experienced. I collapsed on top of Liam as soon as I was spent and buried my nose in the crook of his neck.

Liam wrapped his arms and legs around me, so I must not have been too heavy. We stayed that way for a long time, his hands caressing my smooth scalp while our breathing evened out and returned to normal.

"I hope I was worth the wait." His voice sounded unsure, which wasn't like Liam at all. Maybe I wasn't the only one afraid of screwing up the thing we had building between us.

"I couldn't have dreamed up anything more perfect than what we just shared. Thank you," I said before I lowered my mouth for a long, languid kiss. "Will you stay with me?" I asked sometime later.

"There's no place I'd rather be." His honesty and lack of pretense was sexy. Liam didn't want to play games, and I was past the age where that was remotely appealing. "It's the least you can offer since you didn't even buy me dinner before having your way with me." He sniffed haughtily, but the sassy look in his eyes let me know he was only teasing. His playful banter had my heart rate increasing again.

"I'm a helluva guy, right? If you're really lucky, Liam, I'll let you make me breakfast to thank me for the good time." Liam laughed at my fake arrogance. "Come shower with me, and I'll let you wash my back." I dropped a kiss on his nose, changing the moment from playful to sweet, then gingerly separated our bodies. I held out my hand and helped him off my bed. Thoughts of a wet, soapy Liam had my cock twitching like it might be ready to go again.

Shower fantasies paled in comparison to the real thing, though. I ran my hands all over his wet, lean body while silently begging my dick to behave because we were both tired after a long day. I gave myself a good scrub when I was done taking care of him and shut off the water. We wore matching sleepy grins while toweling off and getting back into bed.

I turned off the bedside lamp once Liam was cuddled up next to me with his head lying over my heart. I gave a short whistle, and Charlie came running into the room and jumped onto the bed. He greeted us with a reprimanding *woof woof*, then circled three times before he curled up at our feet.

Liam chuckled into my chest. "I guess he told us."

"He sure did."

I dropped a kiss on Liam's forehead and closed my eyes, feeling content for the first time in my adult life. I couldn't undo twenty years of thinking in one night. It would take time before I automatically reached for his hand or dropped a kiss on his sweet mouth in public, but that was a goal I wanted to work toward.

As I lay in the dark, I sent up a thankful prayer to my granddad before drifting to sleep.

CHAPTER
Fourteen

Liam

I SLEPT LIKE THE DEAD WRAPPED UP IN THE WARM COCOON OF JACK'S arms. I had never spent the night with a guy before, and I discovered just how much I loved being the little spoon. I could get addicted to having Jack's thickly muscled legs pressed against mine. The warmth of his breath on my neck sent electric shivers down my spine. The strong arms around my waist didn't make me feel imprisoned; they made me feel safe and wanted.

At some point in the early hours of the morning, Jack had gotten up and taken Charlie outside. He brought the nip of the early fall morning on his chilled skin when he got back into bed and curled around me, but it didn't take long to warm him back up. Soon, his morning wood pressed against the curve of my ass, and I couldn't resist pushing back against it.

"You should sleep," Jack whispered huskily in my ear, but his roaming hands didn't encourage snoozing. I wanted to push him to his back and climb on top to ride him again, but instead, I undulated my ass against his erection and relished the feel when I was rewarded with his slick precum on my skin. "Okay, Ace." I loved his nickname for me.

Jack reached around and slowly stroked my erection up and down, rotating his wrist at the crown every few passes. I moaned loudly, unashamed at the reaction he stirred within me. I loved the way he turned me inside out, and I'd be damned if I tried to hide it from him. It was obvious by the bites to my neck and shoulder that Jack was just as turned on as I was, and I hoped my uninhibited reaction to him revved him up even more.

"I want to be inside you again so badly just thinking about it has me ready to blow," Jack growled. "But you gotta be sore this morning." I was tender, but I would gladly take him again.

He wasn't the only one in jeopardy of coming at any second. Jack's cock squeezed between my ass cheeks, seeking the entrance it so badly desired. I rolled over onto my stomach, presenting my ass to him. Jack pushed my legs apart before fitting himself between them. He reached for the lube on the nightstand before spreading my cheeks and drizzling the cool liquid into my crease.

"No penetration this morning," he whispered in my ear as he bent over my back.

Jack rubbed his dick between my cheeks, and I cried out in need every time his cockhead brushed over my sensitive hole.

"Jack." His whispered name was part curse and part plea. I wanted to feel him inside me again so badly that I shook with need.

Jack gripped my ass tightly in both hands, and I loved the dominant action. He sped up his thrusts, and his breath hitched in his throat. "You felt so damn good last night, Ace." Oh, that sexy growl mixed with a sweet endearment was a lethal combination. Jack's rocking motion rubbed my erection against his sheets, and I was in imminent danger of spilling all over them.

Jack lowered his mouth and nibbled at my neck as he chased his orgasm. The slick, hot glide of his steely length faltered as he got closer and closer to the edge. Jack slid his arms beneath my chest and lay against my back, holding me tight as he rutted against me in earnest.

"I'm going to come," I warned.

"I'm right there too, Ace. Come hard for me and let me hear it." Jack sank his teeth into my neck, and I blew all over his sheets while roaring his name. It was only a few short thrusts later before I felt his hot seed spill between the cheeks of my ass and on my lower back. He moaned my name reverently as he continued to thrust, riding out his orgasm and rubbing his cum into my skin.

Jack collapsed on the bed beside me, and I rolled into him, snuggling my head beneath his chin. I knew I should get up and clean myself off, but I honestly wanted to wear his mark and smell him on my skin just a little longer. I thought I might regret the mess once it dried, but right then, the beating of his heart beneath my ear was lulling me back to sleep.

It looked like late morning when I next woke. The first thing I noticed was that the bed was colder without Jack lying next to me. The second thing I observed was a giant glass-walled shower off to the side of his bedroom. I'd been much too focused on Jack the previous evening to pay much attention to my surroundings and studied the shower with fresh eyes. Three of the walls were constructed from clear glass with the last wall heavily frosted glass. I was guessing the sink and toilet were on the other side of the frosted glass for privacy. The enclosure looked more like a piece of modern art than a shower.

Multiple shower heads and jets were attached to both ends of the enclosure, and I had to wonder who Jack had in mind when he'd designed the bathroom. My train of thought derailed the minute Jack turned and locked his green eyes on me. The object of my desire stood beneath the spray, letting the water rain down on his gorgeous body.

He crooked his finger at me, and I nearly knocked myself out on his nightstand when my foot got tangled in the sheets and I stumbled in my haste to reach him. My face heated with humiliation, but Jack's wicked smile made me forget my embarrassment. It seemed Jack liked me tripping over myself to get to him as much as he liked pleasuring me.

He met me at the shower door and pulled me in tight against him as he walked us backward beneath the hot spray. Our mouths met in a passionate foray of tongues, teeth, and lips. How had I lived so long without this? Jack's touch, his kiss, consumed me and turned me completely inside out for him. I wanted to know everything about Jack besides this crazy chemistry that burned between us. I didn't want something that would fizzle out a month or two down the road. He made me yearn for forever.

Jack slowed our kisses until we ended in a few innocent pecks. Water droplets hung from his long eyelashes when I stared into his mesmerizing gaze. The same awe I felt was reflected in his tender expression, and I rejoiced that I wasn't in this alone. Our dicks were dueling swords as if we were two Musketeers, but we both ignored them as if we'd silently agreed that we needed a different kind of bond just then.

Jack cupped my face in his large hands, his thumbs tracing over my cheekbones. "There will be plenty of time for us to discover each other's bodies, Ace. I need more from you." He dropped more kisses on my lips, then said, "Tell me everything. I want to know your kindergarten teacher's name, your first crush, your first kiss, and the name of your first dog. I want to know you better than anyone else knows you." It might not have been a declaration of love, but it had the same effect on my heart.

"I want that too," I said, tracing my fingers over the face I'd adored since we'd first met. I wanted to be the one Jack turned to when things got dark in his life, and be the beacon of light that gave him hope to fight through his battles. I had seen the dark shadows in his eyes lighten since we'd met, but they still lingered sometimes. I wanted to help him cast them out forever. It was probably too soon to confess that to him, plus I was afraid it was too deep for the light conversation we were having. "And I really want to check out your tattoo?" The request seemed innocent enough.

Jack dropped his hands from my face and turned around so I could get up close and personal with his dragon. I had to hold back a giggle as the double entendre registered in my brain. My giggle stuck in my throat, however, when I noticed the intricate details of the dragon. "It's beautiful," I said in awe. That level of talent blew me away and my eyes had a hard time figuring out where to start. I placed my hand on his back and traced the outline of the beast. "Why a dragon?"

Jack tensed beneath my touch for a millisecond before answering, "It was what my Ranger team called me." His words were spoken quietly and with reverence. It was then that I noticed the names and dates hidden among the scales on the dragon. I knew immediately those names belonged to his fallen brothers, and it broke my heart to know how deeply their loss had hurt him. I kissed each name and date as I discovered them as if they were wounds I could heal. Jack's muscular back trembled beneath my lips with every kiss. I slid a hand around him to cover his heart.

"I'm so sorry," I whispered.

Ten names spanning several years and probably many missions. If only I could find a way to shoulder some of the burden he carried. Jack covered my hand, and I realized maybe my small gesture had brought him some comfort after all.

I suspected Jack wasn't one who easily spoke about his pain. He had always seemed so stoic and reserved. I would need to be patient and understanding. I wore my heart on my sleeve and openly communicated how I felt, which was why keeping my identity from Chase for so long and fighting my growing feelings for Jack had nearly eaten a hole in my stomach. Jack would probably pull inside himself and put up a wall when times got tough. I would just need to find a way to scale the barrier to get to him.

We stayed that way for several minutes, giving and taking comfort from one another without a single word spoken. It felt wonderful to just breathe with Jack and not feel pressure to fill the quiet with words. I was quickly learning that a touch could do and mean so much more than words.

Jack's growling stomach interrupted the peaceful moment and made me laugh. "Let's get out and get dressed so I can cook you breakfast to thank you for last night," I said against his broad back, not even trying to hold back my sassiness.

Jack turned and pulled me into his arms again, staring down into my eyes. "I can take you out to breakfast, Liam. We don't have to hide away. I'm not ashamed of us." If my heart hadn't already belonged to him, it would have right then.

"I know." And I really believed that. "I'm just loving being in your space, and I don't want to leave yet." I smiled to show him how happy he made me. "Plus, there's just something about making a meal for someone to show them how much you care." Jack's eyes turned greener as unspoken emotion welled up inside him. Good or bad? I wasn't sure until a beautiful smile split his face. "How do you feel about pancakes?"

"I love them," Jack replied enthusiastically as he shut off the water. He handed me a towel before grabbing one for himself. I stood staring, mesmerized as he ran the towel all over himself until my body pebbled with goose bumps as the steam began to dissipate. Jack's eyes met mine, and I thought I heard a soft growl emanating from his throat. "Liam." His voice was a dark warning to get moving or pancakes would be delayed. Would that really be such a bad thing?

I borrowed a pair of Jack's too-big sweats and a T-shirt. I loved the feel of his clothes against my bare skin and tried to ignore the semihard erection that sprang up when I put them on. I turned my focus to finding the ingredients I needed to whip up light and fluffy pancakes while Jack started a load of laundry, including mine from last night. It seemed so normal and domestic, and it felt so right. I had expected to be nervous about the morning after, but I wasn't.

"Tell me about your family." Jack had reentered the kitchen area and was leaning against the counter, drinking a glass of orange juice I had poured for him. "What are they like?"

I poured batter onto the hot griddle pan. "My mom met my dad when I was four years old. She had answered a job ad for a receptionist at a new car dealership in town. Mom had been working a few part-time jobs, and I spent a lot of time with my grandparents while she tried to provide for us. She wanted a full-time job so she would have evenings and weekends with me. Mom got a lot more than just a job when she applied," I said with a smile. I loved hearing my mom and dad talk about their love-at-first-sight beginning. "I can't remember a single day after when Jamie wasn't present in my life. He was a father to me long before the adoption took place. Jamie was the one who taught me how to ride a bike and cast a fishing line." I laughed as a memory occurred to me. "He was also the one who talked to me about safe sex."

"He sounds like an amazing man," Jack said. "What's your mom like?"

Bubbles began to surface on the pancakes, so I slid the spatula beneath them and turned them over. "She's all kinds of awesome." I didn't try to mask the obvious adoration I had for the woman. I told Jack about my coming out experience and made him laugh. "My mom is compassionate and caring, but she's also tough. It's her house and her rules," I said with a mock sternness in my voice. "She never had to speak a harsh word or raise her voice."

"Sounds like my dad," he said.

I slid the cooked pancakes onto a plate and turned off the stove. "My sister, Leah, is an adorable but brilliant teenaged brat. She's already taking college classes while she's still in high school."

"Impressive."

"Yeah." It was the one place I didn't feel like I fit in with my family. Everyone was so settled on their goals and how to achieve them. I just kind of flitted around for a while, trying to figure out what I wanted to do with my life. I finally figured out that creating food was my passion, and I wanted to go to culinary school. I just needed to save money to make that happen.

"Where'd you go, Ace?" Would I ever get tired of that cute endearment? No, I knew I wouldn't. "Did I say something to upset you? You got this cute little frown on your face, but I'd rather see an adorable smile." He said he wanted to know everything about me, that he wanted to know me better than anyone else. That particular insecurity was known to only me, and I could easily give it to him. So I told him over pancakes and orange juice how everyone else's accomplishments made me feel irrelevant. "Are your parents unwilling to help you pay for culinary school? I'm not trying to be nosy or critical, but it sounds like they could afford to help you out, even if it's a short-term loan." Jack's brow was furrowed in concern, which I thought was freaking adorable.

"They've offered a few times." My confession earned me a raised brow and a slight scowl. "My dad built his business from the bottom up along with my mom's help. He started with very little and carved out a wonderful life for himself, one he doesn't take for granted because nothing was given to him."

"Ahhh." Jack's frown was replaced with a look of respect. "I understand how you feel, and I think it's admirable that you want to do it on your own terms and at your own pace."

"You do?" I asked.

"Yes, Liam. It's also what I did with my bar, so I know exactly how you feel." Jack leaned over and softly kissed my lips. "Mmmm, sweet. You taste like maple syrup. It's a good flavor on you." I leaned closer and tried to lure him in for more kisses, but Jack just shook his head. "I have something to show you first. Are you finished eating?"

I honestly could have eaten a few more pancakes after the previous night, but I was too eager to see what he wanted to show me. I rose from my chair and followed him back to his bedroom. He dragged a military-style trunk from the corner of his room over to his bed. He sat down and patted the bed beside him for me to do the same. Jack whistled, and Charlie came running into the room and jumped up onto the bed.

"This locker belonged to my grandfather, and no one knows about its existence except for me and now you. I want to share this with you, Liam." I knew how much Big Jack meant to him, and I was floored that he was willing to share this with me. I wasn't sure what was inside the box, but it must have been an awfully big secret if Big Jack kept it to himself. With anyone else, I would have joked about it being body parts or a severed head, but I knew it was not the time for my snarky sense of humor. Whatever was in the locker was important to Jack, therefore it was important to me.

CHAPTER
Fifteen

Jack

THE NEXT NIGHT I SAT IN MY OFFICE AND WATCHED WHAT WAS HAP-pening in the bar through the monitors instead of being present. I couldn't be out there with Liam, not with the smell of his skin so fresh in my nostrils. I had never met anyone I wanted to consume until Liam entered my life. I couldn't keep my feelings out of my eyes or my actions. I'd give anyone who looked longingly in Liam's direction a death glare. I hadn't given a lot of thought to the boss-employee part of our relation-ship, but I—we—needed to tread carefully to avoid issues with the other employees and the patrons. I couldn't ruin his tip-earning potential be-cause of my new feelings of possessiveness. Liam wasn't a possession or a trophy I had won; he was a human being with feelings, and he deserved to be treated accordingly.

I admired Liam's independent spirit and his insistence that he do things without handouts from his family. He had a strength in him I didn't know existed, and I found it to be a big turn-on. I was beginning to realize Liam had a lot of layers to him, and damn if I didn't want to slowly peel them all back one by one.

I also loved how he'd let his raw emotions show when I'd told him about my granddad's final letter to me and the contents of the locker. With Liam cuddled by my side, I was finally ready to look at the pictures Big Jack had kept of him and Jeremiah. Liam touched the photos reverently as tears ran down his face. It was beautiful how much he cared about someone he hardly knew because of how much I loved my granddad.

"We should try to find out if Jeremiah is still alive," Liam had said passionately. "We don't have to just knock on his door and out him to his family or anything, but he should know how much Big Jack loved him. Maybe he doesn't have any of these pictures and would like some of them. I mean, look at them, Jack. They were so in love." Liam held up a picture of the two men standing in front of their M4 Sherman tank with their arms wrapped around each other, both wearing matching grins. I had flipped the picture over and seen that it had been taken a few weeks before they'd been deployed to Normandy.

"You think?" I wasn't sure stirring up memories from the past would be a good thing for Jeremiah. I had no idea what path his life had taken after the German army surrendered in May 1945. What if I accidentally caused the elderly gentleman emotional harm?

"We could at least find out if he's still alive," Liam said. "If he is, we can approach his family first to make sure it would be okay for us to visit. We can just say what good friends they were and not reference their intimate relationship." I didn't miss how Liam kept saying *we* in regard to the search for Jeremiah. It thrilled me more than I was able to express at the moment. "Ben's brother, Bevan, is a private investigator. We can get his phone number from Xavier or Ben and see if he could maybe help." There it was again—*we*.

I couldn't resist Liam any longer. I brushed away the tears he'd cried for my granddad's lost love and set the journals and pictures back in the locker. Poor Charlie was sent to the living room, and I made very slow, very sweet love to my Liam. I felt our connection in every fiber of my being, but words failed me. I could only show him how he made me feel and hoped it would be enough.

I sat back in my desk chair, perplexed that I was the only man in my Irish family who couldn't communicate his feelings very well. My dad, my granddad, and my brother had no problem telling people how they felt, but I had always been more reserved. I guess if I added my aloof nature to the secret I had been carrying around for twenty years, I ended up with a recipe for a knuckle-dragging Neanderthal who grunted when he should be talking.

I knew that wouldn't fly with Liam. He'd be patient with me, and he'd never expect me to change my personality to suit him, but he'd want me to talk and tell him how I felt about things. Hell, I hadn't even thanked him for making us breakfast until we had almost fallen asleep later that night. I had a lot to learn. I would work very hard on making communication a reality because I knew one thing after just a few short days: Liam Connelly was made for me.

Yes, I had some issues to work through, and I would. I admitted to myself that the twelve-year age difference worried me, but I'd work through that too. I told myself I wouldn't worry about Liam waking up one day and deciding he wanted someone closer to his own age because all the worrying would rob me from the present, and I wouldn't waste one second of our precious time together. Had Big Jack and Jeremiah taught me nothing?

I watched as Liam and Trevor interacted on the monitor. Trevor had been better since our talk, but I still felt the tension between him and Liam. It was as if Liam anticipated snappy comments while Trevor feared saying anything out of worry he'd piss me off and lose his job. Firing Trevor wasn't something I wanted to do, but I'd be damned if I let him screw up the chemistry of our team. I watched as Trevor pointed down to the opposite end of the bar from where Liam was working. Liam looked over, and his entire body stiffened. He casually removed his bar towel from his shoulder and started to walk to the other end of the bar.

I hit the remote to switch cameras so I could watch him. I should've felt like a voyeur, but my gut told me Liam was about to face something unpleasant. His posture became stiffer when he stopped in front of a toothy asshat at the bar who grinned at Liam like he was his long-lost love. I knew in my heart that I was looking at the guy who'd made Liam feel like an unwanted, dirty secret. *Kenner.* It was all I could do to stay in my seat, but Liam wouldn't appreciate any posturing, grandstanding, or chest thumping out of me. My guy would want to handle it on his own like he did everything else—at his pace and in his own way.

Liam's stiff posture didn't relent, and even Trevor looked concerned as he walked away from the pair. I should've given Liam the privacy he deserved, but I couldn't look away. There was an obstinate side of me that needed to see if Liam still harbored any feelings for the guy.

I tried to be objective as I studied my enemy's appearance. He was tall, blond, and very handsome. This stranger was the epitome of every toothpaste commercial I had ever seen and dressed the part of a spoiled, rich guy. I knew better than to judge a person by their appearance and the circumstances of their birth, but I didn't want to be objective and fair when it came to Liam's heart and happiness.

By all appearances—and by appearances, I meant this Kenner guy's lustful gaze—he wanted Liam back. Well, that was too damn bad because Liam was mine. *All mine.* Liam didn't seem receptive to anything Kenner had to say because his posture remained stiff and unfriendly. Liam leaned a little over the bar and crooked his finger. The asshole's grin grew impossibly wider as he tilted forward to get closer to *my* Liam. I didn't have time to get jealous because Kenner's grin immediately turned into a grimace within seconds.

"That's my boy," I said out loud when Liam walked away without a backward glance. I felt a stupid grin splitting my face, and I didn't care. Charlie gave a *woof* from his couch, thinking I was talking to him. "You're my boy too. There's plenty of room," I said, tapping a spot over my heart. Charlie made a doggy groan and might've rolled his eyes if he could.

Charlie was used to it being just the two of us, but it seemed like he loved Liam almost as much as I did. *Love.* It was too soon to tell him, too ridiculous to even ponder, but it was true. I was head over heels in love with Liam Connelly. I just had to wait until the time was right to confess my feelings.

I could almost hear Big Jack's voice telling me there was no time like the present. If Granddad were here, he'd tell me to can the excuses and tell Liam how I was feeling. Big Jack would remind me to love him with everything I had because tomorrow was never guaranteed. *Surrender your heart.* Blurting out my feelings the same night Kenner had shown up at the bar would've looked suspicious as hell.

Liam went back to work his side of the bar and didn't glance down at the opposite end once. I shamefully watched on the monitors but consoled myself that I didn't go out there and make an ass of myself. Well, not until Country Club Kenner got lippy when Trevor reached a point where he refused to serve him more alcohol.

Trevor held up his hands as if to say he didn't want any trouble, but Kenner's mouth moved a mile a minute. I couldn't hear his words, but I didn't need to because Kenner's facial expressions and body language said it all. He was being told no, and he didn't like it. It was the same reason why he didn't leave right away when Liam had rejected his advances earlier. He was biding his time because Kenner wanted Liam back and Kenner was the kind of guy who always got what he wanted.

"Not this time, pal," I growled as I strode out of my office. I felt Liam's eyes on me as I walked behind the line of barstools filled with patrons. I lightly tapped Country Club Kenner on the shoulder when I really wanted to grab him by the back of the neck. I wanted brownie points for my restraint. "It's time for you to leave, buddy." My voice was firm and fair and held no hint of the resentment and disgust I felt. "Call him a cab, Trev."

"Yes, sir."

Kenner turned around, raking his eyes up and down my body with a lecherous glare. "Aren't you a long, tall drink of tap beer?" Since Kenner had been knocking back the top-shelf liquor, I wasn't sure if the guy was insulting me or complimenting me.

"Not interested, pal." I kept my voice calm and controlled.

"Seems to be the consensus in this shithole," Kenner said, looking around in disdain. Then he locked eyes on Liam and smiled lewdly. "Although, you do hire beautiful bartenders." I sensed Liam was watching our confrontation, but I didn't dare look at him. I'd give too much away, and it would only make it more difficult to get Kenner out of my bar and into a cab. "He's still so beautiful," he said wistfully. "I used to lose myself inside him every chance I got. I blew it, though. I had hoped I could tell him I was sorry, and he'd give me another chance. My life sucks without him."

I was starting to feel sorry for the guy, knowing I'd be miserable if I'd blown my chance with Liam too. Then the dickhead opened his mouth and obliterated any ounce of sympathy he'd garnered.

"Maybe I could just talk him into a fuck for old time's sake," Kenner said. "Keep your liquor, barkeep. I'll just sit here and drink soda until the bar closes, then I'll have Liam take me home with him."

"That's not going to happen, buddy." The growl in my voice must have caught his attention because he swung his drunken eyes toward me.

"It's not?" His question came out slurred.

"No, it's not." I moved closer until only he could hear me. "Liam is coming home with me. He's mine, and I don't share. Ever. Have I made myself clear?"

"Crystal," Kenner said with a leer. "You want to keep that greedy, tight hole all to yourself. Can't blame you," he said, then hiccupped.

I'd never wanted to plow my fist into someone's face as badly as I wanted to hit that piece of shit, but I held back. It wouldn't be fair for me to pound the shit out of him in his drunken condition, but all bets were off if he ran his mouth like that sober.

"Get out of my bar while you still have the ability to walk on your own," I snarled. "Don't ever come back here again."

"I'll walk him to the door," I heard Trevor say from behind me. "I got this, Jack, if you'll take over for me while I put him in the cab." I was grateful for Trevor's intervention. I nodded my agreement and walked away from Kenner before I did something I knew I'd regret.

I met Liam's anxious gaze as I rounded the bar. I wanted to kiss him but settled for placing my hand at the small of his back, hoping it eased his tension. Liam leaned into my touch for a moment, but the heat from his body calmed my racing heart.

I had no idea if Liam was coming home with me after work. I wanted to go all caveman and toss him over my shoulder, take him to my cave, and mark him with my scent. Christ! It seemed like I was regressing from my earlier vow to converse more. Sure, communication came in many forms, but I had meant using my mouth to talk.

It didn't take Trevor long to return to the bar, and I went back to my office. Charlie met me at the door because he sensed my stress. I scratched his ears and back like I always did, and he helped calm me down. I vowed to do some actual paperwork instead of stalking Liam through the monitors like a lovesick fool.

The bar closed at two, and I waited to see who brought the tills to my office so I could process the deposit. The tingling up and down my spine told me it was Liam before he even knocked on the door. He walked in without waiting for my response. Our gazes met and held while he set the tills on my desk. Instead of leaving like he used to, Liam walked around my desk to stand beside me. I scooted my chair back so I could get a better look at his face, and Liam climbed onto my lap, straddling me.

My hands went to his waist and automatically pulled him tighter to me. I looked up into his hazel eyes and saw the same heat that burned through my body. Liam lowered his mouth to mine and kissed me stupid while I gripped his hips up and pulled him closer. He broke the kiss just as quickly as he'd started it and gasped for air for a few seconds.

"Tonight, I'm going to introduce you to your prostate," Liam declared, then rose from my lap and smiled wickedly at me.

"Hell yes." It was all I could manage to say because my brain was overloaded with images of Liam with his finger or cock in my ass. Both were incredibly sexy options, and I was eager to surrender my body to his explorations. "Hurry up and close down the bar," I demanded with a swat on his ass.

I whistled happily as I put the deposits together and locked them in the safe. Charlie remained on the sofa, but he'd pinned his ears back like he was mortified over my scandalous behavior. "Get used to it, pal." I would fight tooth and nail to keep feeling like I did just then—hopeful and ridiculously happy.

CHAPTER
Sixteen

Liam

I CAUGHT TREVOR'S SLY SMILE WHEN I RETURNED TO THE BAR. I GAVE him a saucy little finger wave and got back to work, grateful that the tension between us was gone. I had to be mindful that Jack was my employer and not just my lover. I couldn't just go into his office and jump him any time I wanted. I nearly cringed when I recalled the declaration I'd made in his office. *Ask a dude if he wants you to fondle his hole, don't just assume!*

Thankfully, Jack seemed to be turned on by my declaration, and I wondered if he was curious about more than a prostate massage. Would Jack consider letting me top him? I couldn't stop thinking about the feel of him wrapped around my cock. That line of thinking spelled trouble since I was still surrounded by the crew. I shifted my focus to something that would deflate my burgeoning arousal. *Kenner.*

Did he really think he could waltz in here after all this time and sweet talk me back into his bed? Was I so pitiful that I couldn't possibly find someone to love in the nearly four years since I'd walked away from him? Did Kenner really think I'd shove aside the humiliation he'd caused me for a quick, dirty fuck?

"You've wiped that same spot for several minutes, honey," Mel teased, interrupting my irritating thoughts. "Who was the jerk who came in earlier?"

"Ex." My reply was succinct and dripped disdain.

"Ahhhh," she said knowingly. "They're like assholes, baby doll. We all have them, and they all stink."

We laughed at her accurate comparison briefly before we went back to our tasks. The quicker I finished my task, the faster I returned to Jack and Charlie. My excitement mounted with every step we took toward his loft. I wouldn't let my nerves get the best of me and make our exploration awkward. I'd let things progress naturally and let Jack tell me what he wanted.

Charlie jumped onto the couch as soon as we reached the loft and looked at us broodingly before sighing deeply and closing his eyes. Jack took me by the hand and led me to his room where we unhurriedly removed our clothes between kisses. I wrapped my hands around his erection and playfully tugged until he followed me to the shower.

"I smell like wings and beer when I'd much rather smell like your soap," I told him. "Later, I want *your* scent all over my skin."

"God, you slay me," Jack replied.

The hot water felt nice but not nearly as good as Jack's warm, wet skin pressed against mine. I kissed him hungrily and roamed my hands up and down his back before grabbing two handfuls of his tight, muscular ass. I slipped a finger between his cheeks and teased him with featherlight caresses along his crease. Jack panted into my mouth, and his grip tightened on my hips, silently encouraging me to be bolder.

I wanted to do more but not in the shower. I wanted to see him sprawled across his bed when I trailed my tongue along the same path my fingers had just taken. I broke our kiss and stepped back, reaching for his bar of soap. I was so caught up in his lustful gaze that I lost my grip on the bar, and it fell to the shower floor and slid behind me. Jack looked down at the soap, then back at me with a wicked grin on his face. He cocked his brow, daring me to pick it up.

I dropped to my knees in front of him and forgot all about the soap with his erection so close to my face. I wrapped my lips around his dick and enjoyed the way his breath hissed between his parted lips. I reached between his legs to palm his firm sac while I continued to suck as much of him into my mouth as possible, never once breaking eye contact. I wasn't going for a pretty seduction. I wanted raw and dirty responses from him, and I got my wish.

I begged Jack with my eyes to take what he needed from me. I wanted to trigger the same caveman persona I'd witnessed in the bar. Jack fisted his hands in my hair and gave me what I craved, but he kept his thrusts controlled and even as if he was worried about hurting me. His big body shook all over and lusty growls escaped between clenched teeth as he fisted my hair tighter.

My dick begged for friction, but I ignored it in favor of pleasing Jack. He was getting close. His thrusts became sharper and erratic, his nails scored my scalp as he chased his climax. I breathed through my nose, relaxed my throat, and fondled his balls.

"Liam, I… Fuck me! So good… don't want it to end." His thrusts lost any sort of rhythm, and his balls grew taut in my palm. "Pull back," Jack commanded.

No way. I gave my head a slight shake, letting him know I was there until the end.

"Liam!" His hoarse shout echoed off the shower walls as he came. I swallowed his essence while Jack rode out the last of his orgasm. He eased his dick from my mouth and collapsed back against the glass wall. "That… was…"

"Sexy and incredible?" I suggested when Jack ran out of breath. I fumbled around on the shower floor until I came up with the soap, then rose to my feet with a happy smirk on my face. Jack watched me roll the bar of soap in my hands until they were good and lathered. "I'm not done with you," I told him as I returned the bar back to the ledge. I washed the front of him from top to bottom, taking special care with his sensitive cock. I soaped my hands again and gestured for him to turn around by circling my finger in the air.

Jack smiled wryly but said nothing as he turned. I took my time running my soapy hands all over his muscular back. I stood on my tiptoes and bit his neck, eliciting a grunt from my sexy man. I eased my soapy fingers along the crevice between his lush ass cheeks.

"Liam." My name was a whispered plea, but for what, I wasn't sure. Did he want me to stop? Did he want more?

"I want to taste you right here," I said, circling his tight pucker with my finger. "Will you let me?" Jack answered me with a grunt, then spread his legs, giving me better access to the treasure I sought. I wanted to linger there but decided to wait until I had Jack laid out before me like a buffet on his bed. I finished washing him, then gave myself a quick once-over while Jack watched my every move. I was careful not to touch my cock too much because I didn't want to ruin all my plans.

I loved the feel of his eyes on me as we toweled off, and I raked my gaze over the length of him as well. I couldn't imagine a time when I would look at him and *not* find him beautiful. It wouldn't matter to me if he quit working out tomorrow and went soft around the middle. The real man— the one who lived beneath the beautiful body and handsome face—was more precious to me than his looks or physique.

Jack held out his hand, and I went to him without hesitation. He kissed me with a soft tenderness I never would've expected from him, and all my wishes for the caveman disappeared. This was so much more than a kiss between two men; it was a union of souls so profound I expected the earth to move.

I pulled back from our kiss and playfully guided Jack backward until his legs bumped into his bed. "On your stomach," I commanded, pushing him down. Jack scooted up toward his pillows and lay on his stomach.

I climbed onto the bed, then remembered to retrieve a condom and lube. I set them aside, then sat astride Jack's hips so I could massage him. I needed him good and relaxed for what I had planned.

I loved the play of muscles beneath my hands and the blissed-out sighs that escaped his lips. I made a mental note of which spots pulled the most reactions from him for future use. I massaged along his spine and scooted down his body until I was kneading a tight knot at the small of his back. Jack spread his thighs and I fit myself between them.

Once I worked the knot loose and had him nearly boneless, I began to massage his firm ass cheeks. I had expected a slight hesitation or at least a little tension, but all I got was a deep masculine groan that he'd muffled with his pillow. I swatted his ass playfully and said, "I want to hear how I make you feel. No hiding it from me."

"I love your sass," Jack rumbled, "but hell if it doesn't make me want to take you over my knee and spank your ass red."

"Really?" I don't think I saw that coming. "Okay." Jack raised his head and looked at me over his shoulder. It was hard to say who was most surprised or turned on by that particular idea. With Jack's eyes still on mine, I scooted down in the bed until my head hovered over the round cheeks of his ass. Goose bumps pebbled his skin the second my breath ghosted over his flesh. "If you don't want—"

"I do." Jack nodded for emphasis. He bit his bottom lip when I licked my lips to moisten them.

I placed tender kisses and love bites all over his flesh, loving the feel of his need vibrating beneath his skin. Jack reached down and sifted a hand through the strands of my hair. It felt so good that I nearly closed my eyes, but I didn't want to lose our connection.

I placed the tip of my tongue at the top of his crack and pulled his cheeks apart, exposing his hole. I heard his breath hitch as I slowly licked down until I reached his tight bud. I flattened my tongue and licked up and down several times, stopping to tease his opening with each pass. Jack's ass cheeks flexed and he rutted against the sheets. I amped up my seduction by getting my thumbs to join in the fun. I used them to pull his creased flesh tighter so I could tongue it open. Jack dropped his head forward onto his pillow as if it was too heavy to hold up any longer.

"Liam," he moaned loudly. "Fuck, that feels... so damn good. I never... Jesus," he shouted when the tip of my tongue penetrated his ass. "Ace," he keened as I rimmed him until his hole was pliable and greedy. I kept teasing Jack until he begged, "Fuck me. I want to feel you inside me."

I dropped a kiss on his rosette while reaching for the condom and lube. I kept tonguing his ass with teasing licks until my cock was fully sheathed and lubed. I poured some lube on my fingers and eased one inside his welcoming hole. As tight and hot as he was, I wouldn't last long.

I prepared Jack as lovingly as he had prepped me the night before, then placed the head of my dick at his entrance. I held my breath when I pushed in far enough for my crown to breach the snug ring of muscles, forgetting to breath as they clenched my dick in a heated chokehold. Jack pushed back against me, and I groaned as his tight channel swallowed my dick inch by inch.

Jack bucked his hips beneath me once I was fully seated, but it wasn't an attempt to dislodge me, not at all. The action was accompanied by whispered words. "Love me, Ace."

It wasn't the first time I'd topped a man, but it was the first time I'd topped a man I loved. It felt completely different, just as it had the first time I'd accepted him inside my body. I'd had loveless sex before, but now I knew how it felt to make love. There was no comparison, and I would never settle for anything less than what Jack gave me. I moved slowly in and out of him until I felt my orgasm building to a crescendo.

"More, Liam. Harder." Jack's voice was strained as he begged. He slid a hand beneath his body, and started stroking himself. Next time, I would take him face to face so I could watch his strong hand working his cock while I pegged his prostate. "So close," he cried, and his body tensed beneath me as he came.

Jack's ass squeezed my cock so hard I couldn't hold back any longer. I pulled out of him, quickly removed the condom, and stroked myself until I came all over his ass. I painted his flesh and loved that he would wear my scent all over him. In two short days, I had become a complete Neanderthal.

I picked up the condom from his bed and threw it away in the bathroom trashcan, returning with a warm washcloth. Jack remained quiet while I cleaned us both up, then gingerly rose to his feet and crossed the room. All my energy left me, so I tossed the washcloth on the nightstand and sagged onto the bed.

Jack opened a closet somewhere on the other side of the room, but I didn't turn to see what he was doing. I heard his bare feet pad back across to the bed. Jack walked over to me and placed his hand beneath my chin, raising my head so I had to look into his eyes.

"Can you stand up long enough for me to change the sheets, Ace?"

"Be quick," I told him sassily, earning myself a quick slap on my ass once I was upright. I gasped at the sudden sting on my flesh. Suddenly, I was starting to feel more alert.

"Huh-uh," Jack said, shaking his head. "You might make my heart feel sixteen again, but my body doesn't agree." I pouted for a few seconds before helping him strip the bed and remake it. "I'm going to need to start taking vitamins to keep up with you." He sounded playful, but I still looked over to see if he was serious. Did our age difference bother him?

"Hardly," I snorted. "I suppose I should start working out more since you're in much better shape than I am."

Jack put an arm on my hand to still me. I looked up at him and found him frowning at me. "I think you're perfect just the way you are, and I don't want you to change anything."

"I wouldn't change anything about you either, including your age." I gave him a pointed look and saw a knowing smirk when he realized I had set him up to make my point.

"That spanking is looming closer and closer," he growled and pulled me into a hug.

"Promises, promises," I returned in a singsong voice as we settled back in bed.

Jack whistled for Charlie and turned off the light. It was a routine I was more than willing to get used to. "Liam," he said right as I was about to drift off in his arms. "I want to hire Ben's brother to find Jeremiah. I've been giving what you said a lot of thought, and it feels right to try to find him. If he's alive, I want to give him that photo of the two of them standing in front of the Sherman tank. If he's passed on, then I'll rest easy knowing they're together again."

"I'll get Bevan's phone number from Xavier tomorrow so you can talk to him whenever you're ready." I burrowed even closer because Jack Murphy was the stuff that dreams were made of, and he was mine, all mine. God, I had fallen for him hard and fast. It was both scary and exhilarating at the same time.

"Thank you, Ace," Jack whispered sexily into the night. "Will you come with me?"

"Of course." I'd go anywhere with him.

Jack turned onto his side facing me, holding me tight against him. I nuzzled his chest hair with my nose before I tucked my head beneath his chin. I couldn't get any closer to him unless I crawled inside him. I should've felt too trapped to sleep, but I felt safe in Jack's strong arms. The sound of his heart lulled me to sleep, and I found myself in the exact same position when I woke the next morning.

CHAPTER
Seventeen

Jack

I MADE AN APPOINTMENT WITH BEVAN ST. CLAIRE FOR LATER THAT week. I was excited to begin the search for Jeremiah, but my enthusiasm was tempered by my relentless need for Liam. He had chosen to go to his own apartment instead of staying with me the last few nights, claiming he didn't want to wear out his welcome. Liam wouldn't change his mind no matter how many times I assured him that would never happen.

The quiet solitude of my loft was no longer welcoming and relaxing. I missed the vibrancy Liam had brought into my life and home. Even when he was quietly reading, he put out a comforting vibe that hummed along my skin. As much as I missed him in my bed, I felt his absence most in the kitchen, where he liked to tinker and experiment with food. I simply missed breathing the same air as him.

Thus, I was grouchy—yet determined—as I drove to his apartment to pick him up. I hadn't gotten my physical or emotional Liam fix in a few days, and I was putting my foot down later that night. He would be coming home with me, or I'd follow him home. I *would* have him in my arms all night long.

My crappy mood evaporated as soon as I pulled up and saw Liam step out of his apartment building. His dark jeans made his legs look really long, and he paired them with a deep red Henley, a stylish brown leather jacket, and a scarf. I hadn't really noticed a lot about guy fashion until Liam. He had an effortless way about him that made him look fashionable without being fussy.

The early October sun shone down on him and brought out the streaks of gold in his hair. I knew from experience that those lighter strands would turn darker as fall turned to winter. It was probably pathetic that I had harbored these little details in my heart instead of stepping up and admitting how badly I wanted him sooner. I couldn't change the past, but I sure as hell could live out my heart's desires instead of secretly hoarding them like a dragon.

"Hi," Liam said with a huge smile when he got inside my Jeep.

I grabbed his scarf in my fist and tugged his upper body over the console, kissing him with every ounce of miserable longing I had felt the last few nights. Our kiss was so fierce it was almost brutal, and neither of us could get enough. My body burned with need and want. My balls felt swollen from the need for release because using my hand just wasn't going to be enough, not after having Liam.

Our embrace was getting out of hand in a hurry, so I reluctantly pulled back from his tempting lips. "I would've come up to get you," I told him once I caught my breath.

"Then we would've been late," he replied, running his hand along my scruffy jaw. It made me want to peel off his scarf and rub my rough jaw along his neck until I marked him as mine. "I've missed you too." I loved how he could read me when I struggled to verbalize my thoughts. He made me want to be more than I thought I could be.

"So much, Liam." Our eyes stayed connected for several long moments, and I was certain my smile was as sappy as the one he wore. "Charlie and I have been two lonely bastards without you." God, it was the fucking truth. Charlie had been giving me pitiful looks as if he was begging me to go find Liam and bring him back. I wouldn't be letting my dog down that night. "I have to warn you, Ace. I've got you now, and I'm not turning you loose. I'll throw you over my shoulder and drag you off to my cave so fast you won't know what hit you."

A sexy smile lit up Liam's face. "You make me so damn hot." He reached between his legs and adjusted himself to get more comfortable. I wasn't sure how he was going to get comfortable in those tight jeans. I couldn't wait to pull them off, although I doubted we would get much farther than the entrance table. I only needed to work them down to his knees to access what I craved. "We better get going or it won't matter to me that we're in your Jeep in broad daylight. The things you could do to me while I held on to the roll bar. Mmmm, I don't think I'd even notice the nip in the air."

I nearly swallowed my tongue. We had twenty minutes to get to Bevan's office, but it was suddenly the furthest thing from my mind. Instead, I was trying to think of a private place where I could pull off, remove the top, and give Liam the fucking his eyes were begging for.

"Later, baby," Liam promised in a soothing tone. "I've missed you just as much. I haven't slept worth a damn, and I've learned my lesson. You'll have to throw me out if you want me to leave from now on."

"Never going to happen." I put my sunglasses on, shifted my Jeep in gear, and headed to Bevan's office. "I'm not going to tell him there was a sexual relationship between my granddad and Jeremiah," I told Liam after a few minutes of comfortable silence. "I don't think it's necessary for Bevan to know that in order to find Jeremiah, and I feel like it would betray Big Jack's confidence." I reached over for Liam's hand before continuing, "It feels right telling you, but I don't plan to tell anyone else. The only exception might be Noah."

"Noah?"

"He's my PTSD therapist," I explained to Liam. "He's pretty casual since most of his patients are alpha-type soldiers who probably aren't comfortable talking about their feelings with a psychiatrist." I looked over at Liam and gave him my innocent face. "Not me, of course. I'm the height of enlightenment."

"Uh-huh, except the part where you grunt and carry me over your shoulder to your loft and unleash your inner caveman on me," he said with a raised brow and a smirk. "I'd hate to see how you were before Noah got a hold of you." I stiffened because I wouldn't have wanted him to see how I was before Noah and Charlie had worked their magic on me. "Jack, I didn't mean that the way it came out. Damn." He growled in frustration. "I would've wanted you then just as much as I do now. You never would have been broken or damaged to me. I would have seen beneath the trauma and still found you." Liam sounded like he was on the verge of tears, and that wouldn't do.

"Liam"—I squeezed his hand—"I know you didn't mean anything hurtful by your remark. Honestly, I'm glad you didn't know me before I got help. I don't ever... I *won't* ever go back there again. It was the darkest, deepest pit in hell, and I refuse to drag my loved ones there with me again. Big Jack found Noah for me and practically dragged me to his office, and I am thankful that he did every single day." I glanced over and found Liam still watching me. "Noah helped me through the darkest times of my life, and he's become a friend. After I read Big Jack's letter, I needed someone to talk to, and it seemed natural for me to tell Noah I was gay. His encouragement helped me face up to my feelings for you. Once I held you in my arms, I knew I had to be the man you deserved and tell my family the truth." *Maybe I did have a little Irish poet in me after all.*

Liam brought our joined hands to his mouth and dropped a kiss on the back of mine. "I'm grateful he gave you the push you needed to be honest with yourself and the rest of us."

"I haven't shared any of Big Jack's journal entries with anyone else."

My voice was raspy with emotion. "That's just for us. Noah only knows about the letter Big Jack wrote to me before he died."

"Thank you for including me in something so special." Liam cleared his throat before continuing, "I agree Bevan doesn't need to know they were in love. It isn't our story to tell." Liam got me like not many did.

I pulled up in front of Bevan's building and parked the car. I shut the Jeep off but didn't make a move to get out right away, and neither did Liam. Once again, the way Liam used *we* and *our* when talking about Granddad's revelation and the search for Jeremiah moved me deeply. The words weren't forced or contrived; they just naturally rolled right off his tongue because they were spoken from the heart. That's why they meant so much to me.

I almost blew the special moment when we stepped out of the Jeep and Liam reached for my hand. I tensed up, and he pulled his hand back, his body stiff at the perceived rejection. *Get your shit together, Jack.* I stopped on the sidewalk and reached for Liam's hand, tugging him around to face me. I kissed him right there on the crowded sidewalk, not giving a damn who was around or who it might upset.

"I'm not ashamed of who I am or how I feel about you," I said just in case the kiss wasn't enough. "I'm a work in progress, Ace. Twenty years in the closet," I reminded him with an expression I hoped mirrored the one Charlie gave me when he was in trouble and wanted forgiveness.

"You're forgiven, Jack." Liam rose onto his tiptoes and kissed me quickly before linking our fingers and tugging us toward the building. Once inside, he smiled politely at the receptionist. "Hello, we have an appointment with Mr. St. Claire."

"Are you the Murphys?"

"Um… he is." Liam blushed cutely, and I couldn't help but chuckle. *Liam Murphy.* It had a nice ring to it.

"I'm sorry," she said looking back and forth between us.

"No problem. I'm still trying to make an honest man out of him," I teased, hoping to ease her embarrassment. Liam scowled mockingly at me, and I shot him a playful wink.

"Bevan will be with you in just a few minutes," she said with a laugh. "Would either of you like something to drink?" We both declined and took a seat in the lobby.

"Chase and Xavier are practically brothers," I said. "So, does that make Xavier your brother too?"

Liam cocked his head while he pondered my question. "I'd be honored to be Xavier's brother if he'd have me."

"I'm sure he'd be just as honored to have you as a brother." I opened my mouth to say more, but Bevan's office door opened, and he stepped into the lobby.

"Hey, guys," he said cheerfully. "Come on in."

I'd only seen the guy once when Chase and the gang had held Ben's birthday bash at the bar. Bevan had been reserved and a little distant. I had recognized the signs of disillusionment in his dark blue eyes, and I wondered at the cause when Ben seemed so happy. Then I noticed the way he'd watch the happy couples around him, and I knew exactly what ailed him. It was the same way I felt watching Liam while he worked in my bar. I longed for Liam the way I'd suspected Bevan longed for love.

There was a notable difference in his demeanor and his face had transformed from disconnected to engaged. I noticed three framed photographs on the credenza behind his desk as I sat down in the chair in front of him. The first was a large group shot of Ben and Xavier, Bevan with a dark-haired beauty, a man who appeared to be their father with his arm around an attractive woman, and a ginger-haired guy. I didn't know who all the people were, but they appeared to be on a boat and having a great time.

The photograph in the middle was just of Bevan and the dark-haired woman who I suddenly recalled was Xavier's sister, although I couldn't remember her name. Bevan had his arm wrapped around her shoulders and she was leaning into him. They looked happy and in love, and that was most likely the reason for the change in Bevan's demeanor. Love did that to a man.

The final picture was much smaller, and it looked like an ultrasound picture of a baby, but I wasn't exactly sure what the hell I was looking at. I looked back at the picture in the middle and noticed the woman's pregnant belly. I had been so zoned in on their smiling faces that I hadn't noticed she was expecting.

"How's Ellie feeling?" Liam asked, and I knew he was talking about the woman in the photos.

"She's doing great," he replied with a happy smile. "Not much longer now. Only eleven more weeks. We're all getting excited to meet little Sofia."

"That's a lovely name." Liam sounded wistful, and he grinned from ear to ear.

"Thank you. So, what can I do for you guys today?" Bevan asked, bringing us to the reason for our visit.

"My grandfather passed away recently. After his funeral, I found some photographs of him and a good friend from his army unit. They lost touch after the war ended in 1945, but my granddad still thought highly of his friend up until the day he died. I was hoping you could help me find him. I'd really like to shake his hand and tell him"—my voice broke briefly—"how much his friendship meant to my granddad. Also, I thought he might want some of their photos to keep for himself."

"I'm very sorry for your loss, Jack. I'd love to help you look for your grandfather's friend. Wow," Bevan said excitedly, "this is so much better than a cheating spouse case." We laughed at his joke, which helped me regain control of my emotions. "Tell me everything you know about your granddad's friend, starting with his name. And, if you have it, I'd especially like to have his army unit number, and I will do everything I can to track him down for you."

Bevan opened his laptop and asked me questions for several minutes while taking notes. So far Granddad's journals hadn't mentioned where Jeremiah was originally from or anything about his family. I had to wonder if they spent every second focusing on each other and not the life that was waiting for them when their dreams crashed and burned to the ground. I told Bevan I'd let him know if I discovered anything else that might be helpful.

I felt lighter and happier after we left Bevan's office. We were doing something good for two men who had loved each other and never had a fighting chance at the kind of happiness I was building with Liam. I would never take my freedoms or this man for granted. To prove it, I reached for Liam's hand first and earned a smile that melted my heart.

CHAPTER
Eighteen

Liam

"**T**HESE ARE THE CUTEST BABY BOOTIES I HAVE EVER SEEN," Chase cooed as he looked over the broad selection. We were picking out baby shower gifts for Ellie, and I could already tell he was going to go overboard.

"That's what you said about the other pair you just picked up and put in the shopping cart." I loved teasing my brother whose heart was as big as he was. "I thought you had a list of things she wanted," I said as I looked at a rack of infant dresses. I had to admit some of the outfits were the cutest things I had ever seen. It was hard to imagine my baby sister had ever been small enough to fit into such tiny clothes.

"I do have a list, and I'll buy a few things from it, but I can't seem to stop myself from buying stuff like this. I mean, seriously." His big brown eyes lit up with love and awe as he held up a tiny pink-and-gray-plaid dress with a matching headband. "Sofia is going to look amazing in this dress," he said and added it to the cart.

Chase pushed the cart toward a display of cute little baby towels. "They're so soft," he said as he ran his hand over a set with pale yellow ducks on them. "Towels and washcloths are on her list," Chase said with a wink. He added the duckies to the cart and a baby elephant set too. "Jacob loves bath time so much, and he has several of these." There was no disguising how much he wanted a baby of his own. His best friend, Ava, and her husband had had a baby about two months ago. Brandon and Ava had named Chase and Gray little Jacob's godparents, and it was a role they took very seriously.

"So, what's been up with you lately?" Chase said.

"You mean beside me gaining a brother and a boyfriend in the same week?"

Chase snorted. "You didn't just gain a brother and a boyfriend," he said. "You've gained a whole community."

And I was so damn lucky to have them. "Well, my ex-boyfriend showed up at the bar and caused some trouble," I said.

"Whoa." Chase followed up his one-word response with a low whistle. "Is the guy still among the living?"

"Yes," I said, then snickered. "Jack's caveman reaction was fucking hot, though."

"I bet." Chase grinned wryly. "Did you argue afterward or something?"

A blush heated my skin as I recalled what had happened afterward. "Or something."

Chase snickered and said, "You should see the blissful expression on your face right now. Gram would be so proud." His eyes widened. "Speaking of Gram, did I tell you she would be joining us for lunch?"

"Um, no."

"I asked her to come and formally meet you." He broke into an evil laugh that had more than a few heads turning to look in our direction.

"Sorry to throw you under the bus, but I figured I'd give her a new pet project so Xavier and I can have a break."

"*I'm* a pet project now?" I tried to sound offended, but my laughter ruined it. "Thanks a lot."

"Xavier's coming too, so she'll probably go easy on you."

We paid for our purchases, then headed over to a Mexican restaurant where Xavier and Gram were already waiting. Gram stood and gave us all hugs, but I knew right away something was wrong. She wasn't her usual vibrant self. Her worry lines and pinched lips told me she had something heavy weighing on her mind.

"Chase and Liam, I need to tell you something." Gram picked up her glass of ice water and took a long drink.

"Easy there, tiger," Xavier teased. "You'll get brain freeze."

Gram abruptly set the glass on the table, and said, "Matthew Rivers stopped by my villa at the retirement village well over a year ago. I don't remember exactly when."

"Gram, you never told me." Chase sounded shocked and hurt. "Why?"

"Honestly, a rage came over me like I'd never experienced before, and I didn't give him the opportunity to speak. I told him I blamed him for my daughter's death and slammed the door in his face. He didn't tell me he was dying. He didn't tell me you had a brother," she said in a pleading voice. "I would never have kept a brother from you."

"Gram, I don't know what to think," Chase said. "I know you'd never hurt me deliberately, but he was my father, and he wanted to atone for his mistakes."

"It just shows how selfish he was," she nearly spat. "What kind of man waits until he's dying to apologize to his sons for abandoning them? Where was his remorse the past twenty years when it could've mattered? Who does that? A self-centered son of a bitch, that's who."

Silence fell upon our table. "She's right," I said, finally breaking the silence. "It was a horrible feeling to meet our dad just to find out he's dying. I mean, he had a cab waiting. A cab, Chase. Gram is right, who the hell does that? 'Hey, I'm your dad. We never met, and I can't stay because I'm dying. Find your brother.' *Poof!* Then he disappeared into the night in his cab."

"Sounds like a horrible cable movie," Xavier said. "I hope they don't buy my music. I don't want to be associated with that kind of thing."

Everyone chuckled except for Gram. "Please forgive me, Chase."

Chase stood up and walked to his grandmother. She rose to her feet, and he pulled her into his arms. "I know you'd never do anything to hurt me. I have Liam, and for that I will be thankful, but otherwise, I don't care about Matthew Rivers."

All the tension and worry faded from Gram, allowing her sparkle to shine through. We placed our orders and were probably two minutes into eating fresh chips and salsa when Gram turned her shrewd eyes on me. "So, sweetie, have you let that hot stud Jack Murphy catch you yet?"

"Um…" I looked at Xavier and Chase, but there would be no help coming from those two jackasses. Instead, they fist-bumped each other and sat back in their chairs with matching grins.

"He looks like a pirate. Have you seen the way he looks at you? My lord." She began to fan herself.

"He's my… um… We're dating. Yes, dating." My statement was met by a scowl from Gram and unmanly giggles from my two older brothers.

"*Dating*? Honey, please tell me there's more than that going on."

I wasn't sure if I should crawl beneath the table and hide or run for the exit. "Yes, ma'am," I finally said.

The two jackasses across the table were all gloating smiles until Gram turned her laserlike focus back on them.

"Chase, when are you going to give me a great-grandbaby?" Chase opened his mouth to speak, but nothing came out. She turned her eyes on Xavier, and I saw him shrink down in his chair a bit. "And when are you going to make an honest man out of Ben?" I gave them the same shitty little grin they had given me while I was being interrogated. It was hilarious now that the shoe was on the other foot.

Afterward, I went back to Jack's loft where I had my second big surprise of the day. Jack's mother was standing in his kitchen coaching him while he stirred something delicious-smelling in a large pot. "You just need to let it simmer for a few hours, and you'll be ready to go."

"Hello," I greeted them softly. They both spun around, and two sets of eyes stared at me in momentary surprise.

"Some guard dog you are," Jack said to Charlie, who had flopped down at my feet for a belly rub.

"Hello, Liam. How are you, sweetheart?" Claire Murphy removed her apron and laid it on the counter before she came over and gave me a tight hug. "I'm so glad you got back early so I could see you before I had to leave."

"You're leaving already?" I didn't want her to go. This woman was very important to Jack, and I wanted to get to know her better.

"I have theater tickets for tonight with my sister. I'm staying with her for a few days, and I'd love to get to know you better while I'm in town." She looked lovingly at Jack before turning back to me. "You're so important to my boy, and I want to know all about the guy who snagged the dragon's heart."

"Mom," Jack sighed as a slight blush creeped up his neck.

"I'd love that," I said honestly. "I'd love to cook a meal for you before you head home."

"That sounds perfect." Claire kissed me on the cheek and stepped back. "I really must be going." She gave us both hugs and kisses once more before she left.

"What's going on?" I asked Jack, sniffing the air. "It smells like marinara sauce."

"I wanted to cook you a special dinner and asked for my mom's help since she was in town." Jack walked up to me and placed his hands on my hips. "She might be Irish, but she makes the best spaghetti and meatballs."

"Thank you so much." His sweet gesture warmed my heart and other regions. "Do we have a while before dinner? I ate a pretty big lunch, and I wanted to work some of it off."

"Couple hours," Jack said casually. "You want me to take you to my weight room and put you through the paces?"

"If by that you mean bending me over your equipment and fucking me, then yes."

"I love the way you think, Ace."

CHAPTER
Nineteen

Jack

I ADDED THE SPAGHETTI NOODLES TO THE BOILING SALTED WATER and gave the meatballs and sauce a good stir. I took a look at my mom's note about toasting the bread with homemade garlic butter that she'd helped me prepare. I was just going to buy a frozen loaf and bake it in the oven, but she insisted I make it fresh for Liam.

I smiled to myself as I thought about my beautiful man sleeping peacefully in my bed. I wasn't sure what had been said during his baby shopping and lunch date with his brothers and Gram, but he'd come home randy and ready to fuck and I had the claw marks on my back to prove it.

I sliced the loaf of Italian bread in half and spread the garlic butter liberally—as my mom instructed—on both halves and placed them on a cookie sheet. I checked my notes for the oven temperature, and I noticed it said low broil. *What the fuck was a broil?* I'd used the oven for frozen shit, but I'd never had to broil anything. I felt an urge to wake Liam up so I wouldn't mess up his special dinner.

I was studying the buttons on the fancy oven when my phone rang on the counter. Without thinking or seeing who was calling, I hit the speakerphone button and answered the call.

"Hey, Dragon," Sully said. "How's it going?"

"Hi, Sully," I replied. "It's going pretty good, but I'm trying to figure out how to use the broiler option on my oven." I felt stupid confessing how inept I was in the kitchen. "I see a bake and a self-clean button but not a broil."

"Wow, you sound so domestic." I only heard genuine surprise in Sully's voice, no judgment or disgust. "Are you making your boy dinner?"

"He's not my boy, Sully. That sounds kind of gross. He's a grown man," I said wryly.

"Okay, fair enough. You're making your boyfriend dinner?" I laughed at his attempt to get it right and appreciated the lack of awkwardness in his voice. He had accepted what I'd told him and that was that. "You don't like the term boyfriend either?"

"I do, but I'm not sure it works to describe how I feel. It sounds kind of juvenile, you know?"

"What then?" Sully asked. "Lover?"

"That's too cheesy," I said after rolling it around in my brain for a few seconds. "I honestly can't think of a word to describe our relationship. It seems deeper than any generic label I could slap on it."

"Soul mate?" Sully suggested.

"Warmer."

"Damn, I hope you were smoother when you told the guy you're in love with him. I mean, that drama queen display at the cabin was over the top." I felt a shift in the air, and my body responded to Liam's nearness before he had even made his presence known. Sully was oblivious and kept talking. "I have an announcement to make," he said mimicking my voice and my confession at the cabin. "I'm in love." He sighed dramatically on the other end of the phone, but I was too busy paying attention to the pair of hands snaking around my waist and sliding up my chest. "With a guy," Sully said with dramatic flair.

I felt Liam's hot breath falter against my shoulder and his body went rigid where it pressed against mine. I realized then that he'd overheard Sully teasing me about the way I'd come out to my family, which included a confession that I was in love. Something that I had not told Liam—the man I'd confessed to loving. Liam recovered from his surprise and retaliated by twisting my nipples.

"Ow. Fuck!"

"What's wrong, Dragon. Burn yourself?"

"Um..."

"Dragon will have to call you back, Sully. He has some serious esplaining to do," Liam said, doing a bang-up impersonation of Ricky Ricardo's heavy Cuban accent. I never would have guessed Liam was an *I Love Lucy* fan, but he sure had that famous line down pat. Liam reached over and hit the button on my phone that disconnected the call. There were several long moments of silence where we just breathed, then he said, "Is it true? Did you tell your family you're in love with me?"

I turned and looked into Liam's gorgeous hazel eyes. Maybe spaghetti and meatballs on a Wednesday night wasn't the most romantic way to confess my feelings, but it would have to do. "I did tell them I'm in love with you. I made a grand statement to the entire room just like Sully said. I even had the big dramatic pause he teased me about just now."

Liam's smile was so brilliant, and I regretted not saying the words to him sooner. I cupped his face in my hands.

"I am in love with you," I said. "I can't say for sure when it happened, I just know it did. You captivated me from the very first day we met. You woke something inside me that I could no longer deny. That lust turned into love long before I tasted your kiss or knew what it felt like to be inside your body or lie with you in my arms all night. I didn't need anything physical to know what was in my heart."

"Wow." My sassy Liam didn't have much else to say, which was probably a first since I'd met him. He closed his eyes for several moments, and I hoped it was because he wanted to pull my words into his heart and hold on to them, to absorb them into his body and imprint them on his brain. I also feared that he didn't feel the same way about me, but if he gave me a fighting chance, I'd win his love at any cost. Then he opened his eyes, and the joy I saw in their depths told me all I needed to know. "I love you too, Jack. I probably have from the very beginning."

I saw his lips tremble, and I couldn't resist pressing little kisses to them. I felt like every sacrifice I'd made and hurdle I'd jumped had led me to this moment, and I was never more grateful that I had waited for him. I may have given my body to others before him, but I had never given my heart.

Liam's stomach growled loudly, causing his eyes to widen in embarrassment. "Help me figure out how to broil this bread, and we'll be ready to eat. Damn it!" I'd forgotten about the spaghetti noodles boiling on the stove. "I hope they're not ruined." I stirred the pot to break up the giant clump of pasta in the water. I checked the time on the stove clock and saw they still had two more minutes to cook. "Oh man, the spaghetti will be done before the garlic bread is ready. How do people get this timed out right?"

"Can I please help you?" Liam's soft voice didn't hold an ounce of mockery. "You went to so much trouble. Let me help you finish it up."

"Okay," I agreed without hesitation. The last thing I wanted was to ruin our dinner. "First, help me figure out how to broil this bread. Where is the broil button? I'm such an idiot."

Liam studied the fancy stove and scowled. "You're not an idiot. The designer of this stove is, though." Liam pushed the menu button a few times and found the broil option. "There," he said after he chose the option for low broil. He slid the pan into the oven and stepped back. "Do you have any vegetable oil or cooking spray?" I handed him the can of cooking spray and watched as he hit the water with a few squirts of it. He put the pasta spoon back into the water and stirred, separating the noodles far better than I had.

"Huh, that's an easy fix," I said.

I loved the domesticity of setting the table, serving food, and chatting about our days while we ate. I was afraid my dinner would taste horrible, even though I'd followed my mom's instructions step by step. It turned out well, and I was pretty damn pleased with myself.

"So good," Liam said, licking his lips. If he didn't stop, I'd work up a totally different kind of appetite. "Huh-uh," he said, shaking his head. "I recognize that look, and you're not having your way with me until I'm good and stuffed." He cocked his head to the side, realizing how dirty his statement had sounded. "Eat," he said as he pointed toward my plate with his fork.

"Okay." It was hard to chew food wearing a stupid grin on my face, but I did the best I could. "Ace, I'm not always good with words," I said a few minutes later. "I made this dinner because it's what my mom always did to show her affection. This was my favorite dish, and I wanted to make it to show you're important to me."

"I love it, Jack." His earnest expression matched the sincerity in his voice. Liam was an open book, and I loved that about him. There was no subterfuge or games. Just Liam. "I wish I knew your mom was coming, though. I would've been home sooner."

"She'll visit before she returns to West Virginia. I can't wait for my family to get to know you better." I'd meant what I said. They were going to love Liam so much. "What do you want to do tonight?"

"How about story time?" Liam suggested. "I'd love to know what happens next for Big Jack and Jeremiah." He must have felt my hesitation at moving forward in the journals. "Jack?"

"Ace, we're getting close to the part in the journals where the guys were deployed on D-Day. I'm not sure how graphic the descriptions are going to be, and it might trigger a PTSD episode. I want to know their story too, but I don't want to catch you by surprise. I can sleep on the couch when we get to that part if you're worried I might hurt you in my sleep."

Liam stood up and shoved his chair back so quickly it startled me. I scooted back too, and he climbed onto my lap. "Jack," he said, cupping my face, "I love all of you, not just some of you. If you don't want to read it, then we won't, but don't you worry for five seconds that I will somehow view you differently if you were to have a PTSD episode. You have me and Charlie, and we'll help you through it. Tell me what to expect and what to do to help you, and I'll do it."

"I'm not sure how to explain it, but I'll try." I rubbed a hand over my shaved head while I searched for the right words to say. "I can tell you that the dreams feel so real that I can feel the reverberations of the explosions, feel the sand in my face, and smell the blood of my fallen brothers." Liam looked at me with compassionate eyes. "I shake and sweat violently and sometimes I thrash around. I've never shared a bed with someone during an episode, so I don't know how I'll react if you touch me. Some men have gotten extremely violent and have woken up to find themselves choking their loved ones. Ace, I don't want to hurt you. The dreams aren't as intense as they used to be. Therapy and Charlie have worked wonders, but I can't be sure I won't hurt you."

"I'm sure, Jack."

"Okay, but if you wake up to find me in the midst of a night terror, move yourself to safety and let Charlie do his job. Will you promise to do that, Ace?" Liam nodded his agreement. "Let's do it, then." I pulled him to me for a long, hot kiss. Liam poured us both a glass of wine while I retrieved the journals. I clicked on the gas fireplace and snuggled on the couch with him by my side. "I love you," I whispered into his hair, "so damn much." He opened his mouth to repeat the words to me, but I kissed him instead, long and deep. I pulled back slowly and looked at the blissful expression on his face. Liam's eyelids finally fluttered open, and he gave me the smile I loved so much. "Ready?" He nodded, and I opened the journal to where we'd left off.

It was getting harder and harder to find alone time with Jeremiah as we neared deployment to the European front of World War II in April 1944. One night, we were finally able to find a quiet spot, and I made love to him for the first time. It had taken months for us to make the final leap because we knew there'd be no turning back once we did.

Holding Jeremiah in my arms was the sweetest moment of my life. We were facing so many uncertainties, but all of it felt so far away when I held my soul mate close to my body. If I had truly known just how much I stood to lose, I would have held him closer for a lot longer.

Instead, we were afraid of getting caught and the repercussions we faced if that happened. Neither of us wanted to let go, but we didn't have a choice unless we wanted to have our lives ruined. In some part of my mind, I had to have known he was slipping away from me, that I was going to lose him forever, but I refused to listen. I wanted it all, and I foolishly thought I could find a way to make it happen.

Oh, Jeremiah. I wish I had told you how much I loved you. I thought we had more time.

Liam sniffled and curled closer to me, tucking his head under my chin. His hot tears soaked through my shirt. "So sad," he whispered.

"I know, Ace." My heart broke for the two men who'd loved each other so much but had never said the words. Hell, that could've been me without my granddad's intervention. I couldn't imagine how hard life was for gay men back then. It made me so appreciative for the people who fought so hard for the rights I hadn't even thought I wanted to claim. It also furthered my resolve to find Jeremiah at any expense. If he was alive, I wanted him to know just how much Big Jack had loved him. It was the least I could do for both men. I looked down at Liam in my arms. *We,* I amended.

That night, I held Liam a little closer and fought off sleep a little longer. I couldn't get my granddad's heartbreak out of my mind. There wasn't anything I could really do to fix it, and I hated that helpless feeling, but I could live my life in a way that would make my granddad proud. I would claim all the rights he had been denied.

CHAPTER
Twenty

Liam

I T HAPPENED LIKE JACK SAID IT WOULD. HE WAITED ABOUT A WEEK before reading further in Big Jack's journal, and then I understood why he hesitated. Jack was afraid he'd have a PTSD episode, and I wouldn't be able to handle it, regardless of what I'd said. Probably somewhere in his alpha brain was the fear that I would somehow see him as less of a man while he was in a vulnerable state. Like with all aspects of Jack, I needed to be patient and understanding.

I was sound asleep curled up next to him and was awoken by a cold dog nose pressed against my cheek. Charlie sensed what was happening to Jack before he made his first sound of distress. Later, I would marvel at the miracle that was Charlie, but right then I only wanted to help him bring Jack comfort.

I reluctantly removed myself from Jack's arms, even though they tightened around me as if he didn't want to let me go. I had hesitated for a few seconds after Jack tried to pull me back, but Charlie whined softly like he was pleading with me. I promised Jack I would move out of the way and let Charlie do his job, so that is what I hesitantly did. I kneeled on the bed and watched as Charlie moved in beside Jack.

I watched helplessly as Jack began to mumble in his sleep. His words were indecipherable, but the rawness of his voice told me he was in a dark, scary place. The mumbling was followed by trembling as a layer of sweat began to cover Jack's skin. Tears ran unchecked down my face because I wanted to go to him, to comfort him, but I had promised I wouldn't. Jack was more afraid of hurting me than he was of revisiting his own personal hell. I kept my promise no matter how badly I wanted to break it.

Charlie began to nudge Jack's neck with his nose and whine. It wasn't Charlie's normal whine. It was deeper in tone and seriousness but not quite a growl. He pressed his furry body tight against Jack's and continued to nudge and whine until Jack was finally still and quiet. I wondered what it was about Charlie that could safely rouse him from a night terror when the touch of a human could be perceived as a potential threat. It was just another mystery about how the brain worked and how it processed stimuli. Whatever the reason, I was so grateful for Charlie.

"Good boy, Charlie." Jack's voice was thick with sleep and distress as he scratched his dog's ears. "Best boy ever." Then he looked over at me. It was hard to make out his expression with nothing lighting the bedroom except his digital alarm clock. I desperately needed to know he was okay. Charlie had done his part, and now it was my turn. Charlie jumped off the bed and exited the room with a *woof* as if he was proud of himself or maybe it was a doggy version of an eye roll because he knew what was going to happen next.

"Hi," I said softly as I tentatively straddled Jack's lean hips. "Are you okay?"

Jack raised a hand and gently wiped away my tears. "I'm better than okay." I saw him swallow hard in the dim light before he spoke again. "Will you shower with me? I want to wash the remnants of the dream away." He didn't have to ask me twice.

I took the soap out of his hand once we were beneath the hot spray. Washing away the sweat and the lingering pieces of his dream were things I could do for him. I lovingly soaped and rinsed his entire body before he spoke again.

"The nightmares aren't as severe now." Jack pulled me against him and held me tight. My body reacted to his closeness and the slick glide of water on his skin, but I ignored it. "Thanks to therapy and Charlie, I'm able to handle them so much better. And now I also have you. It's a wonderful feeling to know you've seen me at my most vulnerable and aren't afraid or disgusted." Hot, intense eyes looked at me with such naked adoration that I could barely breathe.

"You do have me, and I was never afraid or disgusted. All I wanted to do was help you, even if that meant doing nothing while Charlie worked his magic." The mood had started to shift in the shower from somber to sensual as the presence of willing, naked flesh made its presence known. I gave him a wicked grin seconds before I kissed him and let my hands slide around to cup his firm ass cheeks. "And I will do anything to make you feel good right now."

"Anything?" He cocked a brow and offered me a suggestive smile. He started backing me up until I was almost against the wall.

"Anything," I affirmed.

"Let's play, shall we?" The wickedness in his eyes should have worried me a little, but I knew I was safe with him. Jack would never hurt me, but I couldn't help but wonder what he was planning. He captured my mouth in a hot, possessive kiss and completely obliterated my train of thought. "I love you," he whispered hotly against my lips after he broke our kiss for air. "I'm not sure how I deserve a man like you, but I promise I won't take you for granted. I know I'm not always what you need me to be, but I'll continue to try harder. I *will* get there, Ace."

I saw his arm move in my peripheral vision, but I was too lost in his eyes to give it much thought. "I love you too. We'll get there together."

The words of love rolled off my tongue naturally and were met by his radiant smile. This time they were also met with a jet of hot water spraying my ass. I wasn't prepared, and I jumped in surprise, which quickly turned into lust when Jack gripped my ass, spreading my cheeks wide so the jet could massage my hole.

"Too much? I can adjust the pressure if it's hurting you."

"Mmmm. Not too much." It was surprising but very sexy. Jack reached behind me with one hand and maneuvered the nozzle so it teased up and down my crack before he left it aimed at my entrance.

"You unravel me, Liam, with every touch, every sigh, and every kiss. I wanted to think of a way to unravel you just a little too." Jack's big hands firmly massaged my cheeks while the jet continued to tease my pucker.

"It's working."

My head felt so heavy suddenly, and I let it fall back against the shower wall. Jack lowered his head and began alternating kisses and bites along my neck. I gasped when he marked my collarbone with a love bite. I loved when he claimed and marked me. I couldn't get close enough to him to ever suit me, so wearing his mark of possession centered me.

I cupped Jack's face and stared into his eyes. "I want to get tested so we can make love without anything between us."

"You want to feel me bare inside you?" The rough timbre of his voice told me how turned on he was. "You want to take me bare too?"

"Yes."

Jack said nothing more, choosing to show me how he felt with his touch and his kiss. He shut off the jets behind me and reached for the condoms and lube he kept on a corner shelf away from the shower spray. I took the condom wrapper from him and proceeded to suit him up. Jack spun me around, and I presented my ass to him, bracing my hands on the shower wall.

He took his sweet time stretching me open, teasing and torturing me like he always did. He never rushed, which I appreciated, but there were times I wanted to feel a little more bite when he entered me. I expected him to press his cock to my pliable opening, but instead he turned me back around. I'm sure I looked confused, but it didn't last long.

Jack hoisted me up, and I automatically wrapped my legs around his waist. The cold press of glass against my back was the exact opposite of his body heat warming my chest. The fact that he was about to wall-bang me in the shower sent my lust soaring to stratospheric heights. I gripped his biceps with my hands as the slick glide of his cock filled me. It was an awkward position but not an uncomfortable one, and I found myself wiggling on his dick.

Jack pulled my hips out a little from the glass wall and began to stroke slowly in and out. I loved the strain and flex of his biceps beneath my hands as he took me. I loved his height and bulkier build but never more than when he manhandled me so easily.

"You want this without condoms, Ace? You want to feel me spill deep inside you, marking you as mine?"

"Please." The image alone had me ready to come. I wanted to close my eyes and give myself over to the fantasy, but I couldn't look away from his intensity. "I need it." I did need to feel marked and claimed by him. I didn't know why, and it wasn't something I had ever wanted before Jack. I didn't know where the need came from, and I decided I wasn't going to question it. There was no harm in wearing his little love bites or the feel of his release inside me as long as we were safe and got tested first. It was our business what we shared privately.

"You drive me wild, Liam. Just when I think I have you figured out, you go and surprise me again."

Jack increased his thrusts, and his grip on my ass tightened exponentially. He teased the taut skin of my stretched hole, stimulating the nerve endings and sending flames licking through my core. Jack widened his stance, pushing my thighs even farther apart. His strokes became long and hard as he drove us toward the finish line. I was incapable of speech by that point. I had to let the whimpering sounds clawing their way out of my throat do all the communicating for me.

"I'm close, Ace. I want us to come together."

I let go of one of his biceps, knowing he wouldn't drop me, and stroked myself to the same rhythm of his thrusts. "Jack." His name sounded like the plea it was. I needed a closer connection. More of him. All of him. Jack lowered his mouth to mine and kissed me, knowing exactly what I needed.

My ass tightened around his cock as my control splintered and my orgasm erupted inside me, spilling over my hands and against his stomach. Jack was right there with me, growling into my mouth as he thrust a final time and filled the condom he wore. I felt the heat of his release through the barrier, but it wasn't enough. It would never be enough with him.

Jack and I washed up after we caught our breaths and returned to our bed. I had come to think of it as our place in such a short time, probably too short, but I was done questioning every damn thing we did or said. It felt right, and I was going with it.

This time I was the one who whistled for Charlie to return to bed once we were settled in. If the dog resented my intrusion into his life, he never let it show.

"Good boy," I said to Charlie. I gave his ears a good scratch, just how he liked. I found myself tearing up as I recalled the loving way the dog had helped Jack safely come out of his nightmare. I laid my head over Jack's heart like I did every night so that the steady beat of his heart could lull me to sleep.

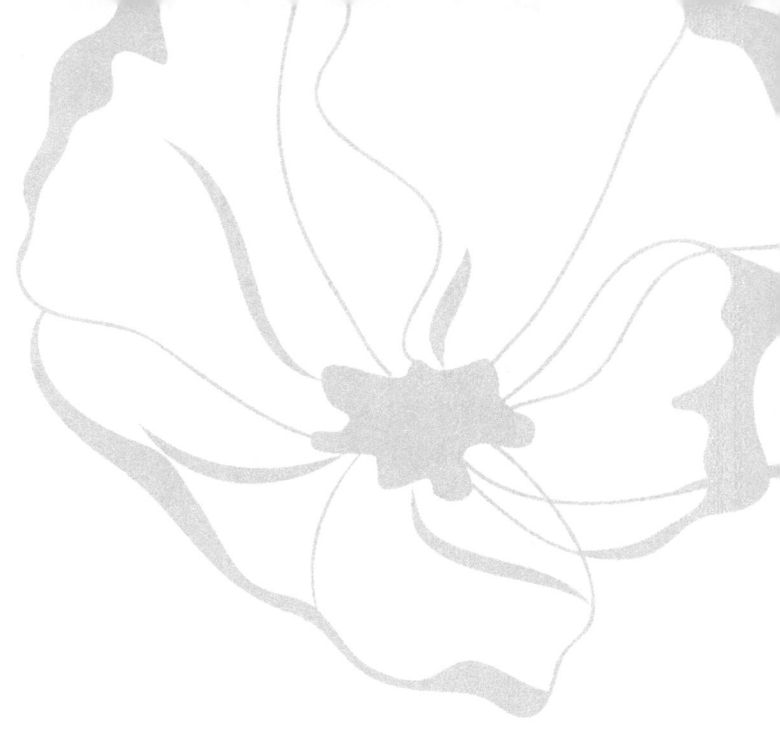

CHAPTER
Twenty-One

Jack

B EFORE I KNEW IT, HALLOWEEN WAS UPON US AND NOT A SINGLE
night passed without Liam sleeping by my side. Thankfully, I didn't
have another nightmare since I'd read Granddad's D-Day journal
entry. That night his words about the horrific deaths of his brothers-in-
arms mixed with my memories of similar deaths. The bloody waters off
the coast of France turned into the bloody sands of Iraq and Afghanistan
in my dreams where I was helpless to save the men under my command.

Either the dream wasn't as bad as the ones in the past, or I had just
become better at handling them. Charlie had brought me out of the nightmare quickly, and I wasn't nearly as shaken as I used to be, but I suspected
Liam being there was a big part of it. His worried face was the first thing I
saw when I'd opened my eyes. I automatically sought him out, and seeing

the love and concern shining in his eyes helped me push away the remnants of the nightmare. Liam obliterated any thoughts of the dream with his loving hands and whispered words of love—not to mention his dirty talk about wanting to feel me raw inside him.

We got tested and had stopped using condoms. I hadn't really expected there to be much of a difference without them, but it was a lot hotter and more intense. I think the difference had more to do with the emotional closeness rather than losing the thin layer of latex. We had entered a phase where we had committed more than our hearts to each other. It felt like forever.

I had taken Liam to West Virginia for a long weekend so he could meet my family as my boyfriend. They already liked Liam from the few times they had met and, of course, my mom had become even more smitten with him since her visit to DC. Liam had made her chicken marsala, and my mom was completely wowed by his cooking abilities. Mostly, Mom loved the way Liam loved me, which she'd told me before she left to head home. I wanted the rest of the Murphy clan to know and love him like I did, and I was certain they would.

We chose to stay at the cabin instead of my folks' house for obvious reasons. I wanted the freedom to make love to Liam in every room of the place. The interior was a lot more luxurious than people might expect. Liam surely wasn't expecting the master bath to have a copper bathtub big enough for two in front of a huge stone fireplace, but he loved the surprise. And I loved sharing it with him.

I smiled at the memories Liam and I had made that weekend. They went beyond sexy times in the tub and how he rode me like a bronco in the back of my Wrangler while holding on to the roll bar. I loved the natural way he fit in with my family and the easy way he spoke and engaged with them. Had I not already been head over heels for him I would've fallen hard right then.

He laughed, he loved, and he made me feel all those wonderful emotions too. I caught the happy gleam in my family's eyes when they saw us bantering back and forth about mundane household chores. I heard my mother's soft gasp when I cupped Liam's face in my hands and kissed him in front of everyone. I realized then that my family had been waiting for that moment for a really long time—the moment I brought home the person I'd share my forever with.

As crazy as it might sound, I wanted to ask Liam to marry me right then, but I held back for a few reasons. I still needed to meet his family, and an old-fashioned part of me wanted to ask his parents for their blessing. Where that had come from, I had no clue. I just knew it was the right step for us. Second, we had only been dating for a short while, and I didn't want to rush him. He loved me. I loved him. I knew I was staring into my future every time I looked into his eyes, but I worried about rushing him. He'd made it clear my age wasn't an issue, and I believed him. Still, I wanted to make sure his parents got to know me and approved before I asked him to be mine forever.

Liam and Chase talked me into a Halloween costume karaoke competition at Bottoms Up. The bar was nearly filled to capacity the night of the event, including all the usual suspects. Liam wouldn't tell me what song he and his brother were going to perform. I pouted, cajoled, and even threatened to withhold sex, but he wouldn't tell me, or it would ruin the surprise. In fact, Chase, Liam, Xavier, and Ben were all hiding up in my loft until it was time for them to come down and perform. I thought they were taking the competition a little too far. The winner got a plastic trophy, not a new car.

My first surprise of the night was when Gram and Lennie showed up. Gram was dressed like Elvira, Mistress of the Dark, and Lennie was dressed up like a 1930s mobster. They both looked amazing.

I had only met Gram on a few occasions, but I'd liked her instantly. She reminded me so much of my granddad with the way she said whatever was on her mind. Of course, Granddad wasn't quite as colorful as Gram.

"Oh my God," she said, fanning herself when she saw my costume. Liam had talked me into wearing a pirate costume—well, at least part of one. I'd refused to wear the skintight pants. I saw the lustful look on Liam's face when he checked out my bulge and agreed to break the pants out for our private party after the celebration. Publicly, I wore a billowy, long-sleeved white shirt that was open almost to my navel. I was feeling too exposed, and Gram's reaction did nothing to make me feel better. "Liam talked you into that getup, didn't he?" She giggled and covered her mouth.

"There's no way on the planet I would have worn this voluntarily." I looked down at the fake sword sticking out of the scabbard at my hip. The black jeans were still tighter than I wanted to wear, but a compromise was a compromise after all. I put my foot down over the knee-high boots, though. I refused to even wear those shiny fuckers privately for Liam, but I had agreed to wear the fake earring and bandanna around my head.

"Have a chat with me for a few minutes before the excitement starts," Gram said. I walked with her to a table while her boyfriend, Lennie, went to the bar to place an order for their drinks. Gram patted the chair next to hers, so I took a seat. I had a feeling no one ever told her no. "You look a lot happier since the last time I saw you at the softball tournament. You've had some pretty big changes in your life, huh?"

I wasn't exactly sure where Gram was going, but I decided to humor her a little. "You could say that."

"But would *you* say that?" she countered with a wink.

"Yes, I would definitely say I've had some big changes in my life."

"I used to watch you watch Liam and think about how sad it was that you denied yourself what you so plainly wanted. Your need for him was so tangible I could see it in the air, cut it with a knife even. I don't know what made you change your mind, but I'm glad you did. Will you indulge a foolish old woman and allow her to give you some advice?"

In all honesty, I knew I was going to hear what she had to say whether I wanted to or not, so I might as well agree to it and make it easier on both of us. I was apprehensive because I didn't know her that well, and I wasn't sure how much Liam had told Chase about us and what either one of them might have passed along to Gram. "You're not old or foolish, but I'll indulge you anyway."

"I think I understand why you were hesitant to get into a relationship with Liam, and that's not because of anything he or Chase has said to me.

They'd never betray your confidence in such a fashion. I'm saying this to you from my own observations of your body language and demeanor, okay?" I nodded for her to continue. "The measure of a man is not the size of his dick or where he wants to put it. A man can't be measured by the size of his wallet, his home, or how many fancy cars he owns. The real measure of a man is his ability to love and be loved. Society doesn't have the right to tell you who you should love or be loved by, and that is what I felt was holding you back. Am I right?" Gram reached over and placed her small hand over mine where it rested on the table.

"Mostly."

"Well then, knock it off." I sat up straighter as her gentle tone turned more militant. "Don't let other people dictate your happiness or define you, Jack. You are a man because you love with all your heart, and you eagerly accept Liam's love in return. It is a gift. Do not waste it."

"Yes, ma'am." My granddad would have loved her.

"Here we go, love," Lennie said, approaching the table with their drinks. "I really love the feel of your establishment, Jack. It doesn't feel like a bar, more like a gathering place for friends."

"Thank you, sir. I'm very proud of it." I rose from my chair, eager to get costume karaoke over with so I could change into normal clothes. "I hope you enjoy the show, although I have no idea what I've let Chase and Liam talk me into with this competition."

"It will be awesome," Gram assured me. I dropped a kiss on her cheek and patted Lennie on the back before I made my rounds to say hello to the gang. I found Bevan and Ellie off to the side. Ellie looked very pregnant and adorable in her pumpkin costume, and Bevan looked ridiculous dressed as Charlie Brown. I went over and said hello to them both.

"Do we look as silly as we feel?" Ellie asked with a grimace. "What the hell was I thinking dressing as the Great Pumpkin?"

"You look cute as hell," Bevan assured her. "I, on the other hand, look like a freaking dork." I shook my head no, but I couldn't keep the mirth off my face. "Wiseass," Bevan said, scowling.

"Enjoy your night," I said with a smile before I stopped by the next table where Miller and Gray sat, laughing and joking. I knew exactly where Chase was, which explained why Gray was without his other half. I couldn't remember the last time I'd seen Miller without JJ, but he was nowhere to be found when I looked around the room. "Stagging it?" I asked Miller. He looked at me with a frown but didn't reply. Why he and JJ tried to pretend nothing was going on between them was beyond me, but it was also none of my business.

"They aren't a couple," Gray said in a mock whisper. "They just hook up at people's houses and spunk up their bathrooms."

"It was one time." Miller's annoyed voice indicated it was a discussion the two friends had had several times. "Just let it go." I recognized the gleam in Gray's eyes and knew there was a fat chance of that happening. I took pity on Miller, who looked miserable.

"Where the hell are your costumes?" I asked, then motioned to my outfit and then to their office attire. I knew what Gray did for a living but didn't have a clue about Miller's profession.

"Just came from the office," was Gray's response.

"It isn't dignified," Miller said with a smirk at my costume. He made me sorry I had stepped in to help him until I saw the teasing glint in his blue eyes. "What's your reward going to be for wearing that getup?" he asked with a wink.

"I'm not telling." I punched him playfully on the arm before leaving to help out behind the bar.

It wasn't much longer before the costume karaoke competition started, and I had to admit Chase and Liam had come up with a great idea. The competitors were serious. They had outfits, dance moves, and the whole works. I enjoyed every act, but I was eager to see what the four Stooges had up their sleeves.

Liam and Chase were up first. My boyfriend, who I loved beyond all others, stood on the stage dressed like Katy Perry while Chase was dressed like the rapper Juicy J. They performed Katy's song "Dark Horse" with Chase doing the rapping. My guy had serious skills as he danced and sang seductively. I found myself smiling while they performed and cheering very loudly when they were done.

The final performance and the hands down best was Xavier and Ben who performed "You're the One That I Want" from *Grease*. Xavier was dressed as Danny and Ben was dressed as Sandy. He'd somehow managed to stuff himself into the tightest leather pants I'd ever seen and wore a black off the shoulder halter top and blond wig. I checked his feet to see if he was wearing high heels, but he was wearing a red pair of Chucks instead. It seemed like he had limits too. Regardless, they gave a flawless performance, and there was no doubt who'd won the competition when it was over.

"No fair," I heard Liam say as he walked up beside me. "They had an unfair advantage with all Xavier's experience in the business." I looked over at him, but it was hard to take him seriously while he was wearing his costume.

The DJ announced that Ben and Xavier were the winners after all the votes had been tallied, which surprised no one. What happened next took everyone by surprise. Xavier dropped to one knee and asked Ben to marry him. The entire pub held their breaths waiting for an answer, which came first in the form of Ben's deliriously happy smile and a jerky head nod.

"What's your answer?" someone from the crowd asked.

Ben grabbed the microphone from the DJ. "Yes."

The crowd cheered for the newly engaged couple. All their close friends, myself included, gave them hugs and slaps on the back. Well, all except Miller who mentioned something about another couple biting the dust. There was no malevolence in his words, so I had to wonder if he was really against monogamous relationships or if he just said he hated them out of habit. I guessed time would tell.

Liam changed clothes and removed his makeup before helping out behind the bar. We were slammed for hours, but things finally slowed down around midnight. I went to my office since they had things under control. I kept finding myself glaring at the customers when they looked a little too long at Liam. I didn't want him to think I didn't trust him because I did. I just didn't like guys flirting with him.

Liam brought the tills to my office, and I pulled him onto my lap for what I thought would be a short make-out session. I should've known better to start something in my office because our kisses led to panting and groping. I pulled back before we got too carried away.

"You go on ahead and go home. I'm going to help close the bar, then I'll be up."

"Are you sure?" Liam's face was flushed with desire. Call me an overbearing, jealous bastard, but I didn't want anyone seeing Liam's afterglow but me.

"Absolutely." I kissed his swollen lips one more time and patted his ass. "Take Charlie with you." There would be extra people on the streets tonight. Many of them would be drunk and looking for trouble.

"Come on, boy," he said, sliding off my lap.

Liam headed up to the loft, and I returned to the bar. It didn't take us long to clean and lock up. I thanked everyone for a great night and their hard work. I had an awesome team, and I appreciated them very much. I was so busy thinking about Liam and the way he made me feel, that I didn't heed the warning I had given him about paying attention in the alley. I heard the crunch of gravel behind me just a second before someone swung a blunt object at my head.

Unfortunately for my attacker, I had quick reflexes so the blow landed on my shoulders and not my skull. I spun around and grabbed the metal object just as he was bringing it down again. I used my momentum to shove him backward. I head-butted his sorry ass and sent him sprawling and unconscious to the pavement below. I bent over his prone body and used the flashlight on my phone to see who my attacker was, but I didn't recognize him. A driver from an expensive set of golf clubs lay beside him. The idiot chose the club with the biggest head and still couldn't take me out, not that I was unhappy about his ineptitude.

I dialed 911, then dialed Liam so he would know why I was late. He freaked out when I told him what had happened and rushed down to the alley, even though I'd asked him to stay inside where it was warm.

"I know who that is," Liam said, peering down at the man who was still out cold. "That's Kenner's best friend, Justin."

"Your ex-boyfriend sent this idiot to take me out, Ace?"

"I don't know," Liam said, shrugging. "It doesn't seem like something Kenner would do."

"Looks like we're about to find out." The douchebag came around and panicked when he saw us standing over him. He tried to sit up but thought better of it when he heard a deep, throaty growl. Liam hadn't come downstairs alone, and Charlie didn't appreciate this guy attacking his human, even if the blow hadn't even been enough to give me a headache. I could have been seriously injured or killed, and my dog wasn't taking it lightly. "You'd better lie still until the cops get here, dumbass." Charlie snarled and bared his teeth just in case I hadn't gotten my point across.

CHAPTER
Twenty-Two

Liam

I WALKED AROUND IN A FOG THE DAY AFTER JACK'S ATTACK. WE WERE so damn lucky Justin had sucky aim and that Jack's shoulder had taken the brunt of the blow. It could have been so much worse. I could have lost Jack. I'd been so angry over the attack while we'd waited for the cops to arrive, but that anger turned to fear as the early morning hours ticked by and we waited to hear why Jack had been targeted. Was Justin acting alone? Was it a hate crime?

Detective Sharon Regan called Jack's cell phone at five thirty in the morning to let us know Justin claimed to have acted alone and that they were not going to charge him with a hate crime. According to his statement, Justin had been in love with Kenner for a long time. He had thought his feelings were reciprocated until Kenner became obsessed with getting me back. Justin said Kenner was enraged after he was kicked out of the bar, and getting even with Jack and winning me back was all he could talk about.

Justin had been cast aside and had become resentful of my intrusion in Kenner's life. Apparently, Justin and Kenner had been an item before I'd come along, and they had rekindled their relationship sometime after Kenner and I went our separate ways… if they'd ever stopped in the first place. I had to wonder if Kenner was screwing both of us at the same time, not that it mattered to me anymore.

Justin had decided to punish me by taking away the man I loved. It had shaken me to hear those words through the speaker on Jack's phone. It felt like someone had stabbed me in the heart with a hot poker. Jack took one look at my face and thanked Detective Regan for the update as he reached for me. I went into his arms, and he ended the call as quickly and politely as possible.

Jack was ready to move on from the incident, but I couldn't let it go. Not yet. Jack could have lost his life! To him the attack had been nothing. I mean, look at all the missions he had been part of and survived. He'd seen his good friends lose their lives, so Justin's stunt was merely an annoyance to him. I had never had violence hit so close to home. I tried to put up a brave front, but I lost it the minute Jack disconnected the call and wrapped both his arms around me. Sobs racked my body as I flooded his shirt with my tears.

"I'm okay, Liam. It will take a lot more than that to kill me." Jack ran his hands through my hair and kissed my forehead to calm me, but it didn't work. I clutched his shirt tighter in my fists as images of what could have been played through my brain on a torturous loop, squeezing my heart in a painful grip. "Ace, I'm not going anywhere. I just found you, and I refuse to believe we won't grow old together." Jack tilted my face up to look at him. He caressed my cheek and looked at me with so much love in his eyes that I forgot to be afraid for a moment. "The only way you're getting rid of me is if you ask me to go."

"No," I shook my head fervently from side to side, "that's never going to happen."

"I'm not going anywhere, so let's get tucked into bed and try to sleep for a little while." Jack undressed me slowly before removing his own clothes. I climbed into bed beside him and snuggled as close as I could get, throwing my leg over his thighs. Jack's warm chuckle stirred my hair as I nestled my head over his heart. "I love you." Those were the last words I heard before exhaustion took over, and I fell into a deep sleep.

I woke up a few hours later feeling anything but refreshed. Jack slept soundly beside me while Charlie was curled up at our feet. I thought about taking a shower but decided a good run might be better to get me out of my head. I quietly dressed, grabbed Charlie's leash, and left Jack a note letting him know where we had gone.

The late morning had a chilly bite to it as Charlie and I set off at a brisk walk. Once I felt my muscles had warmed up enough, I graduated to a steady jog and then a full-out run. Charlie kept pace with me every step of the way, and I found his presence both comforting and protective as we made our way along my favorite trail. I realized just how predictable I had become when a familiar figure stood off to the side of the trail at the halfway point. I wasn't going to make eye contact with him or acknowledge him in any way.

"Liam, please stop for a minute," Kenner said, stepping onto the trail in front of me. "I want to explain." It wasn't the pleading expression on his face or in his tone that caused me to stop; it was the need to put him behind me for good. "Thank you."

"Don't thank me, Kenner." My voice was practically a snarl. Charlie sensed my distress and began to growl, causing Kenner to back up a few steps. "Wise decision, asshole."

"I wasn't part of Justin's attack, Liam. I swear it." He held his arms up in a pleading motion. I wanted to believe him. I didn't want to think someone I had once cared so much about would do something so horrible to hurt the man I loved and me in the process. I also knew Justin wouldn't throw Kenner under the bus even if he had been involved.

I stood straighter as I faced him down. "You'd better be telling me the truth, Kenner, because if I find out you were behind the attack on Jack, I won't stop until you're arrested."

"I didn't... I wouldn't," he stuttered. "I've never been a violent person, you know that." Kenner ran a hand through his hair in agitation and blew out a shaky breath. "I used Justin just as I used you, and I have to answer for that. I feel horrible for it, Liam." He was visibly shaking, and the young man I used to be wanted to comfort my old friend, but that would blur the lines I had drawn. I wasn't willing to do that.

"Yes, you do have to answer for playing with people's hearts and using them, but if Justin did act alone, you are not responsible for his actions." Kenner looked at me hopefully. "Justin's actions are those of someone who obviously needs help."

"What's going to happen to him?" I heard fear in his voice, and I wanted to believe it was for his friend and not himself. "Is he going to jail?"

Was Kenner afraid his reliable booty call would no longer be available, or was he actually worried about Justin? Either way, I was furious. He hadn't asked about how Jack was doing. Kenner only cared about Kenner—just like always. "He hit my boyfriend with a golf club. Justin tried to hurt Jack to make me suffer because you wanted me more than him." I was feeling levels of anger I'd never experienced before, and I was starting to fear for Kenner's safety. "Do you know how it feels to have the man you want to spend your life with attacked on his way home to you?" I inched closer to Kenner and Charlie growled louder. "What you're probably most afraid of is that you're going to get outed during this entire ordeal with Justin. You don't want people to know how much you like cock." I laughed in derision as the truth of my accusation was validated by the pallor of his skin. "You're afraid I'll tell everyone all your dirty little secrets, aren't you? I bet you're freaked out over Justin's statement going public."

"S-s-stop," Kenner stuttered. "I'm not like you, Liam. My family isn't understanding like your family, and they'll have nothing more to do with me. They think your *lifestyle* is disgusting and can't believe we were ever friends. I had to deny knowing you were gay to avoid scrutiny I didn't need. Please..."

"The fact that you think I'm capable of such atrocious behavior shows just how little you know me." I looked him up and down, certain I was sneering at him with the disgust I felt. "I would never out you to your family, but I have no control over what happens with Justin or his confession. That is a matter for you to take up with the police department and district attorney." I took a final step until just a few inches separated us. I still saw the fear and uncertainty in his eyes, but I couldn't work up an ounce of compassion for him. "Do not ever show up at the bar again. Do not approach me if you run into me in public. Don't pull a stunt like you did today. I want nothing to do with you."

"Liam, I..." Kenner was cut off by Charlie's ferocious bark. "Okay. Okay." He threw up his hands in surrender and backed up slowly. "I am sorry for everything," he said quietly before he turned around and walked toward the parking lot.

I didn't watch him walk away. I wouldn't give him another second of my time. Charlie and I resumed our run until we reached the final mile where we shifted to cool down mode. The run had done exactly what I'd needed it to, and seeing Kenner had helped revive me too. I guess anger did that to a person. I didn't want to be mad anymore, though. Fury was a useless emotion that only caused bitterness and resentment, and there was no room for either in my life.

Jack was in the kitchen scrambling eggs when Charlie and I walked into the loft. Regardless of what he said, I saw the bruise across his shoulder where the club had come down. If the entire blow had landed on his head, I wasn't certain we'd both be standing in his kitchen right then. The reality of the situation caused tears to burn at the back of my eyes.

Jack heard us enter the loft and turned to greet us. The smile slid off his face when he recognized the look on my face. He opened his arms, and I threw myself into them. "It's just a bruise," Jack said, nuzzling his nose against my temple. "It will fade in a few days." He was right. If I focused all my energy on what could've happened, I would miss what was happening right in front of me, which was Jack about to burn our scrambled eggs.

I rescued Jack and our breakfast while he toasted bread and poured orange juice. "I ran into Kenner during my run." I saw Jack stiffen out of the corner of my eye. "He swore he wasn't involved and, of course, wanted to know what would happen to Justin. Not one time did he ask if you were okay. He's only worried that he'll be outed if the police statement goes public, or I'll tell all and sundry that he's gay." I shook my head, still not believing how little Kenner knew me. I turned off the burner, set down my spatula, and turned to Jack. He was watching me closely with a guarded expression. "I told him I better not see him again. He better not come into the bar, he better not lie in wait for me on my favorite jogging trail, and he better turn away if we meet in public." I blew out a frustrated breath. "I don't think he's to blame if Justin truly acted alone. Yes, Kenner toyed with Justin's emotions, but that doesn't justify Justin's actions."

I saw Jack visibly relax at my resolute words. I wanted him to know Kenner was not a threat to our relationship. I wouldn't go back to that idiot if Jack stopped loving me. "You'll let me know if he doesn't heed your warning." It wasn't a question.

"Absolutely."

"Bevan called with a Jeremiah update," Jack said once we were seated at the table.

"What did he say?" I asked, setting down my fork. I was more interested in Jeremiah than the eggs.

"He's living in a nursing home in Vermont," Jack said quietly, but I saw the deeper emotion in his eyes. "Bevan gave me the address for his grandson, Joseph, who is listed as his guardian. I'm going to send him a letter and ask permission to meet his grandfather."

"Jack, that's a wonderful idea."

"You'll come with me, right? This is our journey together." I loved how much he'd shared with me and how included he made me feel. I wouldn't miss the trip for the world, which was what I told him. Jack rewarded me with a warm smile and a sweet kiss before we finished our breakfast.

I wasn't scheduled to work, and Jack decided to take the night off with me. He told Trevor what had happened and put him in charge of the bar.

Trevor was shocked to hear Jack had been attacked but was grateful the guy hadn't seriously injured him.

We ordered Chinese takeout and spent the night lazing around together, watching movies and our favorite TV shows on Netflix. It was just the kind of evening we needed after the early morning we'd had. I lay on the couch in front of Jack while he snuggled up against my back. I loved the heavy weight of his arm lying across my waist and the feel of his breath on the back of my neck. The crackling fireplace combined with my full stomach made me start feeling sleepy. Thoughts of Jeremiah and Big Jack popped into my head just as I was about to take a trip to dreamland. I suddenly wanted to hear more of their story, painful as it might be.

"Jack."

"Hmm," came his sleepy reply behind me.

"Big Jack and Jeremiah won't let me go to sleep."

"Me either." Jack placed a kiss on the back of my head before he climbed off the couch to retrieve the journal, and I got us both a beer, knowing we'd probably need it. "May I?" I asked, holding my hand out for the journal. Jack handed it to me, and I opened it to where we had last left off and read aloud.

The liberation of Paris only lasted for a week because German resistance was lighter than expected. Perhaps some of the Germans were as sick of the death and destruction as we were. Perhaps some of them missed their families and just wanted to go home too. Paris had been held captive by the Nazis for over four years, and the celebration of Germany's surrender on August 25, 1944, was like nothing I had ever witnessed.

People came running out of their homes and businesses to greet us as we moved through the city streets. Some of the women kissed our GIs and posed for pictures with them. All I could think about was finding a quiet spot to have some alone time with Jeremiah. It had been so long since I'd had him in my arms. I would have settled for just being able to hold him, but I hoped for more.

Luckily, the celebrations were just the distraction we needed to slip away. No one noticed we had disappeared with so many people around. Jeremiah and I made up for lost time, relearning every part of each other until the wee hours of the morning.

A young woman came across us as we were making our way back to our unit. I had just stolen a quick kiss from Jeremiah, thinking no one would be out and about at that time. I saw the knowing look in her eyes and held my breath, waiting for her to say something to us or to out us to others, but it didn't happen. She offered us a kind smile as she walked past. Even then, European views were more open and accepting of homosexuality. During the brief walk back to our unit, I hoped Jeremiah and I could find that acceptance in our own country when we returned.

That hope died the minute we returned and another guy in our unit asked us where we had been. Jeremiah told him we had found a couple of sweethearts who'd made us feel very welcome in their country. I knew why he'd said what he did, but it hurt like hell. Things weren't quite the same between us after that, and had I known then what I know now, I'd have found a way to put my hurt feelings aside and would have spent my energy finding more private moments with Jeremiah.

Hindsight is 20/20 and regret is a ghost who haunts my every waking minute and sometimes my dreams too.

"I know just how he felt," I said softly once I was finished. "Kenner used to do the exact same thing to me." I turned to face Jack. "At least you never did that to someone. The only person you hurt was yourself. You never held someone in your arms and told them you loved them then denied their relevance in public. Times were so different back then, and I'm not judging Jeremiah. I'm just saying I know exactly how Big Jack felt."

"No, I can be proud of myself for not doing that to someone else, but I would've had to lie and deny it if I had fallen in love with a guy just a few years ago. DADT wasn't repealed until my career was nearly over." Jack looked into the fireplace as he rolled something around in his brain. When he looked back at me, I saw a man who didn't regret his choices. "I'm glad I waited for you and that you were my first." He reached over and pulled me onto is lap. "You're my reward for putting my life on hold and focusing on my career. I'm glad others won't have to be in the same position I was in back then, but I don't have any regrets. Fate led me to you, Ace, and I appreciate what we have more because of the journey that brought me here."

I could honestly say that suffering through Kenner's crap had made me appreciate Jack's openness and honesty even more. He made me feel cherished and loved, and it was the greatest feeling in the world. "I couldn't agree with you more, love."

CHAPTER
Twenty-Three

Jack

JUST BEFORE THANKSGIVING, I RECEIVED A PHONE CALL FROM Jeremiah's grandson, Joseph Merritt. He apologized for the delayed response, explaining that his husband had set the letter aside and forgotten about it due to their hectic lives with their careers and three small kids. I had started to believe I wouldn't hear from him, so I was quick to wave off his apology. Joseph's next words, however, broke my heart.

"Granddad is in the advanced stages of Alzheimer's disease and doesn't speak," he told me with a heavy heart. "I've heard many wonderful stories about your grandfather, and I would love to meet you." I wasn't exactly sure what stories he had been told, and I wasn't about to out Jeremiah to him.

"Will it upset Jeremiah if I visit?" My great-grandmother had

Alzheimer's, and even though I was a small boy, I remembered how scared she'd get when she didn't recognize someone who entered her room. I wanted to see the man who'd meant the world to Big Jack, but not at the expense of his well-being.

"You won't upset him," Joseph assured me, "but it's doubtful he'd recognize Jack's name. Who knows, though. There's so much they still don't know about the disease. When would you like to come up to Vermont to meet us?"

Liam and I had three Thanksgiving dinners to attend together so I knew we wouldn't be able to travel to Vermont until early December. I wanted to discuss it with Liam and perhaps plan a weekend getaway. I was confident Trevor could manage the bar in my absence, which was a weight off my mind.

"Let me talk to my boyfriend, and I'll get back to you with our travel plans. It won't be for a few weeks due to our Thanksgiving obligations." I wanted to leave right away, but that wasn't possible.

"I understand all about being spread thin and trying to accommodate both sides of the family. Just give me a call when you're planning to arrive. I'd love to meet you and your boyfriend for dinner." I agreed to call him back as soon as I talked to Liam and thanked Joseph again for allowing me to visit with Jeremiah.

The situation was bittersweet. I'd be meeting the man my granddad had loved until his dying breath, but Jeremiah probably wouldn't recognize Big Jack's name or be able to verbalize the memory if he did. Alzheimer's disease was the absolute worst thing for a family to face.

I was in deep contemplation when Liam came home from a run with Charlie. My eyes took in his flushed cheeks and tousled hair, and my mind instantly switched gears as it often did around Liam, and I found myself wanting to help him shower to get clean—before getting dirty again. I considered myself to be a helpful and considerate boyfriend, especially when nudity was involved. Liam must have seen the sadness in my expression before my thoughts had gone awry.

"What is it?" he asked, coming to sit on the couch beside me. I told him about the conversation I'd had with Joseph, and I saw the same sadness I'd felt reflected in his expressive eyes. "That's so sad," he said once I finished. "Do you still want to go?"

"I do. It feels like closure of some sort for me to meet Jeremiah and give him the picture. I need to do this for Big Jack because he gave me the courage to admit my feelings for you, and I want to honor the love he felt for Jeremiah." I turned to face Liam with a frown. "Does that make me selfish? I've made this about what I want and need."

"You're not selfish, Jack," Liam said, reaching for my hand. "I think it's admirable and beautiful the way you want to honor your grandfather and Jeremiah's love. Joseph is his guardian, and he'd never encourage a visit if he thought it would harm Jeremiah. You have to trust that he knows what's best for his granddad." I nodded because he was right. "Let's get to planning our trip," he said, bouncing up from the couch to retrieve his laptop.

Later, we made dinner together, then planned out our holidays including our Vermont visit. I never thought I would experience the kind of happiness I did when we talked about the different holiday dinners coming up. I was sure spreading ourselves so thin would get old in time but not during our first Thanksgiving together when I had so many reasons to be thankful.

After calling Joseph to confirm our itinerary, we settled in front of the fire to read the final journal entry together. We had slowly read our way through them, neither of us eager to read about their final goodbye. However, that night it felt appropriate for Liam and me to finish their story since we would be going to see Jeremiah in a few weeks.

Allied troops moved into Berlin, and the Germans surrendered on May 7, 1945. The war was over, and a horrific enemy had been defeated. Our unit celebrated when word reached us because everyone was ready to go home. I did too but not without my Jeremiah.

Things had been tense between us since the liberation of Paris, even though almost a year had passed. I still loved him with all my heart, but I stayed guarded when it came to him. I was going to be saying goodbye to him soon, and it would be less painful if someone just reached into my chest and ripped out my heart.

We'd seen so many horrible things on the battlefield, but nothing hit closer to home than hearing about the Nazi concentration camps that imprisoned and slaughtered Jewish citizens, homosexuals, and anyone else the Nazis judged as unfit to live. Jeremiah and I were not in one of the units that had liberated the victims of these camps, but word circulated quickly about the atrocities found. Stories of humans who looked more like walking skeletons, piles and piles of bones, and massive crematoriums. What kind of monsters could do those things to other human beings? And why? Because of fear or because they didn't understand? Whatever the reason, there was no excuse for their cruelty.

I saw the look on Jeremiah's face when we were told about the camps and knew I wore a similar expression of horror. No matter how much we loved one another, we would never be together. People were tried, convicted, and sent to jail for being homosexual in some countries. Some men were told they could choose between chemical castration and jail. What kind of choice was that? I would never allow myself to be the reason Jeremiah was hurt. Maybe some were strong enough to brave the hatred and intolerance, and perhaps in some parts of the United States we would have been accepted but not in rural West Virginia in 1945.

I made my decision to have one last night with Jeremiah once the European battle was over, then I would volunteer for duty in the Pacific. I had no one waiting for me at home, and I wasn't ready to face reality without Jeremiah. Maybe I had a death wish, but my decision was made, and I stood resolute.

Our goodbye was beautiful and ugly at the same time. The final joining of our souls was beautiful, but the tears we cried over defeated dreams were ugly as hell. We sobbed into each other's arms until a few hours before dawn. I made love to him one last time before we returned to camp, then I set about applying for a transfer.

We never said goodbye publicly because neither of us would have been able to hold back our emotions in front of everyone. The memories of the last night *we had in Berlin would have to last us for a lifetime. It would have to sustain the loneliness of a life without a soul mate. I was sure I could love again. I could find a nice girl, settle down, and have a family like what was expected of me. I also was certain the part of my heart I had given to Jeremiah would always belong to him, and no matter how happy I might be in the future, I would always wish for things that could never be and wonder what if.*

Reading my granddad's heartbreak just about killed me. I had survived a lot during my time in the military. I had seen death rip my friends away from me. I had held them in my arms while they took their last breaths, but this was the worst pain I had ever felt. I had never missed my granddad as much as I did in that moment. I wanted to hug him one more time.

"When I was still in high school, our family took a vacation to Europe," I said through my tears. "Big Jack wanted to see some of the memorials that had been built and wanted his family to respect what his generation had gone through to defeat evil." I stopped to wipe some tears from my face. "We went to Normandy and Paris along with several other stops as we made our way to Berlin. I noticed how emotional Granddad was, but I chalked it up to memories of the war. There was something different about his grief in Berlin, though." Liam reached over and caressed the back of my neck when I paused because it had become too difficult to speak. He calmed my broken heart like no one else could, and I continued.

"We set out to see the museums and monuments, and with each visit, he became more and more despondent. I rarely saw Big Jack cry, but I had come upon him with tears streaking down his face a few times in Berlin when he'd been alone. Now I know why. He may not have died in battle there, but his hopes and dreams had."

Liam crawled onto my lap and wrapped his arms around me. I held on to him as if I would never let go. I cried for my granddad's broken heart and because it could have been me. I could've continued to deny who I was and live the rest of my life not knowing how amazing it felt to truly love and be loved.

"I'm sorry," Liam whispered in my ear. "I know it hurts, but we'll do our best to make it right when we meet Jeremiah. I know he might not recognize your granddad's picture, but we can at least try. If nothing else, we can leave the picture with him so they'll be together, even if we're the only ones who know the significance of the gesture." Liam kissed my lips softly a few times before pressing his forehead to my shoulder.

Charlie came over and head-butted my hand so I would scratch his ears. Liam and Charlie gave me the perfect amount of comfort to ease my hurt. Maybe I should have felt ashamed that I was blubbering over my granddad's journals, but I wasn't. Loving and caring about people didn't make me weak; it made me strong. Crying made me human. Loving someone was a risk to my heart, but not taking the risk was the same as not living. I was beyond grateful I had taken the chance and risked my heart—everything—for Liam. He was worth it. *We* were worth it.

CHAPTER
Twenty-Four

Liam

J ACK AND I HAD SURVIVED THE FIRST TWO THANKSGIVING DIN-
ners—his family the Saturday before Thanksgiving and my family
on the actual holiday. The Sunday after Thanksgiving found us at
Chase and Gray's new house. My brother wanted to have a large gathering to celebrate with his friends and family. He knew we would already
be spread thin during the week leading up to the holiday, so he'd chosen
the Sunday after.

Jack and I arrived early so I could help Chase prepare food for the
large crowd that would be arriving later that afternoon. I gave Jack a kiss
and left him with Gray to watch football while I went in search of my
brother. I entered the kitchen and found him leaning over the open oven
basting a turkey.

"Smells delicious," I said, inhaling the delicious aroma of rosemary, lemon, and sweet basil. "Put me to work." I placed my tote on the counter and began to unload the side dishes I had started prepping at home.

"Mmm, cornbread casserole," Chase said, coming over to stand beside me once he returned the turkey to the oven. "You didn't have to bring so much." He shook his head as he looked at the deviled eggs, cranberry salad, and the desserts I had made in addition to the cornbread casserole. "But thank you for helping me out." He wrapped his arm around my shoulders. "I've never cooked for so many people."

"I do hope to be a chef someday, so this is right up my alley." I threw a sly smile his way and stored the food I'd brought in his refrigerator until it was time to do something with it. I looked around his new kitchen and was once again slightly jealous of his setup, especially his double ovens. I drooled over them every time I was at their house.

"Tell me about your dinners with the families," Chase said as he started peeling a large bag of potatoes. I joined him at the counter and helped with the task. It was the one kitchen chore I hated the most when I helped my mom in the kitchen.

"They were wonderful." I thought back over how well Jack had fit in with my family, and I was crazy about his large crew. "His sister, McKenna, announced she's having a baby, so Patrick and Claire will welcome their first grandchild in about six months. They are so excited, and it was a beautiful thing to witness." I smiled when I remembered the happy tears Claire had cried as she'd hugged her daughter and son-in-law.

"That's great news. Is Jack excited too?"

"He is really happy for them." I recalled something Jack's great-aunt Bea had said once the announcement was made and started to laugh. Chase looked at me questioningly, so I enlightened him. "Jack's great-aunt Bea is a lot like Gram but twenty years older. She has no filter, like none." That got Chase's attention. "So everyone is all 'Congratulations' and 'We're so happy for you,' and Bea blows right through that sweetness with, 'It's about damn time. I was beginning to think your swimmers didn't know how to swim upstream or that your undershorts were too tight, and you were strangling them before they had a chance to knock her up.'"

"Wow," Chase said after he had a good laugh. "That does sound like something Gram would say. How'd it go with your family?"

Jack was pretty stiff at first, fearing my parents wouldn't like him, but he'd relaxed and let them get to know him. "Mom is totally smitten with Jack, and my dad admires him a lot. They've bonded over cars, sports, and building their own businesses with nothing but their own two hands while my mom and I worked in the kitchen."

Chase cocked his head to the side and pursed his lips together. "Kind of like what's happening right now?"

"Pretty much," I said, then reached for the next potato. "Leah's eyes had nearly bugged out of her head the first time she saw Jack." A reaction I was getting used to. "She got over it pretty quickly and treated him to her teenage snarky attitude. Why should he be spared just because he was beautiful?"

Chase pointed the peeler at me and said, "And why the hell should our men get out of kitchen duty because they're so good-looking?"

He walked over to the archway between the rooms and yelled, "Neither of you are getting sex for a week unless you get your butts in here and help."

The television immediately snapped off and the two guys nearly trampled Chase to report for duty. Jack even gave a snappy salute before nuzzling my neck until I giggled.

"None of that frisky business," Chase said, slapping the counter.

Jack straightened up and said, "Put me to work, sir."

"You can either finish peeling these potatoes or snap the green beans," Chase told Jack.

"Wait," Gray said with a cute pout. "Why does he get to choose?" Chase lifted a brow and Gray mumbled, "Never mind."

"I can snap green beans in my sleep," Jack said, moving over to the massive bowl of beans.

Chase smiled like the Cheshire cat when he handed over his peeler to Gray, who pulled his husband close for a hard kiss. Chase sighed and stood back. "Looks like you guys have this under control." He grabbed Liam's arm and headed toward the living room.

"Hey, where are you going?" Gray asked.

Chase didn't even slow down. "Taking a well-deserved break with my brother."

"Can you at least keep us updated on the score?" Jack asked.

"No," Chase and I called out.

We sat on the couch and helped ourselves to their abandoned snacks.

"Jack took both of my parents off to the side at different times to talk to them, but he wouldn't tell me what they'd discussed when I asked him about it after we left. He just told me it was a private chat and tried to distract me with sex."

"Did it work?" Chase asked while waggling his brows.

"Yes," I replied, feeling my cheeks turn slightly pink. "I brought it up once more the next day, but he changed the subject."

Chase hummed a few seconds before saying, "He was probably asking them what to get you for Christmas or something. People think quiet guys like Jack don't have a lot going on upstairs, but I say still waters run deep, and he probably has been giving your Christmas gift a lot of consideration."

"Maybe." I wasn't convinced. It was true Jack was a quiet guy, but he was only that way in public. I got to see his real personality, and I selfishly loved that about us. "I don't suspect it's anything bad, but we don't keep secrets from each other." I waved my hand in annoyance at myself.

"You believe in Jack, you trust him, and you are madly in love with him, right?" I nodded. "Whatever he said to them was important to him— something Jack wanted to say or express to your parents about how he felt about you. Maybe he needed reassurance that they approved of your relationship."

Chase's words resonated and tickled my memory of how Jack had once stressed over our age difference. Did he think my parents wouldn't approve of him because he was twelve years older? Chase might've really been onto something, but I would not bring it up with Jack. I trusted him, and I would prove it by not speaking about his conversations with my parents again.

Chase and I dropped the heavy topics after that, choosing to discuss things that made us laugh until we cried.

"We're finished," Gray called out. "Can we watch football now?"

Chase sighed and stood up. "Let's go inspect their handiwork."

Gray had perfectly peeled the potatoes and Jack's beans were so uniform it looked like a machine had snapped them.

Chase kissed Gray's cheek and said, "I guess—"

Jack and Gray scrambled out of the room before Chase could finish. Seconds later, the television came back on and sounds of the game filtered into the kitchen. Gray and Jack must've liked what they saw because they cheered and high-fived each other.

Gray or Jack returned to the kitchen occasionally to steal a drink, snack, or a kiss while we worked to prepare the meal. "It looks like we're feeding an army," Chase joked once we were finished. "Do you think we got carried away?"

"Not at all. Some of us show people we love them through our food."

The other guests started trickling in, but baby Jacob stole the show. Chase practically knocked his best friend over to get to her baby. He made cooing noises and kissed Jacob's little fingers and face for several minutes before he even acknowledged Ava or Brandon.

"Oh, hello." Chase grinned impishly at them before he carried Jacob to the couch where he sat down next to Gray. "Say hi to Uncle Gray, little Jacob." Gray wrapped his arm around Chase's shoulders and pulled him and Jacob closer. The baby brought his tiny fists to his mouth and began to suck on them. Chase looked up at Ava with accusing eyes. "Oh, I see. You brought him over hungry, knowing I wouldn't be able to feed him. You just can't wait to snatch him back from me."

"Moron," Ava replied affectionately. She reached into the diaper bag and pulled out a bottle and a small towel and walked them over to Chase. "I pumped breastmilk so you can feed him."

"You can have diaper duty later too," Brandon offered.

"We're not afraid of stinky poop," Gray replied. "We've babysat our niece plenty of times, and I can tell you that infant poop is a walk in the park. Just wait until he's eating solid food," Gray said, referring to his brother and sister-in-law's toddler, Grace.

"We're now talking about kid poop?" JJ asked when he walked through the front door, wearing a queasy expression on his handsome face. "It's bad enough I have to listen to all you lovesick fools wax poetic about how great monogamy is and see enough face-sucking to last me a lifetime." JJ might be fooling a lot of people with his sarcastic anti-love diatribe, but it wasn't working on me. His words were the same as usual, but his tone and body language were different as if he was just going through the verbal motions but without the normal feeling.

Gray glared at him and opened his mouth to say something snappy right back, but Miller came through the door, and he shifted his focus to his best friend. "House rules," Gray said firmly, wagging a finger back and forth between JJ and Miller. "No jizzing up our new house like you did our old one."

Neither JJ nor Miller looked overly embarrassed, and I wondered how long they had been screwing each other. I bet it was longer than anyone knew. I hadn't been at the party where they'd gotten busted, so I couldn't be sure, but I had witnessed their physical chemistry on more than one occasion. The first time had been when I'd gone shopping for Gray and Chase's wedding gift. The guys had registered at Nordstrom, and I saw JJ and Miller there when I went to pick out their gift, though neither of them had seen me.

I'd watched as JJ compared items on the registry list to some kitchen gadgets he'd been looking at. He was picking up items and looking at them as if he had no idea what some of them did. His confusion was kind of cute and gave away the fact that he didn't spend any time in a kitchen. I was about to help him out, but Miller arrived on the scene. Their interaction started with teasing and laughter but quickly escalated to something else. Miller helped JJ pick something out while grabbing a gift for himself, and then they were off. It was obvious from the phero- mones floating around what they were leaving to do. I almost expected them to find the nearest bathroom for a quickie, but it was Nordstrom and not a bar.

The second encounter was at a nightclub downtown. I'd gone with a group of friends to celebrate a birthday. It didn't appear JJ and Miller had arrived together, but they sure as hell left with each other. I watched them tear up the dance floor together and was surprised by how in tune they looked. It was as if they had been dancing together for a long time, but I was pretty sure they had only met when their best friends had fallen in love.

"Some people are so damn touchy," Miller said to JJ.

"We should wait until they're in a food-induced coma, then jizz up every bathroom in the place." He looked over at me and offered a sym- pathetic smile. "Welcome to the family, kid." JJ stuck his tongue out at Gray and headed to the kitchen with the bottles of wine he'd brought. I wasn't surprised when Miller followed close behind him.

"Definitely don't jizz up my kitchen," Chase said firmly to their re- treating backs. He looked over at Gray while baby Jacob went to town on his bottle. "Who do those idiots think they're fooling anyway?"

Jack wrapped his arm around my shoulders and lowered his mouth to my ear. "Life is so much better when you stop pretending."

I turned my head and kissed him, and our exchange earned a col- lective "aah" from the crew.

Xavier, Ben, Ellie, and Bevan all arrived together a few minutes later. Ellie handed the dishes she had made to Xavier to put in the kitchen, and Bevan helped her into a recliner. "I will probably need a crane to help get me out of this chair later."

"Nonsense," Bevan said quietly, then dropped a kiss on her fore- head. "You're more beautiful today than you were yesterday."

Ben stood behind his brother grinning like an idiot over Bevan's newfound soft side. Love did that to people. I looked over at Jack and found him watching me with a soft smile. Jack had changed and blossomed so much once he pushed aside all his fears and gave himself over to loving me. He held my hand and showed affection without regard for anyone else's opinion. I never forgot to send a thankful prayer to Big Jack for guiding Jack into living a life of truth and openness.

Gram and Lennie showed up last. "You're never too old to make a grand entrance," she said. Chase kept an iron grip on Jacob until Gram arrived, but he gladly handed the baby to her so she could fuss over him. "I want one of these from you two soon." She gave Chase and Gray a pointed look before turning all her attention to the baby.

Chase, Xavier, and I left everyone in the large family room while we finished getting dinner ready. As much as I loved the large, boisterous crowd, I sometimes found them overwhelming. It was nice to have some quiet time with my brothers for a little bit. Soon, everything was ready, and we gathered around to say grace and share the delicious meal. Part way through the meal, Chase said they had news to share with us.

"Gray and I have been talking about starting a family for a little while now. We couldn't decide if we wanted to try IVF with a surrogate or adopt a baby. We also had to figure out what kind of adoption we wanted." Chase became emotional suddenly and cleared his throat before continuing. "Well, it turns out fate made the decision for us." He closed his eyes and silent tears slid down his face.

"Pastor Simms contacted us last month about a young lady in her church who was looking for a couple to adopt her baby privately," Gray said. "She immediately thought of us. Her name is Abigail, and she's a high school senior. She and her family discussed all her options early on, and she decided on adoption. She wants to do it privately because she wants to make sure her baby gets placed with a family she approves of, and this was the only way." Gray's smile lit up the dining room, and he nodded at Chase to finish the story.

"We had a private meeting with Abigail and her family soon after we received the call from Pastor Simms. We learned the day before Thanksgiving that Abigail chose us to adopt her baby." Total silence fell for a few seconds before everyone started talking at once. Chase and Gray laughed at our exuberant responses, then both held up a hand so they could answer the questions being fired at them from all angles.

"Yes, we know the sex of the baby," Gray said, then looked at his husband. "Should we tell them or make them wait?" There was a lot of whining and pleading going on, but Gray just let everyone fuss for a few minutes before saying, "We're having a baby girl."

"We haven't picked out a name yet," Chase told us. "We are still so excited to have been chosen, and we're a little scared."

"Scared?" Gram asked.

"There's a chance Abigail will change her mind once the baby is born," Chase said.

"It sounds like she thought this through pretty well," Lennie offered.

"She definitely has," Gray replied, "but there is always that possibility. Chase and I aren't dwelling on it because we have so much to do in order to be ready for our daughter's arrival."

"Do you need legal help to navigate through the adoption?" Bevan asked. "I had a law practice before I went into private investigating."

"JJ is helping us," Gray answered.

"I can be helpful," JJ said with a casual shrug. It was obvious he was uncomfortable with everyone's eyes on him.

"Of course you are, pookie," Miller said from beside him.

"Pookie?" JJ asked out loud, but we were all questioning it. JJ didn't look like a guy who would use pet names with a lover. "You should know all about my helpfulness, cupcake." There was a bite of something more than sarcasm and teasing in JJ's voice. There was a slight tension between JJ and Miller I hadn't noticed before, but JJ had been MIA during the costume karaoke competition on Halloween, so it had been a while since I had seen them in the same room.

Miller sneered in JJ's direction before looking down at his plate. His face turned slightly pink under our attention. I didn't know what the hell was going on between them or the reason for their sniping at one another, but I didn't like it. I had hoped they would end up together, even if they'd both claimed to be confirmed bachelors.

"Anyway, back to the baby," Xavier said to get our attention back on something exciting. "What kind of legal process do you have to go through?"

"We have to go through the same classes and training that foster parents go through because we'll essentially be her foster parents until the official adoption takes place a few months later," Chase answered.

"How long before Sofia's baby cousin arrives?" Ellie asked as she rubbed her round belly.

"She'll be here in about ten weeks," Gray answered.

"Congratulations, you guys," Ben said. "We're really happy for you." He put his arm around Xavier and pulled him into his side.

"You'll be amazing dads," Ava said tearfully.

"It's why we picked you to be Jacob's godparents," Brandon added. "You guys were born to be dads. I can't wait for our little ones to grow up together."

"We're going to be uncles to two lucky little girls," I said, motioning back and forth between Xavier and myself. I included Ellie's unborn daughter, Sofia, in the equation because, as far as I was concerned, Ellie was my older sister, and I knew she felt the same familial connection I did.

"Best damn uncles in the whole world," Xavier replied. "I'll sing them lullabies, and you can make them organic baby food."

"Deal."

It was then I realized Gram hadn't said much, which wasn't typical. I looked over and saw she was just sitting there smiling contently. She caught my stare and gave me a wink. I saw the happy tears in her eyes, and I realized how joyful this moment was for her. She had raised Chase on her own from the time he was two years old. She'd been his biggest ally and cheerleader all his life, so it had to be so exciting for her to see his dreams coming true.

Jack reached for my hand beneath the table and squeezed it. Jack and I hadn't discussed marriage and kids. I somehow doubted the thoughts had even crossed his mind. We hadn't been dating very long, and he'd made a lot of drastic changes in a short period of time. I was thrilled to be cohabitating with him in his loft. My lease was up at the end of the year, and after discussing it with Jack, I told my landlord I wouldn't be renewing the contract. It was a big move for both of us, but it felt natural. I was confident everything else would fall into place when the time was right.

CHAPTER
Twenty-Five

Jack

L IAM AND I TOOK THE FOLLOWING WEDNESDAY OFF TO GO Christmas tree shopping. I had never purchased a tree for my loft, and Liam had been horrified. I quickly learned my guy was a Christmas fanatic. He had already warned me there would be cookie baking and Christmas music playing throughout the loft when we returned from Vermont. We would be leaving for our trip on Friday and not returning until Monday. Liam wanted the loft decorated for the holiday so when we returned, he could focus on the fun parts like shopping and baking.

He dragged me to three different home improvement stores looking for the perfect tree. He didn't want a live one because he didn't like the thought of a tree dying just for his pleasure. He wanted a very tall, very fat artificial tree that yelled Christmas. Those had pretty much been his exact words.

"Too short," he said of one tree. "Too skinny," he deemed another with hands on his hips and disgust dripping off his tongue. Liam was clearly offended by the existence of such a tree. Up and down the rows we went. Finally, as if some heavenly light was shining down upon it, there stood a tree in all its tall *and* fat glory. "Oh my God! This is the one! I love…" His eyes locked on the price tag and his voice faded away.

"We'll take this one," I said to the overeager store employee who hadn't gotten too far away from Liam at any time while we'd looked at the trees. I had caught him eyeing my guy a few times and tried not to let it bother me. The employee was gorgeous and closer to Liam's age, but Liam was in love with me.

"Jack, no! It's too expensive. I don't need anything that grand to celebrate our first Christmas together. It only matters that we're together." He immediately walked back to the first tree that had offended him. "This one is fine," he said, forcing a smile.

"We're buying that tree." I pointed to the one that had practically given Liam a hard-on. He shook his head, but I wasn't going to be dissuaded. I'd seen the lustful look in his eyes—the one that was usually reserved for me—and I was going to buy that tree for our home. I started walking toward Liam, and he backed up slightly. His eyes widened but not in alarm. He knew he had nothing to fear from me. "We're going to decorate that tree when we get home, then we're going to turn on the fireplace and spread a blanket on the floor, and then do you know what we're going to do?"

"Tell campfire stories? Roast s'mores?" God, I loved his smart mouth.

"Not even close." I pressed my body flush against his and placed my hands on his neck. I caressed his jawline with my thumbs and watched his Adam's apple bob up and down as he worked to swallow. "I'm going to lay you down and…"

"You're all set, sir." Liam's number one fan stood in the aisle with the tree box on a flatbed cart. His evil smile told me he knew just what he had interrupted.

"Thank you." There might have been a tiny snarl in my voice as I stepped back and took possession of the cart. I looked over at Liam while I wheeled the tree toward the register. He was worrying his lip between his teeth. "What?"

"You brought out the caveman, Jack. I can't be responsible for my actions when we get home."

"Yeah?" Liam smiled at the hopefulness he heard in my voice. He wiggled his eyebrows suggestively at me, and I stopped right there in the middle of the aisle. He stopped too and looked at me curiously. I snatched him to me before he knew what was coming and planted a serious kiss on his gorgeous mouth. I didn't give a crap who might be looking. The moment called for a kiss.

"Wow," he said once he pulled away. "I'm not sure what came over you, but I sure enjoyed it."

"You came over me," I replied, then leaned closer so only he could hear my next words. "Well, not yet, but it's part of what I was going to tell you before we were so rudely interrupted by the president of your fan club."

Liam pulled back so he could look into my eyes. "That guy back there doesn't know me. He only wants to fuck me. You love me with every part of you. There's never going to be competition for my heart or my body where you're concerned, Jack." He meant every word he said, which made my heart swell.

"We better get out of here before we get arrested for public indecency." I wasn't even joking either. Liam's patient love had liberated me from a life of unfulfilled dreams. "I'll show you just how much your words mean to me when we get home." I loved that *my* loft was now *our* home. This was the first year a Christmas tree would decorate our space, and I was suddenly eager to put it up. I wondered how he felt about decorating in the nude.

I wrestled the big mother of a tree into the back of the Wrangler while Liam moved the boxes and bags of decorations to the back seat. I treated him to his favorite frivolous coffee drink on the way home, making sure to tease him when he had whipped cream on his face. My jokes might not have been original, but they made Liam laugh and blush. What else mattered?

The two of us managed to drag the huge tree box up the steps to the loft. I cut into the box and began unpacking pieces while Liam and Charlie went down to the garage to get the rest of our things. There were a fuckton of pieces to the tree, but I wouldn't let it discourage me. My mom had purchased a prelit tree that came in three parts a few years ago, but she didn't like it. She liked all the lights, but she never felt the tree looked real. She wanted to manipulate the branches her way, which was almost exactly what Liam had said when we started out on our excursion that morning. Who knew people were so damn picky about fake trees?

"That's a lot of pieces," Liam said, echoing my sentiments. "We should take a break before we get started." I looked up at him and realized what he intended to do during our "break."

"Huh-uh," I said, shaking my head. "It's going to take a long time to decorate this monstrosity, and I have big plans for you later." I turned back to stacking the limbs in piles based on the colored sticker wrapped around the wire limbs that hooked into the base. "The quicker you help me, the quicker we'll get done, then I can turn on the fireplace and drag out the blankets."

Liam jumped into the mess, and we had the tree parts sorted relatively fast. Assembling the tree was a totally different animal. Liam became a completely different person as he formed each branch, stood back, looked at the tree to see if it looked right, and repeated the process. I gave up at some point because he told me I "wasn't doing it right." I popped some popcorn and drank a beer on the couch next to Charlie while I watched Liam work his magic. I was mostly focused on the way his jeans molded to his superb ass and how long his legs looked, but occasionally I noticed how nicely the tree was coming along.

"I feel you staring at my ass, Jack," Liam said an hour into the tree transformation.

"Yup." Why deny it.

"I'm half tempted to really give you something to look at, but you already denied me when I hinted at wanting to get fucked earlier."

"I did not!" I sat up straight, ready to prove him wrong, but I tore my eyes off his ass long enough to see the playful smirk on his face. "You better watch it, or I'll come over there and help you."

"Please don't. I love you so much, but I'd prefer to do this part by myself." I tried to look sad, but I wasn't fooling him. He gave me a knowing smirk and returned to his task. Charlie and I killed an entire bag of popcorn while we supervised. "I'll allow you to help me with the lights since you're so much taller." The superior tone of his voice made me smile. *Allow me?*

"Yes, dear," I replied, earning myself the stink eye.

Liam placed his hands on his lower back and began to stretch. I wanted to go to him to help work out his kinks, but I knew what would happen once my hands were on his body. We still had lights and ornaments to hang. I wouldn't be getting any action anytime soon, but that didn't mean we couldn't have a little fun. "Do you want to play a little game while we finish decorating the tree?" I waggled my eyebrows at him playfully.

"What kind of game?" Liam asked suspiciously.

"I'll find a radio station that's playing Christmas songs, and we'll each pick a word for each other that we hear often in those types of songs. Every time our word is used in a song, we have to take off an article of clothing."

"Okay, but not if the word is in the chorus," Liam said, negotiating, "or we'll be naked before we get the lights out of the boxes."

"How about we unpack all the lights and decorations before we begin our game?"

"That sounds perfect." I saw a devilish grin split his face seconds before he said, "I'd like to up the ante a little bit. There needs to be kissing or touching with every lost piece of clothing. What kind of prize does the winner get, and how do we determine who wins? Is the first person naked the winner or the loser?" The temperature in the living area felt like it had gone up about twenty degrees.

"Baby, I think we'll both be winners in this game regardless of which one of us is naked first. The winner is the person who is still wearing at least one article of clothing."

"Do you accept the changes to the game?" Liam asked. "Can you handle a teasing kiss or touch and stay focused on hanging lights and ornaments?"

"I'm up to the challenge," I said, gesturing at the semierection I was already rocking. Ha! To think I'd been afraid when we'd first gotten together that I might not be able to keep up with him. It turned out that everything about Liam was an aphrodisiac that turned me inside out.

I poured Liam a glass of wine and grabbed myself another beer, then turned on the radio that played nonstop Christmas music. I helped him unwrap all the strands of LED rainbow-colored snowflake lights. The tree would be so bright a NASA satellite would be able to see it.

"I get to pick your word first since I came up with the game," I said smugly. "I pick *bells*."

Liam narrowed his eyes at me, letting me know he'd been considering that word too. "Fine. I pick *snow*."

"I think we shouldn't have to take off more than one piece of clothing per song," Liam tossed out at the last minute. He gestured at the many strands of lights and the various sizes and styles of ornaments we had purchased. "Neither one of us has a lot of self-control when we're naked and within reach of each other."

"True," I agreed. "Okay, no more than one article of clothing can be removed per song. Any other rules?" Liam cocked his head to the side and gave it serious consideration before he shook his head. We agreed the game would begin as soon as the next song came on. I cringed when I heard Frank Sinatra begin to sing "Let It Snow, Let It Snow, Let It Snow."

"Damn my stupid new rule," Liam said, his smile bright enough to light up Rockefeller Center. "You'd be almost naked within the first few seconds." I took off a shoe and tossed it aside before walking to him. He chose a kiss as his reward, so I poured my heart and soul into it. "Oh my," he said breathlessly, staggering back a few steps once the kiss was over. "Whew. Let's get to work, shall we?"

That's how it went. A dropped piece of clothing followed by the hottest of kisses or touches until I was so on edge I thought I might burst. Decorating a Christmas tree had never been as much fun or as frustrating. Of course, I was the one to end up bare-ass naked first. Liam was down to his sexy red briefs—how fitting—when he stood on the ladder to place the star on the top of the tree.

His tight, round ass was right there on display, teasing me beyond control. He stood up on his tiptoes and leaned forward to straighten the star. I was afraid he might lose his balance, so I did what all loving boyfriends would do and placed my hands on his narrow hips to steady him. Of course, they didn't stay there for long. I slid one of my hands around to massage his bulge while the other teased his tightly pebbled nipples. Liam pressed into me, mewling softly as I caressed his lean body. Unable to stop myself, I leaned forward and nipped his ass through his undies.

"Jack," he cried out my name, but what he'd really meant to say was "More." I slid his briefs down his long legs and tossed them aside. I alternated between tender kisses and playful nips, worshiping the tender globes of his ass. I licked and sucked the little dimples above his cheeks. "Let me down," he pleaded. I stood back but left my hands on his hips as he descended the ladder. Liam turned into my arms as soon as his feet were on the ground. "You said something about a fire, blankets, and laying me down."

I ended up being the one lying on our nest of blankets while Liam raised and lowered himself on my dick. The tree—*our* tree—bathed him in festive lights while the fire crackled and glowed behind him, giving him an almost ethereal appearance. I would never tire of the way he arched his back while he rode me, his head falling back, and his lips parting in ecstasy. I would proudly wear the marks his fingernails had dug into my chest.

Liam snuggled in my arms beneath the blankets once he'd ridden us to completion. Realization of what my grandfather had truly meant when he'd written to me about surrendering my heart came to me just then. I had found that in Liam—the person who showed me what it really felt like to be alive. He was the air I breathed, the blood that pumped through my veins, and the keeper of my heart. I smiled in the flickering firelight when it occurred to me that I was starting to embrace my inner Irish poet.

I had received blessings to propose from both his parents on Thanksgiving Day. I just needed to find the right time to ask Liam to surrender his heart to me. Forever.

CHAPTER
Twenty-Six

Liam

"**D**ID YOU REMEMBER TO LOCK UP?" JACK ASKED HALFWAY INTO our seven-hour trip to Bellows Falls, Vermont.

"Mmm hmm."

"What about the coffee pot?"

"Yes, dear," I said affectionately. "I also made sure we used up the milk before it could expire and set the lights to come on automatically so we're not robbed by bandits while we're in France on vacation." I looked around to the back seat as if I were doing a headcount. "Kevin!" I yelled, doing my best impersonation of the mom from *Home Alone*.

"Smartass." There was no anger in his voice as he reached across the seats and tweaked my nose. "So I'm a little anxious." It was the understatement of the year. It seemed like Jack had a lot more on his mind than meeting Jeremiah and his grandson, though.

"Everything will be under control at the bar while we're away, and we brought Charlie with us. What more could we want?" I asked.

"You're right. I just need to relax and stop stressing about this trip."

"You're amazing, Jack. Have I told you that lately?"

"Just this morning in the shower," he tossed back at me with a leering smile. I loved how confident and happy he had become in all aspects of our relationship since we'd started seeing one another. I'd like to claim a little bit of credit for it, but it had a lot more to do with the nudge Big Jack had given him, which was the reason for this trip.

I knew he wanted everything to go perfectly so he could honor Big Jack's memory and perhaps give his granddad a bit of closure too. Whatever the reason, it was the right thing to do. We were blessed with phenomenal weather for it being December on the East Coast, which usually meant tons of snow. There wasn't a flurry in the sky, and none were predicted over the weekend.

We had just entered New York when Xavier texted to let me know that Ellie's water had broken, and she was being admitted to the hospital. I was sad I wasn't going to be there when Sofia came into the world, but I still felt my place was beside Jack.

"What's going on?" Jack asked after I read the text.

"X wanted me to know that Ellie was admitted to the hospital." I had heard how annoying Chase had been when Ava had been in labor with Jacob, and I wondered if Xavier would be as bad.

"Do you want to go back?"

"What? No!" I loved Jack even more for offering to turn the Jeep around when I knew it was the last thing he personally wanted to do. Had I wanted to go back home, he would have done it. "I'm right where I want to be." Jack glanced at me for a brief second to make sure my expression and words matched. I gave him my megawatt smile as he called it, and he noticeably relaxed. "Are we there yet?"

"Just a little bit farther." His quick comeback made me smile.

We stopped a few times to eat and let Charlie stretch his legs so the seven-hour drive took closer to eight and some change. We checked in at the B&B just before dinnertime. Jack gave me a choice between taking Charlie out for a walk on the grounds or hauling our luggage upstairs. I chose to take Charlie for a walk. The wind was crisp and cold, but I found it to be very pleasant. It reminded me of the time we'd spent at Jack's cabin. The air was so much purer without city pollutants. It was simply beautiful.

One thing I admired about Jack the most was his tidiness. He told me it was because of all the years he'd spent in the military. I found him unpacking our suitcases and placing everything in the drawers or on hangers. I looked around the room and thought the light blue and gray theme was comfortable and not fussy. For some reason, I expected a big floral comforter with about fifteen throw pillows in complimentary colors. Instead, we had a four-poster bed with a subdued duvet with gray and blue stripes and zero throw pillows.

"Very nice," I said to Jack. "It's very quaint and peaceful here."

"It would be beautiful in the fall when the leaves are changing or in the spring when the trees begin to bud."

Joseph and his husband, Brad, would be meeting us downstairs in the restaurant later that evening. Joseph was the one who'd suggested the B&B, and we had no reason to doubt his referral. I wasn't exactly sure how to dress for the meeting, so I chose to go with a nice sweater and dark jeans. Jack paired his black denim with a nice button-down shirt.

We met the couple down in the lobby, and what might have been an awkward first meeting wasn't at all. Joseph and Brad were friendly and welcoming. We had a delicious dinner at the back of the restaurant next to the crackling fireplace. Jack had told me he wasn't sure how much to say about Jeremiah and Big Jack's relationship and would follow Joseph's lead. He wouldn't deny Big Jack and Jeremiah's relationship if Joseph already knew the truth. He just wasn't willing to out an elderly man.

"I made some copies of photographs of our grandfathers when they

were younger," Jack said. "I thought you'd like to have a set for yourself."
I liked the way he segued into it. My guy was smoother than he realized.

"Thank you, Jack." Joseph took the photos, then he and Brad began
looking through them. "Look how young they looked."

"You really do look so much like Jeremiah," Brad told his husband.
"I never really agreed when everyone said it, but I can't deny the resemblance now. That's exactly how you looked when I fell in love with
you—same smile and everything." The two shared a private glance as if
they were the only two people in the room.

"They were so in love," Joseph whispered when he came to the picture of the men standing in front of the tank. "It's so sad they had to hide
who they were. But then again, I wouldn't be here if they had." Joseph
realized what he'd said and looked up suddenly, his face flushed with
embarrassment.

"I just recently learned the truth myself," Jack said, putting Joseph
at ease. "I had no idea Big Jack had been in love with a man. As far as I
could tell, he was very much in love with my grandmother."

"I'm sure he loved her as much as he could love anyone other than
Jeremiah." Joseph smiled kindly. "Granddad told us about your grandfather five years ago. I can't be sure why he told us after all the time that
had passed. Maybe it was because I came out at that time, and he was
showing support or maybe he just was tired of living a lie." Joseph was
physically in the room, but his gaze looked unfocused. "I used to tease
him about double dating, and that's when he told me about his Jack. He
told me he hadn't been strong enough to face a life of ridicule and scorn.
He said he'd walked away from the love of his life because he was a coward. I told him things were different back then and there weren't many
places where they could've lived openly." Joseph wiped a hand over his
face and refocused on us. He struggled to hold back the tears gathered in
his eyes. "I miss my grandfather so damn much. He's here physically but
nothing more." Joseph swallowed hard as a tear slid down his face.

"Joe," Brad said softly, pulling his husband close for a hug. Joe mourned Jeremiah every bit as much as Jack mourned Big Jack, even though Jeremiah hadn't died.

"I'm so sorry," Joseph said finally pulling himself together. "Big Jack just passed away and here I am blubbering away. I'm very sorry for your loss, Jack."

"Thank you." Jack's voice was rough and raw with emotion. I reached for his hand and laced our fingers together beneath the table. "I think your situation is much harder than mine. Big Jack led a robust life up until the last year. The cancer moved quickly, and it didn't take long for him to pass. He died peacefully in his sleep. It's fine if you want to mourn what you've lost with Jeremiah, and don't let anyone tell you differently." Joseph nodded as he wiped his cheeks.

The rest of the night passed without more tears. Brad and Joseph showed us pictures of their kids and made us laugh with stories about parenthood. They were such nice guys, and I found myself wishing they lived closer so we could get to know them better.

After the long day of traveling, the wine, and the crackling fire; time caught up to me. I suddenly found it hard to stay awake. Jack chuckled deeply when I leaned into him and laid my head on his shoulder. "You ready to head upstairs, Sleeping Beauty?"

"Mmm hmm," I replied drowsily.

Our dinner guests laughed and apologized for keeping us up so late after our long drive. As much as they loved their kids, they also loved having a break from them. Joseph told us he would pick us up in the morning to take us to meet Jeremiah. We exchanged hugs—because handshakes felt too formal—and headed up to our room.

Jack took Charlie out one last time, and I eyed the big claw foot tub and wondered if I could talk Jack into a long soak with me. It didn't take much convincing, and I ran us a hot bath. I climbed into the tub and leaned back between Jack's legs, my back to his chest. Jack nuzzled my neck and ran his hands up and down my torso. His movements were more about comfort than sex. We were giving and taking comfort from each other, completely in sync with each other's needs.

Not a word was spoken as we lounged in the tub, even though I felt like Jack wanted to say something. I was certain the evening had been difficult for him. I wanted him to be able to talk to me and tell me how he was feeling, but I wasn't going to push. The following day would be another big day for Jack, and he didn't need any added pressure from me. I wiggled as close to him as I could get, content in the knowledge that he'd reach for me when he was ready.

CHAPTER
Twenty-Seven

Jack

"HERE WE ARE," JOSEPH SAID, PULLING ONTO A LONG, TREE-LINED driveway. The stark, barren branches that hung over the drive were beautiful even in the dead of winter. I couldn't imagine how they'd look in the spring and in the fall. "It's really lovely here, and they take very good care of my grandfather."

"It can't be an easy job," Liam added, "watching all the people you care for slip away. I'm not sure how they do it."

"It takes a special kind of person, that's for sure," Brad added.

My anxiety kicked in as I climbed out of the car and followed Joseph and Brad. I reached for Liam's hand, entwining our fingers together. Joseph stopped to briefly greet the people working the front desk, then led the way to Jeremiah's room.

"I'm just going to wait in the solarium while you visit. The sun is nice and bright today, so it'll be warm enough," Brad said once we'd stopped in front of a closed door. "I don't want to overwhelm him, and I don't want to intrude on a private moment." He patted me gently on the shoulder and kissed Joseph on the cheek before he walked away.

"Should I go too?" Liam asked out of concern for Jeremiah's comfort.

"It'll be okay," Joseph said. "I'll go in first to say hi and tell him I'm bringing you guys in to see him. I doubt he'll have a clue what's going on, but it just feels like the right thing to do." I nodded at Joseph, and he went inside the room, shutting the door behind him.

"Thank you for being here, Ace. I can't imagine..." Liam stood on his tiptoes and pressed his lips to mine, effectively cutting off the rest of what I was going to say.

"You won't have to imagine a time without me or my love," Liam said once he pulled back from the kiss. "No thanks needed."

Joseph opened the door after a few minutes and motioned us inside. My heart thundered in my chest, but a sense of calm washed over me as soon as I crossed over the threshold into Jeremiah's room. It was almost like I felt Big Jack's guiding hand nudging me and whispering words of encouragement like he had when he'd taught me how to ride a two-wheeler. My parents had said I was too young, but he hadn't listened. Big Jack knew I was ready for the challenge—when I was a scared kid trying to find my balance on the bike, when I was a scared man too afraid to love, and now when I stood just inside his soul mate's room at the nursing home. I'd needed his gentle nudge on each of those occasions.

Jeremiah was propped up in bed watching TV. The volume was turned down, but it didn't seem like he cared as much about the sound as he did the activity. I could clearly see the young man he used to be. He was rocking back and forth slightly as if he might be agitated. I looked to Joseph, and he gave me an encouraging nod.

"This is the visitor I told you about, Grandpa," Joseph said slowly, a little louder than his normal speaking voice. "He's Jack Murphy's grandson.

His name is also Jack, and he drove here from Washington DC, to meet you."

Jeremiah turned his head and looked at me. The rocking stopped as soon as his eyes connected with mine, and I had to wonder if just maybe he recognized the green eyes I had inherited from Big Jack. Joseph wasn't the only one who was the spitting image of his grandfather.

"Hi, Jeremiah," I said, approaching the bed. "My grandfather, Jack Murphy, passed away a few months ago, and I found some photos of the two of you from your time together during World War II." Jeremiah held eye contact as I came to stand beside his bed. I had no way of knowing what he understood if anything, but there was something in his gaze—a slight spark.

I reached inside my coat pocket and pulled out the picture of Jeremiah and Big Jack that Liam and I loved so much—the same one that had made Joseph cry the night before. I held the picture up so he could see it. His gaze shifted away from my eyes and landed on the photo in my hand.

"Do you recognize those two handsome fellas?" I asked. I knew he couldn't respond, but I still felt the need to speak to him. Jeremiah held up a shaky hand, and I gave him the picture. He stared at the photo for a long time, then I saw a single tear cascade down his wrinkled cheek. Jeremiah's other hand lovingly caressed the photo, and I knew we had done the right thing by coming to visit. Jeremiah looked at the picture for the longest time before he laid it over his heart.

"He loved you his entire life." The words came out choked with raw emotion, but I needed to say them. I needed to speak the words my grand-dad had never been able to say to him. I took his paper-thin hand in mine. "He never let you go, even when you thought he had. You were with him every step of the way, clear up to the very end. He's waiting for you to be together again when you're called home." Jeremiah gave my hand the slightest squeeze, but I felt the strength fading in his grip. I patted his hand and laid it beside him on the bed, but instead, he placed it over the photo covering his heart. I saw how tired he was, and exhausting him wasn't my intention. "I'll leave you to rest now, Jeremiah. I just wanted to meet the man my granddad loved. Rest easy now, soldier." His eyelids fluttered a few times before closing but not before another tear escaped.

Joseph gave his grandfather a gentle kiss on the forehead before we left his room to find Brad. He was sitting on a bench in the middle of the solarium enjoying the sun shining through the glass walls and ceiling. It was a beautiful space, the sunlight driving away the chill of sadness lingering in my heart after seeing Jeremiah's emotional reaction to the photo.

Brad and Joseph sensed I wanted some time alone with Liam and quietly left us by ourselves. Joseph said he wanted to make sure the nursing staff realized how important that photo was to Jeremiah. He wanted to make sure it was always where his grandfather could reach it or look at it.

Once alone, I pulled Liam into a hug. "I believe what I told him, Ace."

"Which part?"

"That granddad is waiting for him. Grandma got to marry Big Jack and raise a family with him, but Jeremiah gets his eternity. I feel it." Liam raised his head off my chest and gave me a sweet kiss, which warmed me more than the sun. "I'm so grateful I don't have to wait until death to have you."

"Me too."

Brad and Joseph found us in the same position when they returned several minutes later. A few months ago, I would've been uncomfortable showing that amount of affection to another man in public, but it just seemed natural to reach for Liam, no matter where we were or who we were with.

On the way back to the B&B, I asked Joseph for a restaurant recommendation. I wanted something ridiculously romantic so I could wine and dine Liam before I asked him that all important question.

CHAPTER
Twenty-Eight

Liam

J ACK WAS QUIET FOR MOST OF THE AFTERNOON, WHICH WASN'T unusual for him. He spent a lot of time reflecting on things, and when he was ready to talk, he would. We took Charlie for a long walk in the crisp, winter air before we ended up falling asleep. A phone call from Chase to let us know baby Sofia had arrived woke us up. He promised that Ellie and Sofia were doing well, and he would save some chubby baby cheeks for me to kiss.

It was so nice hearing from my brother, and I was looking forward to getting back home and meeting Sofia, but I was loving the long weekend away with Jack. I sensed it was something we both needed.

We took a very long, very steamy shower together before we got dressed and went to dinner. The place Jack had chosen was famous for seafood, and the menu was a bit overwhelming for a mostly beef and chicken kind of guy. I ended up going with steak and lobster while Jack ordered some massive crab extravaganza. I drank most of the wine since Jack was driving, but I wasn't too tipsy to notice something a little more intimate about Jack's behavior. The looks he sent me had me wishing we were eating alone in our room back at the B&B. There were a lot of wicked things I could do with that melted butter.

As soon as the thought occurred to me, a drop of butter dripped off my bite of lobster and ran down my finger. With my eyes locked on Jack's, I licked it from my finger deliberately and slowly. Maybe I should have been more concerned about someone else seeing my behavior, but I only had eyes for Jack. Right then, his gaze told me he was ready to ask for the check, but I wasn't quite done having fun yet.

I slid my foot out of my loafer beneath the table and moved it to caress Jack's ankle before inching up his strong calf and over his thigh until I stopped to press my foot on the bulge between his legs. My naughty actions were hidden beneath the tablecloth. Jack's eyes, however, broadcast just how much my little shenanigans were affecting him. I used my toes to massage him and smiled wickedly across the candlelit table when I felt his cock stir beneath my ministrations.

"Ace." His voice was a soft warning of things I could expect later, but he should've known by then that I liked it rough and dirty. I liked pushing him past his control because I knew, no matter what, he'd never hurt me and would only give me indescribable pleasure.

Jack's big hand covered my foot, and I expected him to pull my foot off his lap so he wouldn't get too aroused in the dining room, but that wasn't what happened at all. Instead, he pushed my foot harder against his semi-erection, thrusting up into it just a fraction. My mouth dropped open when he upped the stakes, and my mind tried to spin out something I could do to top him, but he signaled for our bill before I could make my next move.

"Don't cause me to wreck," Jack warned when he got behind the wheel and started his Jeep. He probably didn't want me touching him, but that didn't mean I couldn't touch myself.

I started out by rubbing my erection through my slacks, but I turned up the heat when I heard a soft growl emanate from his throat. Oh, yes, I wanted to bring out the animal from within. I unfastened my slacks and reached beneath my briefs to stroke my dick. Seeing my hand move beneath the fabric and knowing he was glancing over increased my lust. I wanted to give him a show, but I didn't want to come until he was inside me. I kept my strokes slow and teasing, careful not to stroke too hard or too fast.

"Give me a taste," Jack demanded.

I swiped a pearly drop of precum off the tip and held my finger to his lips. He licked my finger clean like I had in the restaurant with the melted butter. Jack attacked my mouth when we arrived back at the B&B. I tasted myself on his tongue while I refastened my pants and pulled down my sweater to cover my arousal.

"Put your coat on," Jack said, unwilling to let anyone see just how badly I wanted him. All my passion was for his eyes and his eyes only.

We tried not to be obvious as we made our way up to our room, but all bets were off once the door was closed behind us. Our teeth bumped while we kissed, and nails scored aroused flesh in our attempt to disrobe one another and toss the clothes to the floor.

Jack pulled the duvet cover to the foot of the bed and laid me down, covering me with his hot, hard body. I eagerly spread my legs to make room for him while he kissed me long and deep as if he were trying to make a point with his kiss. I was hot and impatient, wanting to feel his hard length stretch and fill me, making me feel complete and whole. That is what his love did for me.

He was just as eager to claim me as I was to be claimed. He reached for the lube and set about stretching me. I bit his shoulder, urging him to take me and take me hard. It must have had the desired effect because he was pushing into me seconds later. I couldn't get enough of the burn and stretch of him entering me. The discomfort never lasted and only pleasure would follow.

"Like this?" Jack asked, beginning to stroke long and deep inside me. "Is that what you wanted, Ace?"

"Yes," I replied, eyes rolling back in my head when he pegged my sweet spot. "Just like that."

"You love to feel me inside you, don't you? Long and hard or soft and slow doesn't matter as long as I'm feeding your greedy hole."

"Yes." It was getting hard to focus on his words. He kept aiming his dick at the target, hitting the bull's-eye with every thrust home. His thrusts got longer and harder, and I began to claw at his back.

"Open your eyes and look at me, Liam." I did as he asked. "Do you want to feel me like this forever?" My head felt so heavy but I managed to nod. "I need to hear the words."

"Yes, Jack."

"Say you'll be mine forever." Jack lifted my legs higher up his torso and dug his knees into the mattress, driving into me at a furious pace. My eyes started to close again as my orgasm loomed near. "Open them."

"Yes." I answered both his question and his demand. I reached between our bodies to stroke my cock, my need to orgasm becoming painful.

"Marry me, Liam."

"Yes." I realized what he had just said—not asked—and my response. My eyes widened, and my hand stilled on my cock. Jack grinned wickedly at me and began to pound into me with renewed purpose. He nailed my prostate one more time, and I came all over my stomach.

"Mine now," Jack growled with possessive glee as he rode out his orgasm, never taking his eyes off mine—not even when he came. Jack collapsed on top of me when the last waves of his climax faded.

"Wait a minute," I said out loud, needing to clarify what had just happened.

"Nope." Jack raised his head to look at me. "You said yes, and there's no taking it back."

"So you really asked me to marry you?" A touch of disbelief had creeped into my voice. The wry smile that spread across his face told me I hadn't imagined his proposal.

"I didn't *ask* you to marry me. I *told* you to marry me."

"During sex? I can't be responsible for what I say during sex." I narrowed my eyes at him like I was none too pleased, but my heart was pumping a lot harder than it had during any orgasm.

"You said yes, and I'm holding you to it." There was not an ounce of apology in his arrogant gaze.

"Jack, what am I supposed to tell people when they ask how you proposed?" I playfully punched him in the shoulder. "Do you really want me to tell them you *told* me to marry you while you were pounding my prostate like a prizefighter on fight night?" Jack's big body shook with mirth before laughter burst from his chest. "I'm being serious, buster."

"Buster?" That only made Jack laugh harder, which made me laugh at the ridiculousness of the situation. Beneath the amusement and disbelief was a whole lot of happy, though. This beautiful man wanted to share his life with me, and I was honored he'd asked me—told me—even if his method was highly inappropriate and scandalous.

"Seriously, babe. You need to do it properly so I have a story to tell. It doesn't have to be storybook quality, just G rated."

"Okay," Jack agreed after much laughter. He slowly pulled out of my body and kneeled beside the bed. "Liam…"

"Seriously? You're going to ask me to marry you while your spunk is dripping out of my hole and I'm coated in my own? The only two people who would find this remotely appropriate are Aunt Bea and Gram." But then I ruined my indignation by shaking the bed from laughing so damn hard. "I'd rather tell the fucking proposal over the spunky one." Jack laid his head on the edge of the bed and laughed along with me. "You're going to have to try this again, and do it right." I tried for an arrogant, upper-crust tone, but it only made us laugh harder.

"Okay," Jack said, rising to his feet. "Let me think up a more romantic proposal, and I'll get back to you."

"When?" I wanted to tell the world I belonged to him.

Jack shrugged and scratched his head. "This is the best I could come up with after two weeks, so you might be waiting a while."

"Two weeks? You've been wanting to ask me to marry you for two weeks?" My voice rose along with my surprise.

"Longer really, but that was when I asked your folks for their blessing." Jack looked embarrassed that he hadn't come up with something better, but I was stuck on the fact that he'd asked my parents for my hand. How fucking cute was that?

"Thanksgiving," I said, light bulbs snapping on in my brain. "That's what all the sneaking and secrecy was about. That's why you didn't want to discuss it. Hell, I thought you were plotting Christmas presents." I sat up and cupped his face in my hands. "Fuck a serious or romantic proposal." Jack raised his brows. "Yes, Jack Murphy, I will marry you."

I kissed him then. Regardless of how or when he asked, the answer would always be yes. I didn't need a fancy, romantic proposal. I just needed it to be real, and that was exactly what he'd given me.

The next morning, Jack brought us breakfast in bed on an antique silver tray. He set the tray on the bedside table and lifted the stainless-steel dome off one of the plates to reveal Belgian waffles with fresh strawberries, crispy bacon, and fluffy scrambled eggs. In addition to the food, there was a carafe of coffee and two glasses of orange juice.

"Marry me, Ace."

Tears filled my eyes because he was giving me a proposal I could talk about. I thought I couldn't love him more, but I was wrong. I was learning every day that there was no limit to my love for him. Every day, my heart expanded more and my love for Jack grew. I could search for the rest of my days and never find another who made me feel as loved as he did. That didn't mean I wouldn't tease him a little.

"Well, now that I've had time to think about it," I said, scrunching up my face in concentration. Before I knew it, he had pushed me onto my back and was straddling my hips. He dug his fingers into my ribs, knowing how ticklish I was there.

"I fucked a yes out of you last night, and I'll tickle one out of you right now," he said, digging his fingers into my flesh and making me wiggle out of control. "What's your answer?"

"Yes!" My shout echoed around the room. Jack smiled like he'd won an amazing prize. "My answer will always be yes."

CHAPTER
Twenty-Nine

Jack

L IAM AND I CAME BACK FROM VERMONT A DAY EARLY SO WE could visit with Ellie and baby Sofia. We made a stop at the Vermont Teddy Bear Company so we could buy a special gift for the little lady on our way home. I hadn't thought much about teddy bears before, but it sure was soft and cute.

Ellie looked exhausted when we arrived but was happy to show off her little bundle of joy. Everyone else had already dropped by earlier in the day, so we got to enjoy a private visit. "She was so worth all the pain," she said, rocking a sleepy Sofia.

I hadn't quite figured out the dynamic with Bevan quite yet. I knew Ben a lot better than Bevan since we played on the softball team I sponsored over the summer. I had heard enough bits and pieces from Xavier,

Chase, and Liam to know Bevan wasn't Sofia's biological father, but that was impossible to tell given the smile that lit up his face when he looked down at the baby in Ellie's arms.

Bevan gently lifted Sofia from Ellie and placed her in Liam's arms. I loved watching Liam holding babies. He was so gentle and loving as he checked her little fingers and toes. For the first time in my life, I could actually see myself with a family of my own. Liam gently kissed Sofia on the forehead and tried to hand her to me.

"I don't know," I told him. I had never held a baby, and she looked really fragile. "I don't want to drop her."

"You won't drop her," Liam replied, smiling indulgently at me. He placed her in my arms with her head cradled in the bend of my elbow. Charlie came over and sat by my knees, curious to see what I held in my arms. He'd press his nose to her blanket, then jerk back when she moved.

I looked at Sofia's innocent sleeping face and felt tugs in my heart I hadn't expected. She was going to be one much-loved little lady. "You sure are a beautiful little girl, Sofia. There will come a time when Uncle Jack will need to look pretty damn menacingly at boys who show up at your front door to take you out."

"I'll thoroughly vet the boys and their families, and you can literally scare the crap out of them with that same scowl you use when some guy stares too long at Liam." So everyone had noticed how badly I wanted Liam, except Liam. "Hey, were you able to get in touch with Joseph Merritt?" Bevan asked.

"Actually, we just came back from a visit with Jeremiah," I replied. "It took Joseph a little while to get back to us, but we planned the trip as soon as he gave us the okay." I told them about Jeremiah's medical condition and how touching it was when he seemed to recognize the photo. "I can't thank you enough for helping me to make that possible, Bevan."

"I was happy to do it. Truly."

Liam held the baby one last time before we gave her back to her mama. We didn't want to stay too long because it was obvious they were all exhausted. We were tired from the long trip back and were eager to get home and crawl between the sheets.

On our way home, I realized we hadn't told Ellie and Bevan our news. I started questioning the way I'd proposed to Liam. As much as we laughed and teased about it, he was right about my proposals being inappropriate. We definitely couldn't tell our friends and family the story. Was that why he hadn't said anything? Should I have waited until I had a ring? I knew guys gave girls engagement rings, but is that what guys did for other guys? It seemed like my proposal was FUBAR. Then I remembered that Xavier hadn't given Ben a ring when he'd proposed, so maybe it wasn't a requirement.

Liam went upstairs with our luggage while I waited outside so Charlie could do his final business for the night. I expected Liam to either be in the shower or in bed by the time I returned, but instead, I found him standing in the kitchen beside his early Christmas present. I had forgotten Chase had overseen the installation while we were away given all the excitement over meeting Jeremiah, my impromptu proposals, and meeting Sofia.

"Jack, you shouldn't have bought me something so expensive." Liam ran his hand lovingly over the red bow Chase had tied to one of the double oven's handles.

"Why not? I saw the way you drooled over Chase's the few times we've been over there, and I knew it would make you happy. Besides, you weren't impressed with the way your cookies turned out, though I thought they were perfect." Liam cocked his head to the side. He was biting his lip, which meant he was nervous or fighting back tears he felt he shouldn't cry. I never wanted him to hold anything back from me. I'd never think less of him because he showed his emotions. In fact, he was a bigger man than most. "I want you happy, Ace. Deliriously so. God knows I don't always say the right things, and sometimes I don't say anything at all. It's just the way I'm wired, but I am trying to do better. There are times I just want to show you how much your happiness means to me."

"Jack." I loved it when he whispered my name so lovingly.

I dropped to one knee in front of him. "Marry me, Liam."

A bubble of laughter escaped him followed by the sweetest smile I'd ever seen. "Already asked and answered, sir."

"Say it again. I need to hear it. We'll go pick out rings tomorrow if that's what you need for this to feel real to you." I hoped he could see my yearning for a future with him in my eyes. "I want to tell our families and friends that we are taking this step together. They might look at us a little funny for moving so fast, but we know it's right for us."

Liam tugged my hand until I stood. "I don't need a ring until our wedding day, but if you want me to wear one before then to show I'm taken, I will. Is that what you want?"

"Yes." I hadn't known that was what I wanted until he'd phrased it the way he had. I did want him wearing my ring, even if we weren't married yet. In my heart, we already belonged to each other.

"It's settled, then," Liam said. "We'll pick out rings and wear them to show our commitment. How are we going to tell everyone? Who do we tell first? Our parents?" Liam pursed his lips in concentration.

"Why don't you bake a cute cake or cookies in the form of an announcement, and we can text it to everyone all at once."

Liam's eyes widened. "I love that!"

"You do?"

"It's fun and quirky," he said. "Besides, how would we decide who to tell first? Our extended families are huge!" He clapped his hands playfully. "I need to start planning." Liam headed toward the kitchen but paused suddenly. "People will notice our rings."

I snatched his hand and pulled him behind me toward the bedroom. "Tomorrow will be soon enough to plan and put things into action. Tonight, we make love and go to sleep." A thought occurred to me on the way to the bedroom. "I still need to come up with a proposal we can repeat. Sex proposal, cum proposal, breakfast in bed proposal, and now double oven proposal," I said, naming all my attempts. "I suck."

"Mmm, you suck so very well," Liam purred. And just like that, all my sleepiness disappeared.

The next morning, Liam and I went to the mall to pick out our rings. There were so many to choose from, and it was a little overwhelming, but our salesperson, Candace, was very helpful without being pushy. "Are you looking for matching rings or would you like something different for each of you?" she asked.

"Different," we both said.

"Okay," Candace replied. "Let's rule out the metals you don't like."

"I'm not fond of yellow gold," Liam replied, then looked at me for my thoughts.

"I'm not fond of it either."

"All right," Candace said, "we've made a lot of progress with just that decision." She put the trays with the yellow-gold rings back in the case, but it still left several to choose from. "We can always have the rings custom made if you don't find a design you like in your preferred metal."

Candace went through each metal option until we ruled out all of them, except titanium. We worked our way through the trays of titanium rings, which were all beautiful, but none seemed to fit our personalities. I was starting to get discouraged until Candace pulled out a tray of rings with etchings on them, several with Celtic symbols, and my heart immediately skipped a beat.

"Oh, look at this one," Liam said, holding up a ring that had a dragon etched in flames all around the band. It was surprising that someone could get such intricate detail on a wedding band. "It's perfect for my Dragon." I nodded quickly, suddenly feeling very emotional.

I continued to look through the selection for a ring that better suited what Liam meant to me. Our rings would be forged of the same metal, but the symbols should match what the other person meant to us. Liam would wear a dragon to represent me, but I wanted to wear something that embodied my Ace. Then I found it, a band with beautifully etched Celtic hearts all the way around the ring. "My Ace of hearts," I said, holding it up for Liam to see. He smiled approvingly and leaned in for a quick kiss.

"Let's get you both fitted," Candace said cheerfully.

CHAPTER
Thirty

Liam

I KEPT LOOKING DOWN AT THE RING ON MY LEFT HAND AND RECALL-ing the way Jack's eyes had lit up with love when he'd slipped it onto my finger in front of all the customers and sales staff in the store. I thought it was sweet Jack wanted to create a proposal I could proudly tell our families about, even though I loved his original proposal the most. I didn't need fancy or formal. I wanted real, and that was what I got.

I sighed happily and looked around the mall to see if Jack was on his way back with our coffees. He had left me sitting at a pretty table for two while he went to get our drinks. He spoiled me in the sweetest ways. My eyes landed on my sexy guy as he made his way back to me, but he wasn't alone. I sat up straighter as my eyes raked over the handsome stranger walking beside him. I didn't care for the way he smiled at Jack or the obvious ease Jack felt in his company. They looked like they knew each other really well, and I suddenly felt insecure.

He gave you a ring. He asked you to marry him. He bought you a double oven. Stop the nonsense! The smile on Jack's face when he pointed his coffee cup in my direction eased my mind further. This man was seriously in love with me, and it was obvious he was proud to introduce me to the stranger, who smiled disarmingly at me.

"Sorry for the long wait," Jack said, dropping a kiss on my lips as he handed me my cup. "I ran into Noah at the coffee shop and brought him to meet you."

"Oh." I put my drink down, stood up, and hugged Noah. I caught the man off guard and he staggered back a step before he returned my embrace. Suddenly, it made sense why Jack had been so pleased to see him. No wonder they looked familiar with one another. "It's so nice to meet you," I said, pulling back. I bit my lips to keep them from trembling. Without Noah, I wasn't sure I would even have been there with Jack. Would Jack have taken the tragic turn so many returning warriors with PTSD took? Tears burned behind my eyelids at the thought of a world without Jack in it, but the presence of his ring on my finger helped me shift my focus away from the what-ifs.

Noah grinned widely, looking a little flushed over my exuberant greeting. "It's nice to meet you too, Liam."

"Let's move to a bigger table so you can join us," I said.

Noah looked at his watch, then said, "I would really love to stay and chat, but I'm meeting someone for lunch." I couldn't tell from his tone if his lunch date was personal or professional. "Maybe some other time?"

"Sure," I replied with a nod.

"Congratulations on your engagement." He looked at Jack and added, "You deserve this happiness."

"Thanks, Noah," Jack said.

We waved him off and settled at the table. I didn't think I really wanted to wear rings before our ceremony, but that had changed as soon as Jack had mentioned it the night before. I loved the feel of his ring on my finger and loved how mine looked on him. I reached over and traced a finger over the metal band that represented our commitment to one another. I laid my left hand over his and angled it so both our bands were visible, then snapped a picture with my phone.

"We better get home soon so I can set our plan into motion because I don't think I can take this ring off just so no one will notice it," I said. "I plan on taking it with me into the afterlife."

"I'm not taking mine off either." In his eyes, I saw how affected he was by my words. "Will you send me a copy of that picture so I can have it too?"

I texted him the picture as we made our way out of the mall and into the frigid cold December morning. I shivered beneath all my layers and Jack pulled me into his side, wrapping his arm around my shoulders to offer his body heat.

He turned on his preferred radio station once he started the Jeep. The song switched over on the station from a honky-tonk song to a ballad. I expected Jack to drop the gear shift into drive, but he didn't move. I looked over at him and found him staring at me.

"What's wrong?"

"This song always makes me think of us. It's even the ringtone when you call me, did you know that?" I shook my head. I hadn't known Chris Young's "Who I Am with You" reminded Jack of us or that it was my designated ringtone. It was a beautiful song, and listening to the words about a man wandering through life lost and alone did sound a lot like Jack before we met. Tears threatened to spill down my face by the time the song reached the chorus.

"It's a beautiful song," I said once it ended, and I wiped my damp eyes with the back of my hand. "I have a song for you too."

"You do?" Jack's eyes lit up.

"Yep, let me play it for you." I turned down the radio and searched through my music until I came to the right song. I hit Play and the beginning of Sir Mix A Lot's "Baby Got Back" came through the speakers of my phone. Jack's eyes widened when he recognized the song, then he pulled me into a headlock and proceeded to give me noogies while I laughed about the shocked look on his face.

"You think I have a big ass?" Jack's growl only made me laugh harder.

"Muscular." I tried explaining my way out of it. "Makes me want to take a bite out of it."

"That's slightly better," he said, still not appeased. The noogies turned into tickling when he dug his fingers into my upper thigh. "I love how ticklish you are. It seems like suitable torture for an imp like yourself."

"Let me play the real song that makes me think of you and how you make me feel. I even have a secret ringtone for you too." Jack leaned back and narrowed his eyes at me suspiciously.

He released me and pushed a button on his steering wheel. "Call Liam," he said when his hands-free menu came on. Jack smiled when he heard Ed Sheeran crooning "Kiss Me" through my phone.

"It makes me think about our first kiss," I told him. "It was so full of promise and passion, but I was afraid it would be the only kiss I got from you. I figured it was just curiosity or a slip of control but would never be more. I was afraid to hope."

"You have me now, Ace." He gestured to the ring on his finger. "We just need to decide when we want to make it legal."

"Let's get through the holidays first, then we'll start making wedding plans. Sound good?"

"I guess," he grumbled and shifted the Jeep into drive.

"Are you ready for the chaos?" I asked Jack as my finger hovered over the Send button on my phone. Jack's finger was doing the same. I'd baked a variety of sugar cookies, then decorated them to say various things about love and marriage. I arranged them around a larger center cookie that read Liam Said Yes in big, bold letters.

"Let's do it on the count of three," he said. "One, two, three..."

We pushed the Send button at the same time and braced ourselves for hours of phone calls and texts. We had made a list of all our friends and family members to send it to, and it didn't even take a minute for both of our phones to go off. We talked, laughed, texted, and celebrated with our friends and families for hours. It was fun, exciting, and so damn exhausting.

When it was all over, we curled up together on the couch in front of the tree with Charlie and Big Jack's photos and journals. I hated that Jack's granddad wasn't physically present to share our joy, but he was there in spirit. So many of Big Jack's good traits flowed through Jack's blood, and I was blessed to have him by my side for whatever life threw at us.

We decided to read the rest of Big Jack's journals to honor his life and celebrate the happy times, not just the sad ones. I couldn't wait to read what Big Jack had thought the first time he'd held his grandson in his arms, but we had a while before we got that far. Jack cracked open a journal and began to read about Big Jack's return home after the war was over. It was obvious he had tried to put his sorrow behind him and focus on the things he thought he could have instead of the things he thought would never be. As sad as I was that Big Jack didn't get his happily ever after with Jeremiah, it was hard to be too upset when I had Jack beside me. Like Joseph had said when we'd met, he and Jack wouldn't be there if things had worked out differently. So as sad as I was for Jeremiah and Big Jack, I focused on what Jack believed, which was that eternity was reserved for them. I found a lot of comfort in those thoughts as I laid my head on Jack's shoulder and let his voice, and his beloved grandfather's words, wash over me.

CHAPTER
Thirty-One

Jack

I F THANKSGIVING WAS HECTIC, THEN CHRISTMAS WAS AN OUTRIGHT zoo. It felt like we had someplace to be every single weekend while we rang in the holidays. I would've hated all of it before I met Liam, but he'd changed the way I saw the world and the people in it.

My favorite weekend was when Hunter and Sully had come to DC for a visit. Liam was fidgety and nervous like I had never seen him. He wanted everything to be perfect and was afraid they wouldn't like him because he was so different from us.

"Ace, you've fluffed that same throw pillow ten times," I told him. I went to him and pulled him into my arms. "Relax, Liam. They're going to love you, just like everyone does."

"I'm not some alpha hot stud like you guys," he had told me. I used my thumb to smooth the frown lines that marred his brow. "I don't like sports all that much. I prefer wine instead of beer. I wear skinny jeans and have product in my hair." He started ticking off reasons they might not like him, so I covered his mouth with my finger to stop the flow of words.

"You're incredibly sexy just the way you are. You love music and so do they. The guys like wine sometimes. And I love your skinny jeans and hair." I ticked off my counterpoints. "More importantly, they're going to love how much you love me. Isn't that what you want for your friends?" At his nod, I said, "Then please stop worrying and relax." The tension eased in his lean frame and he melted against my chest.

I'd been absolutely correct about Sully and Hunter. They were taken with Liam right away. It helped that Sully broke the ice by referring to Liam as the dragon's prince. Liam took to the nickname instead of being insulted and started making bawdy jokes about what it took to tame the dragon. Where Sully and Liam bonded over jokes, Hunter spent time with him in the kitchen helping to prepare food. Hunter thought it was awesome that Liam would be starting culinary school in the spring. I had forgotten how much Hunter liked messing around in the kitchen and had a sudden vision of Liam and Hunter owning a restaurant. The idea had merit, and I made a mental note to bring it up to Liam later.

It meant so much to me that my two closest friends were so open and accepting of my life with Liam. As much as I loved Hunter and Sully, I was glad I didn't have to choose. There wouldn't really be much of a choice because Liam was my present and future. He was and would always be my lover and best friend.

Liam had gone Christmas shopping with Chase on the final day of Hunter and Sully's visit. They seemed disappointed that he wouldn't be hanging around with them before they left, but Liam felt like we needed some alone time, just the three of us.

We watched some football and ate pizza, but it didn't take long for Hunter and Sully to let me know how they felt about Liam and his presence in my life. I knew without them saying anything, but it was nice to hear the words anyway.

"I've never seen you this relaxed or happy, Dragon," Sully told me.

"It's nice to see," Hunter added. "You deserve happiness."

"Everyone deserves this kind of happiness, fellas," I corrected. "I hope you both find it someday. If you do, surrender your hearts. You won't regret it."

My favorite holiday party was definitely the one Chase and Gray threw for their ever-expanding extended family. Everyone was there wearing the ugliest freaking sweaters they could find in hopes of winning a trophy that would get passed around each year. This was the first year, and everyone wanted to be the first winner, including me. Liam had found a knitted reindeer sweater in my size that he'd embellished by wrapping mini lights around the antlers. There was a tiny battery pack in the waistband of the sweater that annoyed me, but I wanted to win the damn trophy so I could display it on my mantel until the next year.

I should've known I wouldn't stand a chance going up against Gram. She wore a sweater that was so gaudy and obnoxious it hurt the eyes but no one could look away. The theme of the sweater was The Twelve Days of Christmas, and it had every single character mentioned in the song scattered all over the sweater in glitter. I gracefully bowed to the queen.

I had one stipulation during all the Christmas chaos, which was that Christmas Day would just be for us and always would be. If we were ever blessed with kids, I wanted to spend the day setting up and playing with their toys.

Liam and I had already exchanged a gift early. I had given him his beloved double oven, and he'd given me something that squeezed my heart until I feared it would burst. He'd had a fire-breathing Celtic dragon tattooed over his heart with the words *Surrender Your Heart* beneath it. As much as I loved all the gifts he'd given me on Christmas morning, the tattoo was my favorite. Of course, I had to wait for his skin to heal before I could trace it with my tongue like he always did with my tattoo.

After our Christmas morning gift exchange, Liam made us a delicious breakfast that I wanted to make a part of our traditions, but I feared my waistline might not agree. I let Charlie have some table scraps since it was

Christmas and because he was the best dog in the world. Santa Paws had brought Charlie plenty of doggy treats and toys, so he was a happy boy too.

Liam and I called my parents to wish them a merry Christmas. I sensed the sadness in my dad's voice, even though he acted jovial. I missed Granddad so much, and I couldn't imagine how hard it was for Dad, who was his only son. There were days I felt guilty knowing things about Granddad that my father didn't, but I couldn't break Granddad's confidence.

Granddad was still on my mind long after I'd hung up the phone. Liam sensed my mood and brought one of the journals to me. It had been a while since we read an entry, and it made me feel better to just hold the journal in my hand.

December 1, 1955

Today was the happiest day of my life. Mary Lou gave me the most amazing gift I have ever received in the form of a squalling baby boy. We had been trying for a few years now and had given up hope of ever becoming parents, but there he was, Patrick Aidan Murphy, named after both our fathers. I wanted to be in the room when he first came into the world, but it wasn't permitted. I guess they thought men who'd fought in wars weren't tough enough to watch their children being born.

Had anyone asked me after the war ended if I could ever feel this happy, I would've said no, but I could never have told them why I felt that way. No one would have guessed I had left most of my heart with another man on a distant shore while fighting tyranny and hate. I never would have thought my heart could be healed, but my Mary Lou found a way.

Holding my newborn son in my arms, I realized the heart is capable of healing and expanding to let new people and experiences into our lives. This might not have been the life I wanted, but it was the one chosen for me, and I would make the very best of it because it is a gift. Mary Lou and Patrick are my gifts, and I will cherish them with everything I have inside me until I take my last breath.

I want Patrick to know unconditional love so he will love in the same way.

I want him to know what it feels like to hold his very own bundle of joy in his arms someday. The best way I can honor Jeremiah is to make sure I love and support Patrick no matter where life takes him or who he loves. That's what being a father means to me.

Welcome to the world, my sweet boy.

"I have one more present for you," Liam said softly when I finished reading. "I debated giving it to you because I was afraid it would make you sad and ruin your holiday. Now, I think it's just what the moment needs." Liam scooted off the couch and bent over next to the tree, pulling something out from way in the back. It didn't matter that I'd already had my Merry Christmas sex this morning, seeing his ass up in the air made me want more. Liam gave me a sexy smile, knowing where my thoughts had gone as he made his way back beside me with a flat, rectangular package. "Here you go." I watched as Liam began worrying his bottom lip between his teeth, but I couldn't imagine why he'd be nervous about his gift.

I accepted the package from him, looking down at the wrapping paper that had nothing to do with Christmas but instead was covered with various types of fish and fishing equipment. "You already gave me too much." But I had to admit, the odd wrapping paper had me curious, so I didn't waste a bunch of time telling him he shouldn't have because he would just insist, then I would accept. I wanted to skip past the BS so I could have more Christmas sex.

Beneath the paper was a large collage of photos of me and Big Jack taken throughout my lifetime. There were pictures of fishing and camping trips, school plays, baseball games, my graduation from basic training, and many, many more. In the center was a picture of him holding me when I was just a few hours old.

"It's beautiful," I said to Liam as I took in every expression on Big Jack's face. "This is so thoughtful, Liam."

"I thought it would look beautiful on the mantel," he whispered from beside me. "That way he can always be watching over us."

"I want to think he's looking down on us right now and smiling over how happy I am. I want to thank him for his encouragement to do the right thing for myself, which led me to you. I will honor him the rest of my life by being the best husband, and maybe someday a father, by following his examples."

I stood up and moved things around on the mantel to make room for the amazing gift. Big Jack's love radiated from every single photo, making me smile. Liam stepped up beside me, and I pulled him in front of me, resting my chin on his shoulder. Granddad had given me the courage, but the man in my arms had made my dreams come true.

CHAPTER
Thirty-Two

Liam

J ACK CLOSED DOWN THE BAR TO THE GENERAL PUBLIC TO RING IN the new year, but we still had a packed house full of friends and family. Everywhere I looked, I saw the people I loved most in the world. They were playing pool, darts, or arcade games, chatting at tables, or taking turns on the stage singing karaoke. Chase and I supplied the food, and Jack supplied the beverages. He made those drinking alcohol surrender their keys unless they'd brought a designated driver with them.

"Happy New Year, sweetheart," my mom said, kissing my cheek. "You're about to experience more happiness than you've ever imagined." I had a feeling she was right. She crooked her finger, and I leaned even closer. "I heard through the grapevine what Jack did for Justin. I think everyone would have understood if Jack wanted Justin to be fully prosecuted for attacking him. It shows what a remarkable, forgiving man he is, and I am honored to be his future mother-in-law."

Jack had talked to the district attorney and had asked that Justin get counseling and community service instead of jail time. Some people thought Jack was being too lenient, but he felt in his heart it was the right thing to do. I was still angry over the incident, and I was having a harder time forgiving Justin, but I supported Jack's decision.

I looked across the room to where Jack was talking to Chase and Gray at the pool table. It looked to me like Chase and Gray were competing against one another again and Jack was somehow acting as referee. Chase would point at the table and say something while Gray countered with his own gestures and words. There wasn't anything heated about their disagreement as evidenced by the ornery matching grins they wore. Most of us had started referring to their little competitions as foreplay. Jack must have had enough because he took their pool sticks away and pointed for them to go take a seat at a corner booth.

"He's really good at conflict resolution," my dad said with a laugh as he came up to stand beside us. "Have you guys picked a date yet?" It was the question everyone had asked, but Jack and I had decided to wait until after the holidays to discuss it. We weren't even sure what kind of wedding we wanted.

"Not yet. We have plenty of time," I replied with a patient smile. I hugged my parents before moving on to circulate around the room.

"Married in Vegas?" I heard Ava ask Gram. She was sitting on Brandon's lap instead of in the vacant seat beside him. It was cute to see how much she still liked to cuddle against him. As she had told me earlier, they didn't have a lot of free time to hang out with friends and cuddle like they used to. She loved being a mom to Jacob but was happy to have a sitter for the night so she could spend time celebrating with her friends and husband.

"That's what she suggested," Lennie said. "I told her she would be miserable without all of you on her special day." He reached over and brought Gram's hand up to his mouth and kissed it.

"He's right. I can't get married without all of you. I'm just not sure what kind of wedding to have," she said with a sigh. "Outdoor, indoor, skydiving," she said with a wry smile. "It just gets so overwhelming."

"What gets overwhelming?" Xavier asked, walking up behind me. I ducked to avoid what I knew was coming, but I wasn't fast enough to escape a noogie. "Making up for lost time," he said, digging his knuckles deeper into my scalp when I tried to squirm away.

"Step away from my man, and no one gets hurt," said my growly-voiced dragon on his way to the rescue. It worked too because X let go and hid behind Ben. "That's what I thought."

"Gram was saying that wedding planning can be overwhelming," Ava chimed in. "How're your plans going, Xavier?" She gave him a pointed look, and we all turned in his direction.

"I'm thinking Vegas," he said smartly, causing us all to laugh. "What?"

"Gram was just saying the same thing," I told him.

"Maybe we should all take a field trip to Vegas so all the engaged couples can get married at once," Brandon suggested, earning a pinch from his wife. "Ow, baby. I was just trying to be helpful."

I visited with them a little longer before the urge to check on the food and circulate struck me. The food was well stocked, and I was just about to head over to visit with Chase and Gray, who had turned their exile from the pool table into an excuse to suck face, when my eyes landed on JJ and Miller. Gone was the tension I'd witnessed between them during Thanksgiving.

Miller had his back to one of the posts dividing the main bar from the game area. JJ was standing so close their chests were almost touching with one of his arms braced over Miller's head. JJ lowered his head and whispered something that made Miller smile wickedly. Miller's smile faded from his lips when JJ stood up straight and looked at him. I couldn't quite figure it out, but I would have sworn something more serious than just sex was happening between them.

"They look like two men trying to fight the inevitable," Jack said as he wrapped his arms around me. "I recognize that look on their faces because I saw it plenty of times when I looked in the mirror. The ship is going down, fellas," Jack said but only loud enough for me to hear. "It's time to sink or swim."

"You have to wonder why they're fighting it so hard." I rested my head back on Jack's shoulder, letting his warmth sink into my body. "I don't understand those two. It's not like we don't all know they're screwing around. What do they have against monogamous relationships?"

"I can't say for sure because I don't know them that well," Jack replied. "Maybe they've been really hurt in the past and that's their defense mechanism, or maybe they really can't see themselves sleeping with the same person for the rest of their lives."

"Hmm, pity," I replied.

"I have a feeling there's a lot more to them than any of us realize. I've noticed a lack of conviction lately when they spew their disgust over our committed relationships. It's not quite as venomous as it used to be." Jack's chuckle vibrated my back.

I kept watching them for a few minutes, unable to look away. JJ started to touch Miller's face but stopped at the last minute. Miller watched JJ's hand as it lowered to his side, then he looked back into JJ's eyes. Miller's expression looked like a challenge, daring JJ to make a move.

JJ didn't strike me as the kind of guy to back away from a challenge, and he proved my point when he pressed his body completely against Miller's and lowered his head for a kiss. It wasn't a peck on the lips either. It was a no-holds barred, toe-curling kind of kiss.

"Looks to me like they've decided to swim," Jack whispered in my ear.

Epilogue

Jack

I RECEIVED A PHONE CALL FROM JOSEPH A FEW DAYS INTO THE NEW year. I could tell by the sadness in his voice during his greeting that Jeremiah had passed away before he even said the words. He hated to tell me the news over the phone, but a massive ice storm had pounded the New England states making it impossible for him to travel to DC to tell me in person. Joseph assured me Jeremiah had died peacefully in his sleep sometime during the night, holding the picture of him and Granddad over his heart like he had every night since I'd given it to him.

My heart broke for Joseph because I knew how much it hurt to lose someone you loved so much. He thanked me repeatedly for giving that photo to Jeremiah because it clearly broke through the disease to trigger a happy memory. Jeremiah was able to have happiness in the last weeks of his life, and that meant more to Joseph than he could express.

Even in the sadness, there was a glimmer of rightness that my granddad and Jeremiah were together again, which was confirmed in my heart when a bright ray of sun pierced through the heavy, gray clouds. I talked to Joseph for a little while longer, letting him talk about the man his grandfather had been and how much he would miss him. We made tentative plans for Liam and me to travel to Vermont in the spring so we could have a private remembrance for the two men.

I stared out the window for a long time after we hung up, watching the sun shine down on the Potomac. Tears of sorrow and joy slid down my face as I said goodbye to two great men but rejoiced in their reunion. "Surrender your heart, Big Jack."

Liam found me standing in the same exact place when he came home from his culinary school orientation. I told him about the phone call and how Jeremiah had died holding the photo to his heart. I held Liam while he cried for two men he hardly knew. That was my Liam—my Ace of hearts. I couldn't wait to make him legally mine.

"I know we agreed to talk about setting a wedding date after the holidays," I reminded him once he stopped crying. "What are your opinions on Vegas?"

He pulled back and looked at me, a smile slowly spreading across his face. "I've never been."

"Hmm, I think we should rectify that immediately. It's beautiful there this time of year. No snow. No slush. No dreary, gray skies." I looked into his hazel eyes so filled with love and promise. "What do you say, Ace?"

"Let's do it."

The End!

Want to be the first to know about my book releases and have access to extra content? You can sign up for my newsletter here: http://eepurl.com/dlhPYj

My favorite place to hang out and chat with my readers is my Facebook group. Would you like to be a member of Aimee's Dye Hards? We'd love to have you! Go here: www.facebook.com/groups/AimeesDyeHards/

Other Books by
AIMEE NICOLE WALKER

Curl Up and Dye Mysteries

Dyeing to be Loved

Something to Dye For

Dyed and Gone to Heaven

I Do, or Dye Trying

A Dye Hard Holiday

Ride or Dye

Curl Up and Dye Box Set

Road to Blissville Series

Unscripted Love

Someone to Call My Own

Nobody's Prince Charming

This Time Around

Smoke in the Mirror

Inside Out

Prescription for Love

Welcome to Blissville Collection (Both M/M Blissville series)

Volume One

Volume Two

The Lady is Mine Series
The Lady is a Thief
The Lady Stole My Heart

Queen City Rogue Series
Broken Halos
Wicked Games
Beautiful Trauma

Zero Hour Series
Ground Zero
Devil's Hour
Zero Divergence

Zero Hour Trilogy Box Set

Matrimony and Mayhem (Continuation of Zero Hour)
The Magnolia Murders
Marriage is Murder

Sinister in Savannah Series
Ride the Lightning
Mr. Perfect
Pretty Poison

Sinister in Savannah Box Set

Savannah Standalone Books
Invisible Strings
Bad at Love

Fated Hearts Series (Second Edition)
Chasing Mr. Wright
Rhythm of Us

Standalone Novels
Second Wind

Coauthored with Nicholas Bella
Undisputed
Circle of Darkness (Genesis Circle, Book 1)

Acknowledgments

I must give a huge shoutout to my editing team, Susie Selva and Lori Parks, for tackling this rehab project with so much gusto and passion. If not for their guidance and cheerleading, the Fated Hearts series probably would've stayed in the vault. Thank you so very much, ladies.

I've been so fortunate to work with Stacey Blake of Champagne Book Design since virtually the dawn of my career. In fact, Chasing Mr. Wright was the first book she formatted for me, so it only seemed right that I tapped her to work on the covers for the second editions. Stacey is a brilliant artist, and I'm always so thrilled to show off her pretties.

And I'm sending so much love to the fans who've waited for the Fated Hearts gang to return.

xoxoxo

About
AIMEE NICOLE WALKER

Ever since she was a little girl, Aimee Nicole Walker entertained herself with stories that popped into her head. Now she gets paid to tell those stories to other people. She wears many titles—wife, mom, and animal lover are just a few of them. Her absolute favorite title is champion of the happily ever after. Love inspires everything she does, music keeps her sane, and coffee is the magic elixir that fuels her day.

She'd love to hear from you.

Want to connect? All her links are in one nifty location. Go here:
linktr.ee/AimeeNicoleWalker

www.ingramcontent.com/pod-product-compliance
Lightning Source LLC
Chambersburg PA
CBHW051242250626
47155CB00009B/3126